Throwaway

Heather Huffman

Booktrope Editions
Seattle WA
2011

Copyright 2010-11 Heather Huffman-Bodendieck

Cover Design by Emily Stoltz
Cover Image Copyright © 2010 Emily Stoltz
Edited by Katie Flanagan

This is a work of fiction. Names, characters, places, brands, media, and incidents are either the product of the author's imagination or are used fictitiously. Any resemblance to similarly named places or to persons living or deceased is unintentional.

ISBN 978-1-935961-24-6

DISCOUNTS OR CUSTOMIZED EDITIONS MAY BE AVAILABLE FOR EDUCATIONAL AND OTHER GROUPS BASED ON BULK PURCHASE.

For further information please contact info@libertary.com

Library of Congress Control Number: 2011913847

Dedication

To Emily Stoltz & Erica Fitzgerald—God blessed me with two amazing sisters through blood and then two more when I met you. I would never have continued writing without your encouragement. This book is possible because of you. Thank you.

Acknowledgements

I have many people in my life for which I am eternally grateful—my husband and children top that list. Adam, Dylan, Blake and Christopher: I love you. Thank you for lighting up my life.

Mom and Dad, I love you both. Always have, always will. Thank you for all you've sacrificed over the years.

Angie and Karen – you're my heroes. Thank you for teaching me the meaning of the word strength and for the years of love and guidance.

To my nieces and nephews, you're all awesome. Don't listen to Uncle Adam; he doesn't really have a favorite.

Emily Hellmer, thank you for your willingness to be the cover model.

John Bartley, thank you for music that inspired a novel.

Emily Cain & Elaine O'Brien—thank you for lending your eagle eyes to the proofreading stage.

And to all the other people who've encouraged me, been a test reader or helped me market this novel, thank you

Chapter One

I t was the kind of gray day that made Jessie glad she didn't have a regular nine-to-five job. She took one look at the overcast St. Louis sky and crawled back into bed. There was no power on earth that could make her grateful for the job she had, but she could be glad for what it wasn't.

She had nearly dozed off again when there was a knock at the door. She reminded herself the roommate she'd been assigned was little more than a scared kid. That fact alone kept her from throwing something heavy at the door.

"Give me five minutes and I'll meet you downstairs," Jessie called to the willowy brunette on the other side before pulling herself out of bed with an exaggerated sigh. She stretched and padded barefoot to her bathroom, cringing a little at the sight of the rat's nest in her platinum blonde hair. She gingerly worked a brush through it, trying to remember the color it had been. Before.

Just like she did every morning, Jessie stared intently at her face in the mirror, searching for any signs of a wrinkle. Her baby doll face and large blue eyes made her look quite a bit younger than thirty-two, but the day when she couldn't mask her age was creeping ever closer.

That was a day she didn't want to think about. Somehow she doubted Spence would put her out to pasture. That sounded much too pleasant.

"Jess, are you ready? I'll walk down with you," Harmony called.

"Sorry. Give me one more minute." Jessie quickly changed for her daily workout. She knew Spence well enough to know that as long as he desired her, he'd keep her around. Her lithesome, leggy body was one card in her favor—even if she was ancient by street standards.

"I made you a smoothie." Harmony was waiting at the front door, holding a glass out.

"Thanks." Jessie took the offering with a smile. "How was class this morning?"

"Fascinating." Harmony lit up and instantly dove into a dissertation on the merits of studying quantum physics over just plain old mechanics. Jessie didn't even try to keep up; she just smiled and nodded.

Harmony was different than the rest of the girls. Even Spence saw that. She was there to pay for school and she'd move on when the time was right. For some reason, Spence would let her. Jessie believed him when he said he would.

Not Jessie. She was a lifer. He'd made that much clear since the day he took her under his wing nearly fifteen years before. She pushed memories of before from her mind, gulping down the rest of her smoothie so she could beat an old lady to the last bicycle.

Jessie pretended not to notice the dirty look she got in return. She'd made the mistake of deferring to age once and the woman had stayed on the bike for a full forty five-minutes. Not this time.

Other than dodging the hate glares from the old lady, Jessie enjoyed her workout. There was something very cathartic about stretching her muscles to their very limits. The sweat, the pain, the test of endurance… they felt good. They cleared her mind.

That evening, as she carefully applied her mascara before work, Harmony settled in on the countertop beside Jessie's makeup bag.

"Do you ever wish you'd gotten married and had kids?"

"Not really," Jessie answered without thinking. "What brought this on?"

"I don't know. I guess I just wonder sometimes if I'll ever get to do those things." Harmony seemed embarrassed by the admission.

"I don't think we're missing much."

"Really?"

"The way I see it, we have a husband. Sometimes we even have several husbands in the same night."

"I don't think a john is quite the same."

"Have you heard how the suburbanites talk about their

husbands?" Jessie routed through her bag for her favorite lipstick. "They count tiles on the ceiling. They make grocery lists in their heads. They think their husbands are too smelly, too fat, too predictable...."

"You can't write off the entire notion of love based on a couple of sexually frustrated moms in Bread Company."

"How do you know I'm talking about those women in Bread Co?"

"I was with you. I heard their conversation, too," Harmony reminded her.

"I bet their husbands are about as nice to them as johns are to us," Jessie got in one last barb before relenting. "But if anyone can find the one love story this world has left to offer, it's you sweetie."

"I think this old world has one up its sleeve for you, too."

"Sure thing." Jessie didn't believe it for one second. She was the very definition of used goods. But arguing that with Harmony wasn't going to accomplish anything beyond hurt feelings, so she let it go.

They locked up and went to hop the Metrolink across the bridge. East St. Louis was much more tolerant of their livelihood than its neighbor to the west. It didn't matter much to Jessie which side of the river she worked on. Her clients were happy to follow her across the Poplar Street Bridge and she liked staying out of jail.

A sleek black car pulled up alongside them and the tinted window slid down. "Ladies, looking lovely as always."

"Hey Spence." Jessie smiled saucily, wondering if there would ever be a day when her stomach didn't tighten just a little when she saw him. She learned a long time ago how to keep that feeling from showing.

"Hey Spence." Harmony's eyes didn't quite mask her own unease.

"Join me for a minute, girls."

"You're going to make us miss our ride." Jessie didn't like the look on his face.

"I am your ride." He motioned for them to join him again and this time they relented.

"New car?" Jessie made conversation as she eased into the seat beside him.

"You like it?"

"It's great."

"What's up?" Harmony didn't seem inclined to discuss Spence's new Mercedes S600. Jessie preferred not to think how many nights she'd worked to buy the car they were sitting in.

"You two get to be part of an experiment." His eyes lit up as if they should be happy with his words.

"How so?" Jessie was almost afraid to ask.

"Downtown is coming to life again. I'd like you ladies to work this side of the river tonight."

"We'll get picked up by the cops in five minutes. You know that."

"Don't tell me what I know." Anger flashed across his face before being replaced with a beseeching expression. "Come on. You are my two classiest girls. If anyone can fly under the cops' radar, it's you. Just go hang out in a few bars tonight. Have a drink or two on me. Get a feel for it. Then we can talk about it tomorrow. Okay?"

"Okay," Jessie agreed hesitantly, her eyes meeting a pair of hazel eyes in the rearview mirror. It wasn't like Spence to be reasonable. He must need something from them. Besides testing the waters west of the bridge, that is. If anyone would know, it would be Vance. As Spence's guard, he'd be privy to what was really going on. If Jessie could get him alone, he'd probably tell her. Friends might be a strong word, but Vance and Jessie looked out for each other.

"Sure, Spence," Harmony grudgingly agreed as well, following Jessie's lead.

"That's my girls." He planted a kiss on Jessie, his hand running up her leg. The car pulled into a garage on the riverfront.

"Looks like our stop." Harmony bolted out the door the second the car was parked.

"See you tomorrow." Jessie was right behind her.

"You girls be careful. And have fun." Spence thrust a wad of bills at Jessie before the car peeled out, leaving the two women to stare at each other incredulously.

"What just happened?" Harmony was the first to speak.

"I have no idea." Jessie shook her head. "He's up to something. He must want eyes on these streets for some reason. Let's stay close to each other, eh?"

"I'm okay with that."

"Tonight, we're just a couple of girls out for girls' night. We'll go dancing, hit a few bars… and we'll go from there tomorrow."

"Jessie?"

"Yeah baby girl?"

"I forgot my fake ID."

"Don't you have another one?" Jessie frowned.

"That was the other one," Harmony admitted, biting her lower lip as she did.

"Alright. Just stick close. But you're not drinking—got it?"

"Fine with me." Harmony wrinkled her nose and Jessie was briefly overwhelmed by just how young her roommate was.

With good enough legs and sufficient attitude, they didn't have much problem getting past the gorillas at the door at Club Aruba. Harmony drank orange juice; Jessie stuck with a light beer.

Despite her concerns that Spence was up to something that was going to land her in jail, Jessie had to admit she was looking forward to a night off. If not a night off, per se, at least a change of duties.

She and Harmony alternated between dancing and hanging out in the lounge, neither seeing much of anything that should interest Spence. No cops, no competition, not even a thriving drug scene that particular night—which was a little surprising. Just a whole lot of drunken kids and desperate looking men. If the desperate looking men had any money, maybe they would interest Spence, but Jessie doubted they did.

It didn't take them long to be sick of Club Aruba. They wandered in and out of other bars. The Drunken Sailor held their interest for a while, but neither knew what they were supposed to be looking for.

"Wanna try Memphis Blues?" Jessie suggested, not really sure why.

"But Spence dropped us on the Landing."

"And we've been up and down it. Call it a hunch. It's not that far."

"You don't think Spence'll be mad?"

"If he is, it'll be at me and he always gets over it."

"I don't want him to hurt you, either."

"He won't hurt me," Jessie replied with more conviction than she felt. Sometimes when she had a night off—a real night off—she'd hang out at Memphis Blues. If she wasn't at O'Malley's, that is. Memphis Blues wasn't too far from their apartment on Cherokee and they had a respectable beer selection and better music. There was something about a good blues or rockabilly beat that could massage away the tension in her body.

"Jessie girl, you're looking fine tonight," the bartender greeted her with a broad grin.

"Hey Chad." She accepted the beer he extended to her. "What can I say? It's girls' night."

"What can I get you, kid?" He nodded to Harmony.

"Ice water with a twist of lemon?" She looked like she'd had enough orange juice to last her for a while.

"Sure thing." He smiled a little and turned his attention back to Jessie. "Wow, really—you look amazing tonight."

"I clean up okay I guess." Jessie tried to shrug off the attention. Maybe this was a bad idea. She usually came in wearing jeans and a t-shirt with her hair in a ponytail. Now that Chad realized she was a girl, she wouldn't be able to hang out undisturbed. Oh well, she told herself, the damage was done. She might as well enjoy the music while she was here.

"You like this stuff?" Harmony frowned a little, surveying the exposed brick and hardwood floors.

"Love it." Jessie tugged Harmony after her. "Let's find a spot."

"I think the bartender likes you." Harmony leaned into Jessie so she could be heard. "He's still watching you."

"Chad? Yeah. I guess there'll be no living with him after this."

"I don't think he's the only one watching you."

"Maybe they're watching you."

"No, I'm pretty sure this guy is watching you. Not that I can blame him. Blues suit you."

"Not sure what to say to that…."

"Wow. He's really cute, Jessie."

Jessie allowed her eyes to follow Harmony's towards the door. He actually was good looking; she grudgingly had to admit that much. It was more than the messy brown hair, angular jaw line, or muscles peeking through his shirt—but she couldn't say just what it was.

He seemed irritated by her presence, though. Not quite as enamored as Harmony would like to believe. She dismissed him with her gaze. "You're imagining things, Harmony."

"Really?"

"Yeah, really."

"Because he's headed this way."

"The bathroom's behind us."

"Oh." Harmony didn't seem convinced.

"Hey." The man in question nodded casually to them, coming to a stop beside Jessie.

"Hey." Harmony suppressed a giggle. Jessie nodded in response, swallowing hard. She had no idea what was wrong with her. Something about this person standing so near left her feeling very...unsettled. But it wasn't the same kind of unsettled Spence made her feel. No, for some reason, she liked the odd electric current running through her.

They were looking at her like they expected a response.

"I'm sorry..." She frowned and tried to clear her mind. "Were you speaking to me?"

"I said, she's good...the musician."

He was smiling at her. Jessie could see the hint of a dimple hiding under his stubble. She closed her eyes briefly before answering.

"Kim Massey—she's great. I'd love to have her talent."

"Can I get you a beer?" He leaned in closer and she couldn't help thinking that he smelled nice. He didn't reek with cologne like Spence often did and he didn't have the sweaty, nervous smell most of her clients carried with them. He smelled... clean... masculine.

She held her beer up as if to say "I'm good," because her voice box seemed to be failing her at the moment.

He disappeared and she felt herself able to breathe for the first time in a while. She took the opportunity to gulp in some air, leaning against Harmony for support.

"What is wrong with me?"

"Haven't you ever been attracted to a man before?" Harmony laughed then froze. "You haven't, have you?"

"Is that what this is? It feels more like a minor stroke."

"You have a crush." A smile twitched at the corner of Harmony's mouth.

"What should I do?"

"Flirt."

"I don't think Spence would like it."

"Spence'll never know. I didn't say marry the guy. Just flirt a little."

"Really?" Jessie bit the corner of her lip in thought. The idea had merit.

"What are you ladies talking about?" That dimple was back again.

"You," she blurted. Maybe the red lighting was playing tricks with her eyes, but it looked like a spark of amusement flickered across his face.

"All good, I hope."

"Very," Harmony supplied with a smile before becoming interested in a group of young men across the bar.

"Minx," Jessie muttered as her roommate sashayed across the room. The man laughed and the sound washed over Jessie like a warm bath.

"Do you have a name?"

"Jessie. How about you?"

He paused briefly before answering. "Gabe."

"Are you sure about that?"

"Yeah, I'm sure." There was that laugh again. Jessie wanted to bask in it; she found herself smiling back at him.

"So… do you come here often?"

"Did you really just ask me that?" Jessie couldn't resist calling him on it.

"Wow, I guess I did. I'm a little rusty at this."

"If it makes you feel any better, I think Harmony has given me up as hopeless."

"Then we make quite a pair."

"It appears we do." A smile toyed with her mouth. If he only knew.

"So... what kind of work do you do?"

Jessie nearly spit her beer out. She was pretty proud of herself when she swallowed it instead and finally managed, "Customer service. How about you?"

"Teacher."

"Really?" Wow, she was a horrible person. She shifted her gaze from him, hoping he wouldn't see the pathetic sorrow in her eyes.

A sleek black Mercedes S600 glided past the window. She didn't need to see the plates to know who it was.

"Sorry, I have to go now." She caught Harmony's eyes and motioned for her.

"Did I say something?" He frowned.

"No, no. I enjoyed meeting you. I just really need to go now." She could see Vance striding across the street as she spoke.

"Can I see you again?" He grabbed Jessie's hand when she would have slipped away.

"I don't know..." Jessie glanced from Vance to Gabe. There was a look in Gabe's eyes that made her breath deepen. A power other than her brain took over and she impulsively wrapped her fingers through the hair at his nape and pulled him to her for a quick but thorough kiss. "Broadway Oyster Bar, night after tomorrow... eight o'clock."

He nodded, a little shaken. Jessie smiled at that and brushed a light kiss on the corner of his mouth before grabbing a now-waiting Harmony by the hand and rushing to meet Vance at the door.

"You're playing a dangerous game, Jessie-girl," Vance warned in a low voice, grabbing her by the arm more gently than it appeared.

"It wasn't exactly planned." Jessie frowned, hoping neither Gabe nor Chad had witnessed her departure.

"Just tell Spence it was only you girls in there."

It wasn't like Vance to advise her to lie to Spence. What exactly was going on that she didn't know?

"Did you ladies have a nice evening?" Spence's voice was smooth as silk, but Jessie recognized it for what it was—bridled fury.

"It was fine. A little boring, but fine. Is there something in particular we're supposed to be looking for?"

"You'd know it if you saw it."

He seemed to be trying to read beyond her words. He peered so closely at her, she wondered for the briefest of moments if he could read minds.

"Do you want us to work Washington tomorrow? Soulard? Or do you want us back on the East side?" Harmony jumped in, turning his attention from Jessie.

"Washington? That's not a bad idea. Start at the casinos and work your way down Washington. We'll make a decision after that."

"Sure, Spence," Jessie agreed more eagerly than she felt. After that, the tension in the car ebbed. Spence seemed satisfied that the girls were just being thorough, and he listened as they described their evening—minus one detail.

That night, after Harmony had gone to bed, Jessie still sat chin-deep in a warm bubble bath. The smell of mandarin curled around her senses; the bath oils clung to her skin. His face hovered in her mind's eye.

A knock at the door startled her. As she wrapped a fluffy orange towel around herself, she glanced at the clock. It was 3 a.m.

"Vance, what are you doing here?"

"I only have a minute." He looked around nervously.

Jessie nodded. She knew Spence watched her comings and goings. He meant it when he said she belonged to him. Someone was usually watching her building and it was just one way he made sure she didn't make any attachments other than those allowed to her.

"That guy in the bar," Vance continued. "The one you were with when I got there. He's one of the reasons Spence sent you down there. That guy's been tailing Spence for a month now."

"The teacher?" Jessie furrowed her brow.

"Honey, that's no teacher. He's a cop."

Chapter Two

J essie wasn't sure how long she sat in her towel with her back to the door after Vance disappeared. He wasn't about to risk being caught leaving Jessie's building in the middle of the night, so he'd left right after dropping the bomb on her.

She furiously wiped away the tears on her cheeks. If this was what having a crush on someone got you, it was just as well she'd never had one before.

After the hurt feelings came anger. It simmered as she dressed for bed and then as she lay in the dark, reliving the evening through the lens of new information. It continued to bubble all throughout her fitful sleep.

By the time her eyes opened to the late-morning sun streaming through her window, rage was boiling over. She wasn't mad at Spence for using her as bait. That was pretty typical Spence.

But Gabe had flat-out lied to her. He'd seemed so sincere. Jessie wasn't about to dissect why this lying man bothered her when so many had lied to her before. If she took too close a look, she might uncover something really unsettling… like the fact that this one bothered her because she'd wanted him to be telling the truth.

She had cared.

"Jessie." Harmony was knocking at her door. "Are we going to yoga?"

"Sure. Give me five minutes," she called out lifelessly.

As much as she would have loved to crawl back under her covers and hide from the world, she knew yoga would clear her mind better than pouting. And she needed a clear mind so she could decide just how best to annihilate Gabe.

The yoga routine did help calm her rattled nerves. The rest of the day seemed to crawl by. Evening finally came and Spence once again showed up to drop Jessie and Harmony off on the west side of the river.

They didn't have to go farther than the casinos to find clients. Jessie was glad she didn't run into Gabe. She's never been ashamed of who she was but found herself holding on to some sliver of hope that he didn't know. Maybe Vance had been wrong.

Yoga might be nice, but Jessie was happy for her weight routine the next morning. She had a little steam to burn off and a long day looming in front of her. Buying groceries would only take up so much of it.

Harmony had a full day of classes, leaving Jessie to her own devices. She killed some time by wandering in and out of the antique shops and thrift stores. She treated herself to La Vallesana for lunch, snagging a seat under a bright blue umbrella to savor her tacos al pastor. Vance strolled across the street from Vallesana 2, apparently engrossed in his lime ice cream.

A smile tugged at the corner of Jessie's mouth. He seemed much less intimidating when licking the back of a plastic spoon. He settled into a seat beside Jessie without a hello; the two sat in silence, enjoying their treats.

"What's he gotten himself into?" Jessie finally asked in a low voice.

"He tried to play with the big dogs." Vance shook his sandy-blonde head. "So far all he's managed to do is get himself in debt and catch the cops' attention."

"So you think Harmony and I are bait to draw out the police?"

"He knows you won't turn him in."

"And I won't be any good to him for much longer."

"I don't know about that… he's been waiting a long time to have you all to himself," Vance seemed to be trying to reassure her. She shuddered a little at the thought. She liked having limited exposure to her boss.

"Does he know Gabe is a cop?" Jessie wasn't sure why she asked.

"That guy's not very good at undercover if he's giving out his real name," Vance snorted.

"So that is his real name?"

"Gabe Adams. St. Louis PD. He started tailing you the minute you got out of the car last night. I think he's after some of Spence's new associates."

"If you know all of that, why is he still alive?"

"At least we know who he is. If he gets removed from the equation, they'll just send a new one."

"Why do you need me?"

"Spence is trying to figure out what they're after... how much they know. He's hoping that by being on the streets, you'll hear something. Worst case scenario, you get picked up by the cops and maybe you'll learn something that way."

"And you're telling me this because...." Jessie wondered against her better judgment.

"You're in a bad spot, Jessie-girl. Don't make it worse. Spence won't let you go—you're his."

"Unless he gets me arrested," Jessie growled. "Then I belong to the state of Missouri."

She'd belonged to the state of Missouri once before and through no fault of her own. She had no intention of being their ward in a new capacity now.

"He doesn't think you'd go away for long."

"That's comforting."

"I'd better go. Last thing I need is for someone to see us together—Spence'll get the wrong idea."

"Thanks for stopping by." Jessie gave him a small smile. "I'll be careful."

She wondered if meeting Gabe Adams for drinks fell under the description of being careful. Probably not, but that didn't stop her from wishing the minutes on the clock would move along a little faster. Even if she did plan to annihilate him, she was looking forward to seeing him. Maybe she could hear him laugh one more time.

Jessie planned her wardrobe with extra care that evening. Her favorite pair of jeans, boots that would make Nancy Sinatra proud and a bra that promised age-defying lift were part of her arsenal. She completed the ensemble with a simple cotton shirt—she didn't want him to think she was trying too hard.

"You look nice." Harmony raised an eyebrow knowingly.

"Don't you have some studying to do?"

"What should I say if Spence calls looking for you?"

"I don't know... tell him I'm working in a soup kitchen or something."

"A soup kitchen?"

"What can I say? I'm a hooker with a heart." Jessie shrugged prettily.

Harmony rolled her eyes and laughed. "I'll be sure to tell him that, too."

"Maybe he won't check up on me."

"Maybe." Harmony didn't seem convinced. "Be careful tonight."

Jessie had opted to keep Gabe's true occupation to herself. There was no sense worrying Harmony more than she already was. She wondered if she'd have to wait long for Gabe to show up.

Turns out he was waiting for her.

"Who was the goon that came to drag you out of Memphis Blues the other night?" He frowned at her as she eased into the chair across from him.

"My brother." She motioned for the waitress to bring her a beer as she spoke. "And hello to you, too."

"Your brother?" He took a drink of his own beer, seemingly considering his next words. "I doubt that. Are you okay?"

"Yeah." She shrugged a little. "My brother covered for me with Daddy, so I didn't get grounded or anything."

"Right." The way he drew the word out spoke volumes. They were silent for a moment, both seeming to consider the lone singer on the stage. Jessie'd seen him around before. He was a young, good-looking guy who appeared to be at least a little tipsy. The line of empty Corona bottles behind him seemed to back that assessment. Still, he was talented and his laid-back demeanor fit the sea-shanty feel of the place. Well, sea-shanty with a White Castle as its closest neighbor.

"So, tell me about being a teacher. That must be fascinating. What grade do you teach?" Jessie drew her gaze away from the yellow, pink and green lights running along the rafters to look Gabe in the eye.

"There's not much to tell."

"What district do you work in?"

"You're awfully inquisitive tonight."

"I just find teaching such a fascinating subject. You know, I've often considered myself a teacher of sorts."

Gabe choked on his beer and Jessie smiled behind her bottle as she took another swig.

"I thought you were in customer service," he recovered nicely, his eyes locked on the graffiti art covering the benches lining the walls.

"You can offer exceptional service and teach someone at the same time," Jessie primly informed him, a hint of amusement in her eyes.

"I'll have to remember that," he said once he'd composed himself a second time. This time, his eyes held hers.

The waitress brought Gabe another beer and took their order. Jessie was grateful for the distraction. She studied the trees peeking through the open rafter ceiling for a moment.

She loved this place, with its rickety tables and walls that were a mixture of wooden planks, stone and brick. She loved that people freely signed their names on the benches and walls. Some of the artwork was really quite good.

Someone at the bar was smoking a cigar and it gave the room a cherry wood smell. A breeze licked her skin, promising a summer storm before the night was over. Conversation resumed but stayed light as they shared a bowl of gumbo. She imagined it was what gumbo tasted like in New Orleans.

"Come on." Jessie stood, grabbing his hand to tug him along behind her after they'd finished their dinner.

"Where are we going?"

Jessie's only answer was a wicked little grin before pulling him to her, their bodies instinctively moving to the music.

"We're the only ones on the dance floor. I don't know that we're supposed to do this."

"He doesn't mind."

"How do you know?" He seemed skeptical.

"Excuse me." She leaned against the stage, immediately capturing the singer's attention. "Do you mind if this gentleman and I dance right here?"

"I'd love for you to dance, sugar," he answered into the microphone. "I know just the song."

"You're my hero." Jessie gave Gabe a look that smacked of "told you so."

And just like that, the music shifted to a slower pace. The new beat demanded her body's attention. It tugged and pushed and pulled like an unseen puppeteer and she took Gabe on the ride with her.

He seemed to have forgotten being self-conscious. The look on his face said he wanted to devour Jessie. Whatever his mind had planned for her, his body was completely malleable to her will at the moment.

What Jessie hadn't expected was how her own body hummed at his touch. Every nerve ending was on alert.

Harmony once told her that when lightning strikes, not only does a current come from the storm, but streamers from objects on the ground actually extend up, attracted by the current. When the charge from the storm meets the streamer on the ground, you have a lightning strike.

She felt like her whole body was one big network of streamers. If they connected right now, she imagined it would feel about like being struck by lightning.

Before she could let herself get carried away any further, she leaned close to his ear, his rough cheek brushing her own smooth one as she whispered, "I think I've figured out what kind of teacher you are... Social Studies."

"Is that so? What makes you say that?"

"I can picture you teaching eager young minds all about things like the justice system. And I'm sure you're the kind of thorough teacher who would be sure to cover the lesser-known facts. Like the entire Miranda statement—not just the 'right to remain silent' stuff you see on T.V."

"Of course," he played along.

"I bet you'd also explain to your students about the difference between a sting operation and entrapment."

"A must-know for eager young minds these days."

"I bet that lecture is a real crowd pleaser." Jessie stilled, her eyes meeting his. She'd meant to level the man. Instead, she found herself appallingly close to kissing him again. Or crying. Both felt like a distinct possibility at the moment.

They stood frozen in place, a breath away from each other and afraid to move in either direction. A war waged within. She took some amount of comfort from the fact that he seemed to be struggling as much as she.

"So... where do we go from here?" He spoke so close to her skin she could feel his words more than she heard them.

She licked her lips and took a steadying breath. "I have no idea."

"Me either."

They might as well have been the only two people in the room. Jessie was keenly aware of her crackling nerves and his every breath. The rest was a blur.

"I think I need a drink." His breath was jagged.

"Me too."

The beer was warm, but it was wet and that was half the battle. Even better, it was something to do that wouldn't get her into trouble.

It didn't seem like the place or time for the kind of talk they needed to have. They sat in silence, letting the music wash over them as they regarded each other. He would occasionally take a breath as if to speak, but would invariably shake his head and sink back into silence.

Jessie's lip twitched ever so slightly.

"What?" he demanded.

"Nothing." She held her hands up. "Not a thing."

"Then stop looking like you want to laugh at me," he admonished before a chuckle of his own escaped.

"Not at you, necessarily," she promised as a giggle bubbled up. With one last look at each other, they gave up the battle and succumbed to their laughter. When Jessie finally caught her breath, she sat back and surveyed him—wishing she could read his mind as she tried to figure out where to go from there.

"Looks like your friend is here." Gabe nodded towards the street. Sure enough, Vance was striding towards the door with a scowl on his face.

"They know who you are." Jessie glanced around to see if the door by the stage was clear. "If my boss catches me here with you, he will kill one or both of us."

"He might try." Gabe seemed all-too-ready for the challenge.

"Whatever, tough guy. I'm not sticking around while you two check to see whose is bigger."

With that, she was out of her seat and headed towards the stage and the door that stood beside it.

"I resent that." Gabe was right on her heels. "I don't need to check."

"Whatever." She rolled her eyes, pausing to glance down the street.

It was clear; she took the chance to dart towards the White Castle as Vance went in the Oyster Bar's front door. She ducked into White Castle and ordered a coffee to kill some time while she surveyed the streets around her.

The Mercedes rounded the corner, apparently circling the block while Vance was inside. The second it was out of sight, she and Gabe went out the restaurant's side door and crossed Broadway. They disappeared behind a large brick building with a painting of an oversized owl and a wizard issuing the peace sign.

Jessie stopped and leaned against the cool brick of the building while she thought about what to do next. Gabe leaned beside her, shielding her from the view of the street with his body. The small act of chivalry wasn't lost on her. Neither was the fact that with him this close, the need to touch him was almost palpable.

"So... do any of your associates spend much time in South County?" He tenderly brushed an errant hair from her cheek as he spoke.

Jessie licked her lips distractedly before answering, "Not usually."

"Come on, then."

He didn't offer any more explanation and she didn't ask for it. He took her fingers loosely in his and led her to his car. She wasn't surprised that he drove a beat up old Jeep. At one point in its life, it was probably red. Now it was faded and looked as if it spent more time off the road than on. It suited him.

She was a little surprised that he was listening to Leonard Cohen. It seemed a bit dark for him... not that she really knew him at all. The music pumping from the speakers pronounced the dice as loaded, the fight as fixed. It was a statement Jessie could get behind at the moment. She hadn't wasted much of her life feeling sorry for herself, but she allowed herself that small indulgence as the road passing underneath took her further away from the city.

Her childhood had consisted of being bounced from foster home to group home and back again and she'd taken that in stride. When the state had kicked her out on her eighteenth birthday with $47 to her name and nothing else, she'd dusted herself off and found a way to survive.

When the means of survival turned out to be less than ideal, she looked for the good in that, too. She'd held her head high when Spence degraded her. She rolled with the punches—proverbial and not.

But this was just ticking her off. She looked up at the stars and mentally asked them if she'd ever done anything to harm the cosmos. Was there a reason she wasn't even allowed the pleasure of a crush? She wasn't even asking for love here... just a crush. It was the minutia of the wish being denied that infuriated her.

"Penny for your thoughts." His hand twitched, as if he wanted to touch her as badly as she wanted him to.

Jessie chuckled at that. "If that's all thoughts are worth, I guess I did land myself in the right profession."

Gabe shook his head, but Jessie could see his grin in the dim light.

"You don't want to know my thoughts," she added. "Hell, I don't even want to be in my head right now."

"I know the feeling."

"So... where are we going?"

"To a little diner the guys took me to a while back. It's open all night and the coffee's good. And no one we know should be there."

Jessie nodded, not really sure what else to say.

"When did you figure out I was a cop?"

"When Vance told me. I'm normally pretty good at picking out the cops. I guess my radar is a little rusty. Would you really have arrested me?"

"Absolutely."

"Really?" Jessie tried not to look hurt.

"I'd like to think so."

"Jackass."

"It's my job."

Jessie merely arched an eyebrow at him. She had ditched her job for him—he could at least lie and tell her he would have done the same. She certainly wasn't going to admit that to him now.

"I should arrest you now."

"I haven't done anything illegal."

"Contributing to the delinquency of a minor."

"I don't like you anymore."

"You like me?" he asked playfully.

"Used to. Maybe. A little bit."

"Used to?"

"Yep."

"What if I admit that I was supposed to take you in after you got Harmony into Aruba?"

"That could possibly work in your favor," she considered, biting the edge of her lower lip rather than smile.

"Come on, I'll buy you the greasiest burger you've ever had in your life." He smiled charmingly at her as he slid the car into the last remaining parking place.

"Sounds appetizing." She didn't even try to keep the sarcasm from her voice.

"You'll love it," he promised as he rounded the car to open her door. The only reason she was still seated when he got there was shock on her part.

"I place my life in your hands," she replied saucily, accepting the hand he offered as she climbed out of the Jeep. A look flashed in his eyes, one that seemed to wonder if there was more to that statement than a joke. Jessie sobered briefly at the thought.

If the smell hadn't given it away, the yellowing wallpaper stood testament to the fact that this little dive was one of the few havens remaining for smokers. It was crowded, but not claustrophobically so. It was more of a bustling atmosphere. A jukebox sat across from the counter, and from it Janis Joplin was reminiscing about Bobby McGee.

"Whatchya' drinkin'?" a waitress called to them before they had even found a seat.

"Two coffees," Gabe called back, his gaze asking Jessie if that was the right choice. She smiled and nodded. Although she still didn't believe him that a greasy burger was a good thing, she found herself liking the place instantly.

Sometimes in life, there are pivotal moments. While seemingly benign on the surface, something within acknowledges that a bridge has been crossed.

Jessie smiled at the waitress who brought their coffee as Gabe ordered their dinner. When she turned her eyes back to his, it struck her that she was crossing just such a bridge. Her life had irrevocably changed on this night.

Chapter Three

There was a certain decadence to the world's greasiest burger, and that's what made it good. Jessie grudgingly admitted as much, earning a grin from Gabe. In between bites, they discussed their current situation in hushed tones.

"So… why didn't you arrest me?"

"I have no idea," he admitted. "Maybe it's because I find you fascinating."

"There's a description I don't normally hear." Jessie smiled at the irony. She wasn't normally the type of person to belittle herself, but there are certain realities in life that just are. One of those being the fact that men like Gabe didn't find women like Jessie fascinating. Men like Gabe didn't usually look much beyond the cleavage, in fact—unless they want to check out her legs.

"You're a hell of a lot purer than most women I meet," he argued. "There's something very true about you. What I can't figure out is why you run around with someone like Spence. Do you really have me that fooled or are you in trouble?"

"I'm not looking for a knight on a white horse to come save me, babe," Jessie scowled. "If you're looking for a damsel in distress, you're in the wrong spot."

"God forbid someone try to help you." His expression was as dark as her own.

"I'm not sure what you want me to do, Gabe." Jessie threw her hands up in exasperation before leaning in to add in a whisper, "I have nowhere else to go."

"Surely there is somewhere else in this great big world for you to ply your trade."

"You really are insufferable, you know that?" Jessie huffed. "And don't call me Shirley."

"Airplane reference... nice." He smiled approvingly.

"It's not as simple as you make it sound," she returned to the conversation.

"Sure it is."

"From your very limited vantage point, maybe. From where I'm sitting—you're asking me to risk my life."

"If you really wanted out, I would help you. I could protect you."

"I'm not sure where to start with that one." Jessie wanted to laugh. Or cry. "First, why on earth would you want to do that? You don't know me. You are nothing to me. You have no idea what you're getting yourself into. Second, are you going to guard me every moment of every day? Are you going to tuck me away somewhere Spence and his crew can't find me? I don't think so. I think Spence is the kind of guy to keep what is his—and I am his."

"When you say you're his" He seemed to be considering his next words carefully. "Do you mean you work for him? Or is there another layer to this that I'm missing?"

"I think I make Spence a lot of money, so he usually leaves me alone. But I'm not allowed to have relationships outside those he permits—friends, boyfriends, any of it. Someday, he's going to retire me and keep me for himself."

Jessie stared intently at her coffee cup. Shame crept into her cheeks at her admission. It was the first time she'd spoken aloud the words everyone seemed to know.

"Do you want to be his?" Gabe's voice was low and gentle.

"No." Jessie's eyes flew to his and her voice rose instinctively.

"I can't not arrest you indefinitely," he sighed. "My boss is really pushing me to bring either you or Harmony in."

"That's what Spence is banking on."

"Really?"

"He wants us to find out what you know."

"And he's using you as bait?"

"Sure. He figures I won't stay in long if I get caught. And he knows Harmony isn't around for long anyway."

"Why isn't Harmony around for long?"

"They have a four-year contract. She's different than me."

"Why don't you have a four-year contract?"

"I wasn't offered the choice."

Gabe took a breath to speak and then let it out slowly. His expression said he wasn't really sure what he could possibly say at that moment. He finally decided on "Well that sucks."

"Yes, it does. Do you want more coffee?"

"Here, I got it." He grabbed the refill pot left on their table and replenished both cups.

"Thanks."

"You want to check out the jukebox with me?" His mood lightened.

"Okay."

It should have seemed odd, to just change the subject from one so dark to the merits of Fleetwood Mac over vintage Alice Cooper. It should have, but it didn't. They stood side by side, not quite touching, as they scoured over the selections on the old machine. When he told her he was playing "Poison" in her honor, she bumped him out of the way playfully with her hip and entered the number code for "Go Your Own Way."

That started a war and each of their selections from that point on was geared to irritate the other. By the time their money was spent, both were laughing.

There didn't seem to be a compromise to be had that night, so they steered clear of the topic that had brought them there. Instead, they talked about their favorites—music, food, seasons. Neither seemed inclined to discuss their past and the future wasn't a good topic either. So they stuck with the present.

Jessie wished she could stay in that place forever—or at least an hour more. But the Pepsi-Cola clock on the wall was telling her that she would have hell to pay already.

"Can you give me a ride back to my place?"

"Sure," he agreed a little reluctantly, grabbing the bill when Jessie made a move for it.

"Let me leave the tip?" she bartered.

"If you must." He stood, waiting for her.

Jessie liked that he knew her occupation and still treated her like a person. Not many people outside the trade did.

"We still haven't figured out what we're going to do," Jessie commented as she stood in the parking lot waiting for him to unlock the car.

"No, we haven't," he agreed, opening the door for her. "Do you have any ideas?"

"You could take your band of merry men down to Soulard and let us have the Landing," Jessie suggested once he'd joined her in the car.

"I don't have a band of merry men."

"I doubt you're all alone."

"It's not going to happen."

"I know. If you have to take someone in, take me. Harmony doesn't need a record."

"Or you could just cooperate with us and let me get you out of there."

"That's not going to happen, either." She shook her head.

"Then we're right back where we started."

"I guess we are." Jessie stared at her reflection in the window, illuminated by passing streetlamps.

"I could always pretend to take you in."

"Spence would check in on me."

"Maybe we could convince him you'd been sent somewhere far away."

"Maybe."

"Does that mean you'll think about it?" Hope crept into his voice.

"Maybe." Jessie turned to study him thoughtfully. "Do you want to go to a movie with me tomorrow?"

"Are you asking me on a date?"

"Yes, I believe I am. That's a first for me, you know."

"I'm supposed to be working."

"Me too."

"What do you want to see?"

"I have no idea. I don't normally go to movies. It just seemed like the date thing to do."

"I'm sure we can find something. Do you want me to pick you

up?"

"Sure. At the corner of First and Lucas. About eight o'clock?"

"How much is this going to cost me?"

"I hate you." She crossed her arms over her chest and scowled at him.

"Just asking."

Jessie felt a little giddy and a lot terrified as she hopped out of Gabe's Jeep and dashed up the stairs to her apartment. Spence would kill her if he caught her, but she had a plan to keep that from happening. He kept tabs on her during her nights off. But when she was working, as long as he saw her on the streets at some point and saw money the next day, he left her alone.

"Where were you? Spence is going out of his mind looking for you." Worry marred Harmony's pretty brown eyes.

"Sorry." Jessie meant it—she didn't want to make things difficult for her friend. "You probably don't want to know where I was."

"You were with that guy, weren't you? The one from the other night. I'm sorry; I never should have encouraged you to flirt with him."

"No." Jessie shook her head. "I'm glad you did. I felt almost… normal tonight. But we can talk about this later. Spence will be on his way. I'm sure he had Vance watching our door. You should go to your room until he leaves."

"I'm not leaving you alone with him—not if he's angry."

"I appreciate the gesture." Jessie took her friend's hands in her own. She knew how much courage it would take Harmony to face Spence. "But that would actually make things worse. The less reason we give him to think something is going on, the better."

"I don't know."

"It would help me if you went to bed. Now if you'll excuse me, I have to take care of one thing before he gets here."

Harmony grudgingly went to her room and turned her radio on. Jessie took the world's fastest shower and threw on a pair of pajamas, then pulled several bills from under her mattress. She had just put the money in the bamboo pedestal bowl that sat on the table in the foyer when her front door burst open and the man himself strode through it.

"Where were you?" he growled, grabbing her arm and jerking her to him.

"What's going on?" She did her best to look confused.

"You traitorous bitch... where were you?" He didn't need to shout; the venom in his voice was sufficient to make her stomach tighten.

"Working."

"Don't lie to me." He spat out the words as he backhanded her.

"The money's in your bowl." She gingerly touched her cheek. Pain radiated from it. "I think that's going to leave a mark."

"Why were you working on your night off?" He was suddenly composed as he plucked the money from the bowl. That was as close to Spence ever got to an apology.

"A regular at the Broadway Oyster Bar recognized me. Asked what it would cost him to forget his ex. I obliged. I thought you would be happy."

"Next time check in."

"Sure." She nodded, going to find an ice pack for her face. "You want us on the west side again tomorrow?"

"Maybe for a couple more nights." He agreed taking a step towards her.

"We can do that." She fought the instinct to shrink from his touch when he leaned over to kiss her cheek. Instead, she closed her eyes and pictured Gabe's dimple.

When she was alone, she sank onto the couch in an exhausted heap. Harmony tentatively stuck her head out the door.

"Aw, Jess, you should have let me stay with you," Harmony exclaimed when she saw the bruise already welling up.

"Trust me—this was better than it could have been."

"I hate that man."

Jessie nodded, not trusting her voice enough to speak. She was suddenly very tired. She didn't protest when Harmony poured her a glass of wine and curled up on the couch beside her.

"So... tell me about this guy."

It was the kind of normal conversation Jessie had always wished she could have and it was exactly what she needed at the moment. A smile tugged the corner of her mouth.

"He has amazing brown eyes—they're almost golden. And when he laughs, I feel ridiculously happy inside." Like a cat with a bowl of milk, actually. But she kept that to herself—it seemed a bit over the top.

"What's he do?"

"He's a teacher." Jessie felt bad lying, but no sense complicating things.

"No he's not." She gave Jessie a knowing look.

"Okay fine, he's a cop. But I bought the teacher line at first."

"That's because you're twitter pated."

"Twitter-what?"

"Didn't you ever watch Bambi as a kid? Wow, you were seriously deprived. What kind of parents did you have?"

"I don't know," Jessie admitted with a small frown. "I don't think I ever knew them."

"I'm sorry."

"No worries." She smiled more brightly than she felt. "What about you—where are your parents?"

"They live in Hazelwood. They think I have a research internship to pay for school. It would kill them if they knew. But— they made too much money to qualify for financial aid and not enough to pay for school. I had two choices: rack up a lifetime's worth of debt in student loans, or work my way through. Plan B seemed like the more fiscally-sound approach."

"You're nuts." Jessie shook her head.

"Maybe it wasn't my most well-thought out decision, but what's done is done."

"True," Jessie acknowledged.

They talked for a while more. The throbbing in Jessie's cheek subsided and the wine succeeded in making her drowsy. She allowed herself the luxury of sleeping in even later than normal the next morning before joining Harmony in yoga.

The day passed like a Salvador Dali painting. Everything seemed distorted, slow and odd, until she was standing in front of her closet, trying to decide what she could possibly wear that would be suitable for the movies and not raise Spence's suspicions. Then the clock seemed to be on fast forward.

She finally settled on folding her skirt over at the waist to shorten it and putting a button-up in her bag. She siphoned more money from her secret stash in the mattress so she could pay Spence for the evening before heading out for the night.

Jessie sincerely hoped she didn't look as nervous as she felt. Harmony chatted with her easily about not much in particular and she took that as a good sign.

"Be really careful you don't pick up a cop, baby girl," Jessie warned.

"Is that a joke?" Harmony nodded in the direction of an old white Plymouth that pulled up at the corner of First and Lucas just as they walked up.

"Don't accidentally pick up any cops," Jessie amended before waving and darting across the street to hop in the car.

"Hey there." His eyes seemed to lap her up.

"Hey." She flushed under his gaze. "Where'd you get the car?"

"I bought it a few years ago. I keep meaning to fix it up and never get around to it. It's not pretty, but it runs great."

"No, it's cool. I like it. What year is it?"

"Sixty-three."

"Good year for cars." She nodded knowingly.

"You think so?"

"I have no idea," she admitted. "It just seemed like the right thing to say."

Once they were on the highway, she maneuvered in her seat to pull her skirt down to a respectable length before sliding the button-up shirt on over the layered tank tops she'd worn out.

Gabe burst out laughing, an incredulous look on his face.

"What?"

"Usually it's the other way around... the girl sneaks out with more clothes on..."

"Ah, I see what you mean." Jessie grinned at the absurdity of it. "I never have been normal."

"Normal is overrated," he assured her. "Have you decided what we're going to see?"

"Haven't got a clue."

"What's your curfew?"

"I think I brought enough to buy me until 1 a.m." She double-checked her wallet to be sure.

"To buy you? Are you paying him for a night off?"

"I'm paying him to think I worked," she corrected.

"I'm not okay with that." He frowned.

"Then pretend you didn't hear it."

"I can't pretend I didn't hear it."

"Then get over it. I don't want you ruining a perfectly good date—you don't want to waste my money, do you?"

"I don't feel right making you pay to spend time with me."

"You aren't the one making me. It's kind of funny, really."

"Funny?"

"Sure… usually people pay to spend time with me."

"You're just full of paradoxes, aren't you?"

"Yep. Look at it this way. People spend money on all sorts of things. Drugs. Alcohol. Some people collect things or overeat. Lots of people spend money on big houses or fancy cars. I don't spend money on any of that stuff. For fourteen years, I've been sticking money under a mattress because I didn't have anything better to do with it and nowhere to go."

"Fourteen years?"

"Now I have somewhere to go."

"How much do you have?"

"A lot. Probably. I don't exactly flip my mattress over to count it."

"And still you don't leave."

"I told you, that's not an option. You're not going to ruin our date by bringing that up again, are you?" She repositioned herself in the seat so she could face him more fully.

"What the hell happened to your face?" he shouted, causing her to regret repositioning herself. A vein was pulsating in his temple. She took that as a sign he was really angry.

"That's not a very nice thing to say," she admonished. She didn't want to be that woman—the one who lied and said she tripped. But she also didn't feel like discussing the truth with him, either. "You're supposed to tell me I look ravishing tonight."

"You do—but I'm going to kill him for touching you."

"I know you're the expert on this kind of thing, but I'm pretty sure the law would frown on that."

"You're not that funny."

"But I'm cute. Come on, admit it. You think I'm cute."

"Yeah, I do think you're cute." That dimple of his flashed again as he grudgingly gave in. "I just don't like seeing you hurt."

He reached out to stroke her cheek with his thumb. She couldn't help leaning into his touch. It felt so warm, so sure.

They wound up watching a romantic comedy. Well, sitting in a theater that was showing a romantic comedy. Mostly they watched each other.

After the movie, they went back to the little diner. Jessie knew she couldn't eat like this too many nights in a row or she'd gain a million pounds. At that thought, she paused to toy with the idea of gaining so much weight Spence wouldn't want her. She quickly tossed it aside as too simple a solution. He'd probably put her on a bread and water diet the minute he suspected what she was up to.

They were careful to leave the diner in plenty of time to get her home before curfew. She'd even grown accustomed to Gabe opening doors for her and paused at her door while he unlocked the car. Only instead of opening the door, he took her face in his hands and lowered his lips to hers.

The kiss was gentle, reverent almost. It made her want to weep. It made her want to sing for joy. It was over as quickly as it began, although she could still feel it the entire ride home.

Chapter Four

The next night he took her to see the Cards. She'd never been to a ballgame before. He brought her an Albert Pujols shirt and a red baseball cap with a cardinal on it. They drank ridiculously expensive beer and ate nachos with the works. They sang and clapped and shouted and cheered.

As much as Jessie loved watching the game, as dearly as she enjoyed his company, what she couldn't get over was the feeling that she belonged to this enormous group of bustling, happy people. She wasn't on the outside looking in; she was right in the thick of the moment. And she couldn't stop smiling.

"You look amazing tonight," he told her quite solemnly after they finished jumping and screaming over a Pujols homerun.

"I feel amazing." She laughed as she stood on tiptoe to kiss him. "Thank you."

"I like seeing you smile." He kissed her bruised cheek and she sobered briefly. He'd gotten a few dirty looks from people who assumed he'd done that to her. She felt like crawling in a hole whenever it happened—the last thing she wanted was for him to experience one moment of discomfort because of her.

Seventh inning stretch shifted her attention back to the moment and she sang "Take me out to the ballgame" with the rest of the stadium, then made a beeline to the bathroom with the rest of the women in the stadium.

As she neared the line, a familiar face caught her attention. It was another of Spence's girls, hanging off the arm of an older man. Something in her eyes said she knew Jessie's face but couldn't place from where.

Jessie ducked behind a large man and walked beside him a bit before veering off to weave her way back to Gabe. Her heart pounded a thousand miles an hour in her chest, but she tried to appear calm as she slid into the seat beside him.

"Are you okay?" Concern etched his face the moment he saw her.

"Absolutely."

"You're a lousy liar. What's wrong?"

"Nothing. The line was really long, so I didn't wait."

"So the pained look is because you have to pee?"

"Don't be crass."

"What? Something's wrong. If you won't tell me then I have to guess."

"I really do hate you sometimes."

"I think that's Jessie-code for 'I'm really crazy about you because you're so handsome'," he informed her.

"You think so, huh?" She grinned, happy he'd been distracted from his concern.

"Absolutely," he mimicked her.

"Grrr."

"Did you just growl at me?" He cocked his head as if deciding whether he'd heard correctly.

"I don't know... maybe."

"So, are you going to tell me what upset you earlier?"

"You're like a freaking bulldog, you know that?"

"I prefer to think Rottweiler. German Shepherd, maybe. Something manly."

"It's not like I called you a Yorkie-poo."

"Yes, it could always be worse... so... what was wrong with you?"

"You know, if you're going to spend the next two innings driving me crazy, we can leave now and beat the traffic."

"Not a bad idea...come on. Let's blow this popsicle stand."

"Really? You're having fun. We don't have to go."

"You're not having fun?" He looked wounded.

"I am. I had a wonderful time," she assured him, before relenting. "I just ran into someone who might have recognized me. I'm starting to worry it'll get back to Spence."

"I can take care of that for you." He did growl, and it wasn't the playful sound Jessie had made, either.

"No. I'm not going to tell you again—stop trying to kill people."

"Why are you protecting him?"

"Who says I'm protecting him?"

"I don't need protecting."

"Ha!" she practically snorted. "You definitely need to be protected from yourself."

"Hey Pot, my name's Kettle."

"I hate you. Have I mentioned that?"

"I love it when you talk dirty to me." He tapped her nose playfully.

"It's a good thing you're cute." She made a face at him.

"Are you going to sit there and yak at me or are we getting out of here?"

"You really don't mind?"

"Nah. I was hoping we'd have time to make out in the car before curfew anyway."

Suddenly, Jessie didn't mind leaving early. In fact, it seemed like a grand idea to her. They walked hand in hand back to the car, stopping for Jessie to run to the restroom while Gabe stood lookout and again to give a five to the saxophone player outside the stadium.

Jessie frowned when she realized they were nearing her neighborhood. He must have been teasing about the making out thing.

"At least you'll be able to get some real work done tomorrow. I won't be able to get away." She didn't like the idea of not seeing him.

"Do you have to work?" He tried to sound calm, but Jessie could tell he wasn't happy.

"No, actually, it's my nights off when I have trouble getting away. I have two nights on and one night off. The on nights Spence doesn't keep track of me—so long as he gets his share the next morning. The off nights, I'm on a pretty short leash."

The cloud that fell over Gabe's eyes spoke louder than any words could. Jessie shrank back in her seat with the distinct feeling she was somehow tainted in his eyes now. She mentally cursed herself for reminding him who she really was.

"So," he began after a long pause. "What are we doing the next night?"

"I don't know. What do you want to do?" Hope fluttered inside her.

"I know a great little corner bar over near Dogtown. Want to grab a bite there?"

"Yeah, sure. Sounds great." Jessie nodded, relief washing over her.

He might have been teasing about making out in the car, but the goodnight kiss he gave sent flames shooting through her. It was fascinating to be so completely and totally overtaken by the need to be touched by another human being—by this human being.

She expected the next day to crawl by. She now firmly held the belief that nothing of interest could happen in between date nights. She was wrong.

The morning passed pretty much the same as any other. After their morning workout, she and Harmony went clothes shopping at Retro 101. She found a cute mini dress and some cowboy boots to wear on her next date with Gabe. It was garish enough for Spence to not think twice about it and stylish enough she wouldn't feel the need to take extra clothes with her. She found a few other treasures before calling it a day. On her way home, she stopped in at the Cherokee Market for a soda.

"Hello sunshine," her favorite Irishman greeted her, kindness and laughter dancing in his warm blue eyes.

"Hey Danny." She smiled and hugged him. "How's the wife and kids?"

"Beautiful as always. You coming to see me tonight?"

"It's Wednesday, isn't it?"

"I didn't know—I heard Spence was fit to be tied today."

"I haven't seen him." Jessie frowned in confusion. "What's up?"

"Word is he is sporting a fresh bruise on his cheek... a lot like yours, actually. Some guy just walked up to him, clocked him, and walked off."

"Really?" Jessie's breath caught in her throat.

"Scared the life outta him, from what I hear." A smile seemed to be tugging the corner of his mouth.

"Well, unless I'm in trouble and don't know it, I'll be there tonight. Tell your family I said hey." She kissed him on the cheek and wandered back to her flat.

Despite living on the same street for fourteen years, she never got tired of soaking up all of its character. How could you not love a place with murals on the sides of buildings and mosaic tile trashcans?

But today, she walked home without seeing her surroundings. What had possessed Gabe to do something so stupid? If Dan had noticed that Spence's bruise matched her own, wouldn't everyone else—Spence included?

Fear that he had made things worse for her mingled with a small amount of satisfaction.

"Spence is looking for you," a Hispanic woman with riotous curls called from the other side of the street as she passed by. It didn't matter how long she knew Marie, every time Jessie saw her, the thought flitted through her mind that the girl had obviously watched Pretty Woman once too often as a child. Marie's riotous curls and thigh-high boots always reminded Jessie of Julia Roberts in that role.

"Thanks," Jessie waved and smiled, pretending her stomach wasn't in knots. If Marie sensed fear on Jessie's part, the story would be all over the neighborhood by the end of the day. The more she could convince people this had absolutely nothing to do with her, the better.

To that end, she plastered a benign look on her face and strolled into her apartment as if she hadn't a care in the world.

"Wow, Spence… what happened to your face?" Maybe it was a little over the top, but Jessie couldn't help it. When she saw the large black mark marring his pretty skin, satisfaction quickly took top billing over fear.

"Who did this to me?" His voice was low and silky.

"How should I know?" She tossed her bags on the nearby couch, refusing to look at the obviously terrified Harmony, who sat curled up in their oversized chair.

"Because my cheek now bears an uncanny resemblance to yours."

"Wow, you're right. But I didn't have anything to do with this, Spence. How could I?"

"What's going on here?"

"I told you—I don't know. Everyone knows I'm your girl. Maybe someone decided to get chivalrous... but I'm telling you, I don't know who did this or why."

Before she knew what was happening, he crossed the distance between them—striking her on the other cheek with a force that caused her to stumble backward.

"Jessie," Harmony shrieked, leaping to her assistance.

"Stay out of this!" Spence shouted.

"Don't hurt her," Harmony pleaded.

"Hey, no worries." Jessie clasped Harmony's hands in her own, trying to calm the frantic teenager.

"Let's see if your boyfriend has a response to that one."

"I'm telling you, there is no guy, Spence. It's just a coincidence."

"I guess we'll see now, won't we?" With that pronouncement, he strode out of the little apartment.

"Sorry about this," Jessie whispered miserably, blinking back tears that threatened to spill.

"You don't need to apologize." Harmony's hands shook as she applied an ice pack to Jessie's newest bruise. "I really hate that man."

"Don't waste the energy."

"Someone should just shoot him. Then you'd be free."

"I'm not going to shoot him... and you aren't either," she added when Harmony got a determined gleam in her eye.

"What if he gets himself shot with some of the crap he's into now?"

"One can always hope, huh?" Jessie smiled.

"What are you going to do about Gabe?"

"Avoid him like the plague," Jessie answered without a moment's hesitation.

"But you're crazy about him. I can tell you are."

"I've survived this long without a man; it won't hurt me to walk away from this one now."

"Don't you ever wish for another life? Have you ever even thought about going back to school or getting a new job or running away to suburbia and raising a couple of kids?" Harmony's speech was an impassioned one, full of all the zeal and innocence of youth.

"I took some classes at the community college once—botany. I wanted to try my hand at landscape design. It's actually why I picked the flat across the street from the Garden Center. But Spence made me quit after a semester. I think he worried I'd get it in my head to leave or something."

"He sucks."

"Yes, he does. But I don't think I'd even know what to do with a family and all that crap. I wouldn't know how to act."

"I bet you'd figure it out. You're a good person."

Jessie didn't bother answering that one. She just patted Harmony's hand and went to get a bubble bath. Her face was throbbing and Jessie wondered if maybe Spence had broken her cheekbone this time. She wouldn't be working for a few nights now. As much as she wanted to go listen to Danny play—his lively Irish folk music would inevitably lift her mood—she should probably hide from the world for a couple of days.

A glance in the mirror confirmed her suspicion; one whole side of her face was swelling. She frowned and sank back into the bubbles. After her bath she'd ask Harmony to fix her up with some takeout so she could pile up on the couch, stuff her face, and watch sappy movies on Lifetime. Spence could just live with less income this week. Served him right.

True to her resolve, she didn't step out of her apartment before Saturday night. Spence had shown up to scream at her, but backed off when he saw her puffy face. Since the blow hadn't been reciprocated, his suspicions seemed to be ebbing. Now he would feel slightly remorseful for his actions and would be looking for a way to make it up to her.

She did change her mind about watching Lifetime when she fell asleep on the couch the first evening and spent a restless night dreaming about Gabe. The second night she relegated herself to mindless reality shows, only to be haunted by Gabe again in her sleep. It was frustrating her to no end that she couldn't seem to get him out of her head. The growing need to see him only strengthened her resolve to not.

She was tired and unsettled by the time she finally returned to work on Saturday night. So it really shouldn't have surprised her when the very first car she got in turned out to belong to a cop.

She cursed herself mentally for being stupid the entire ride to the police station. It wasn't the first time she'd been picked up, but it was the first time in the past decade. She held her head high amid the disdainful looks that so easily dismissed her humanity.

The cop who brought her in dumped her in an interrogation room and left. She was grateful to be alone. Even if there was someone behind the mirror, she could pretend they weren't there. She wanted to hide her face in her hands, to close her eyes and will this rotten world away. Instead, she sat ramrod straight and waited for the show to begin.

Given the fact that Gabe was a cop, she really shouldn't have been surprised when he burst through the door. Maybe it wasn't surprise so much as a shock to the system. Either way, it left her looking like a deer in headlights for the briefest of moments before she recovered her calm demeanor.

It was hard to say who the rage on his face was aimed at. Maybe it would help Jessie get over her ridiculous crush if it was geared towards her. All the same, she wasn't sure she could survive that.

"Are you okay?" He strode towards her.

"Fine, thank you." She gave a barely perceptible head nod.

"Don't pretend you don't know me, Jessie. I've been worried out of my mind about you."

"I can't imagine anyone here would be happy to hear that I do know you," she reminded him.

"To hell with them."

"You don't really mean that. Not really."

"How do you know what I mean?"

"Jessie Jones." A voice full of authority broke into their conversation. "We've wanted to talk to you for some time now."

"So talk." She motioned for him to sit down as if she were inviting him to share a spot of tea at her table.

He began to sit, then realized he'd just handed control over to her and jumped back up with a scowl. Gabe looked away too late to hide his smirk.

"What are you laughing at? You had a week and couldn't bring her in—it took Thompson one night. I wonder… is there a reason for that?"

"Absolutely," Jessie jumped in before Gabe could. "I'm not feeling all that well tonight. It has my brain a little fuzzy."

"Very funny," the man snarled. Jessie knew who this man was without introduction; his reputation on the streets preceded him. Detective Brunner was a cliché—from the waistline that had seen one donut too many to the cocky attitude that probably masked all kinds of inadequacies. "Gabe, you don't want this one. Lord only knows what crawls on her."

Gabe took a step towards Brunner, only to still at the calm in Jessie's voice when she spoke.

"I'm a lot cleaner than your wife."

"What do you know about my wife?" Brunner laughed at the thought.

"Her name is Riley. She's a petite little redhead, although, from what I hear, that's not natural. Trust me—I've heard all about her… and that girl has stuff Ajax won't take off."

Jessie was fairly certain it was words coming out of Brunner's mouth, but all she could make out was angry sputtering. Gabe stopped laughing long enough to grab Brunner when he lunged for Jessie.

Outwardly, she didn't flinch. Inside, she was really glad for Gabe's quick reflexes. He was growling something in Brunner's ear as he dragged him out the door. Jessie could guess what it was. Of course, his chivalry was probably getting her in trouble again as it was prone to doing.

"Jessie, as much as I enjoyed that, you aren't helping yourself here."

"I didn't take Thompson's money."

"Excuse me?"

"It's sitting on his dashboard. I'm never the first one to break the law. Go check it out. Then you can either charge me with a crime or let me go."

"Jessie, I wish you'd listen to reason."

"I'm not sure what you think you can accomplish by keeping me here." She sat back and folded her arms across her chest.

"He hurt you again." Gabe lowered his voice to a strained whisper, resting his face in his hands as if to shield himself from the truth.

"I told you to leave him alone; you'd just make it worse."

"What are you talking about?" He looked up at her, his eyes speaking of great pain.

"He did this to draw out whoever vindicated me."

"I have no idea what you are talking about." He shook his head.

"You didn't punch Spence?"

"I'd like to draw and quarter him, but no—I didn't lay a hand on him. I figured he'd just take it out on you."

"Oh." Jessie wasn't sure if she was disappointed about that or not.

"Hey, if you want me to beat the bastard to a bloody pulp, I'll gladly do it."

"No, no. That's okay. I wonder who hit him."

"If you find out, tell him thanks for me."

"Or her. It could have been a girl."

"Have any ideas?

"No. Harmony hates him, but I can't see her doing that."

"Hey Detective Adams." A young uniform poked his head in the door. "Can I talk to you for a minute?"

"Be right back," he told Jessie.

She had a pretty good idea what the kid was telling Gabe. Sure enough, he came back with a bit of a grin on his face.

"Looks like you're right. No money changed hands. You're free to go."

"Great. Good seeing you." She jumped to her feet, ready to bolt.

"Not so fast." He snagged her hand before she could dart away. "I was kind of hoping you would stick around long enough for us to work something out. If you help us, then we can help you start a new life."

"Sure. Sounds peachy. And what happens when Spence catches me? My face can't take much more of him being pissed at me."

"I'll protect you."

"Sure you will, sugar." She ached to believe him.

"Trust me… please."

She didn't have confidence in her ability to answer so she tore her gaze away from his and pulled free. She managed to hold herself together until she was on the Metro bus and the police station was shrinking in the distance.

Then she did something she hadn't done since she was small child—she cried.

Chapter Five

S pence took some convincing that she'd managed to get in and out of the police station without giving anything away or learning anything in turn. Jessie couldn't bring herself to settle back into her routine just yet, so she bought herself a couple of nights off to go watch a movie by herself.

The second night she stood in line for a free seat at the outdoor theater in Forest Park. Going to the Muny seemed like something a normal person would do with a night off. Normalcy was something she craved more and more with each passing day.

It was the first time Jessie had ever seen Jesus Christ Superstar, and she was instantly and completely drawn in. Maybe it was the music, maybe it was Mary Magdalene, but she barely blinked the entire show.

The music was still wrapped around her like a warm blanket as she rode the bus home that night. The next day after her workout, she scoured Cherokee Street until she found a vinyl of the soundtrack.

Maybe she was no Mary Magdalene and Gabe wasn't, well, Christ, but he was good and Jessie could identify with the yearning and the confusion in Mary's voice.

It was Jessie's night off for real, so she grabbed herself a bottle of wine at the Cherokee Market and spent her evening submerged in a bubble bath, drinking cheap wine straight from the bottle and listening to Andrew Lloyd Weber over and over again. All in all, it was a pretty good night.

The next evening she told herself she couldn't avoid work forever, so she donned the outfit she'd intended for her date with Gabe and hit the streets with Harmony. Spence had stopped giving them rides, but had made it clear they were to stay on this side of the river.

They usually didn't have to look further than the casinos for a gig. This night, Jessie had a customer the second her feet hit the pavement.

"Excuse me, ma'am..." A nervous kid cleared his throat.

"Ma'am?" Jessie arched an eyebrow. "That's a first."

"Would... would you possibly be available for the evening?"

"The whole evening? You sure you don't want to start off with twenty minutes?" She shouldn't be talking herself out of money, but something in her took pity on the kid. He seemed terribly nervous.

"Yeah, sure, whatever."

Jessie felt bad; maybe she'd hurt his feelings. She tried to amend things. "I'm game for the evening, too, sugar. I just didn't want to take all your money."

"No, it's okay."

"So, do you have somewhere in particular you want to go or do you need directions?" Jessie asked as she slid into the passenger side of his Ford Taurus.

"The parking lot on the corner of MLK and First will be fine, kid." A voice came from the back seat.

"Damn it, Gabe." Jessie jumped even as she recognized the voice. "You nearly gave me a heart attack."

"Well, you didn't leave me much choice." He grabbed her by the arm and tugged her down towards him.

"Oh dear." The kid gulped as Jessie's face nearly landed in his lap.

"Are you looking to take over Spence's job?" she hissed at Gabe.

"Easy there, kid." Gabe chuckled at the boy. "I just needed to get Jessie here close enough to talk."

"We were talking just fine as we were," she pointed out.

"Then maybe I just wanted you closer."

"What do you want?"

"Jeffrey here is going to pull into the garage and we're going to get in my Plymouth. I'll tell you the rest then."

"You're a real jerk, you know that." She glowered at him.

"You might have mentioned that once or twice before." He

leaned up and kissed her on the nose. "I missed you."

"It's hard to take you seriously while you're lying in this kid's back floorboard, you know that?"

"It worked, didn't it?"

"I hate you."

"Aw, thanks honey." He grinned devilishly and she rolled her eyes.

It was useless trying to reason with him when he was in this mood. She didn't even try to talk to him again until they were seated upright in his car. Jessie had no sooner opened her mouth to speak than he was pulling her head into his lap.

"Dang it Gabe, knock it off." She shoved at him.

"Calm down darlin'." He swatted away the hands that were swatting at him. "I don't want anyone to see you in the car. It's just until we get out of the city."

She heaved a sigh but stopped smacking him. Without the distraction of a fight, she was keenly aware of the firmness of his thigh under her head and the heat radiating from him. He absentmindedly stroked her cheek with his thumb as he hummed along with the radio.

As much as she hated to admit it, any resolutions to steer clear of him skittered right out of her mind along with the rest of rational thought when he did that. She couldn't formulate the first thought that didn't have anything to do with the longing that was snaking its way through her.

"We're here," he announced as he swung the behemoth into a parking space. Jessie sheepishly sat up; she hadn't intended to lie on his leg the whole way there.

"I don't know that Nick's is such a good idea." She frowned when she recognized the little Irish Pub. "A lot of industry people hang out here."

"But not at this time of night. And if we get inside before the game ends, we can get $2 nachos."

"Oh, well, that's worth risking my life for."

"No one will recognize you... here... wear this." He reached into his back seat and grabbed a cowboy hat, which he plopped on her head.

"Do I want to know where you got this?" She pulled the hat off to study it. It wasn't the cliché ten-gallon kind you normally saw. It was dark brown suede and looked like it might actually have been worn by somebody wrangling a cow or something.

"There are all kinds of things you don't know about me." He winked. "Come on. We'll miss our nachos."

With a look that said she didn't believe him for a second that this was a good idea, she jammed the hat back on her head and followed him across the street into the unassuming corner pub.

"There's our guy—right over there." He grabbed her hand when she would have backed out the door and tugged her towards a booth at the back of the room.

"You didn't tell me we were meeting someone else," she whispered fiercely in his ear.

"We never got around to talking." He gave her a look that was both charming and innocent at once.

"Thanks for meeting us, Carter." Gabe shook the man's hand as Jessie slid in the seat warily.

"Glad to do it," Carter smiled.

Jessie knew she must look like a frightened wild animal, but she couldn't help it. Every warning bell in her head was going off full tilt. Gabe seemed to be trying to silently tell her it was okay. Maybe that's just what she wanted to see in his eyes.

"Carter here is the Captain of our Organized Crimes unit... he's my boss," Gabe explained. Jessie went to bolt but he was in her way and wouldn't budge.

Her eyes accused him of betrayal.

"Just hear what he has to say. If you want to take off when he's done talking, then I'll even drive you home," Gabe whispered against her ear, his warm breath both soothing and sending chills down her spine. She sought his eyes with hers, trying to see the truth in them.

"Don't make me regret this," she sighed and settled back down.

Jessie took comfort in the gentle pressure of his leg against hers beneath the table. She took a deep breath and looked Captain Carter in the eye. "Organized Crimes, huh? Spence really stepped in it this time."

"Did you know he was involved with a local family?" Carter asked.

"No, but I did wonder where he came up with the cash for the Mercedes. He's never been so flush before. What's he running for them? Drugs or girls?"

"I'm not really at liberty to answer that," Carter coughed uncomfortably.

"Girls, huh. So I guess you want me to keep my eyes open for newbies… or are they just passing through?"

"How do you know it's girls?"

"I watched your facial expressions," Jessie shrugged and turned her attention to Gabe. "Are you going to get us those nachos? I want a beer while you're at it."

"Sure thing." He motioned for the waitress. The look of pride on his face made Jessie feel warm inside.

She took in her surroundings while he ordered. A fairly steady stream of college kids filed by, obviously headed for the stairs. There was a certain Irish punk feel to the place. One of the bartenders was a big, brawny guy with well-tattooed forearms and a large tat on the back of his bald head. The other bartender was a cute but gruff-looking girl with short reddish-brown hair tucked under a brown flat cap. There was a kitschy, eclectic mix of stuff above the bar that included a cross, a soccer ball, a piggy bank and a golf bag—along with a lot of others she couldn't quite make out.

The lighting was dim and it was incredibly loud, so loud it was private. She understood why Gabe felt pretty secure they could talk freely without being heard. Jessie wasn't sure she could pick a conversation out of the cacophony if she tried; only the occasional bubble found its way to the surface. It was a good place to blend in and go unnoticed.

Seven televisions lined the walls of the front room, most of them showing the Cards game. A couple played more obscure stuff the majority of patrons could care less about.

The bouncer sat at a small table by the front door, flipping through a book of fake IDs. Behind him, red lights from the train signal shone through the oval window on the wooden door.

Large windows along the front of the place offered a view of the road. The occasional bus would fly by—the first one startled her.

Two beautiful women walked through the front door as if they owned the place and Jessie recognized them instantly. She ducked her face against Gabe's arm, grateful for the hat.

"You know them?" Gabe instantly spotted the escorts. The giveaway wasn't so much the short, flowing dresses with low cut bodices. That was a pretty common sight. It was the perfection of their look—the brightness of the dresses, the impeccable makeup—and their confidence in contrast to the men following behind them that signaled the true nature of their relationship. The women oozed self-assurance out of every pore. The men looked like they fully expected to be thrown out at any moment.

"I told you this was a bad idea," she reminded him.

"They went in the back. You're okay."

"Associates of yours?" Carter's interest was piqued.

"They aren't Spence's girls. Probably RCG girls, but I see them around every so often," Jessie explained. River City Gazette girls were the ones who didn't have pimps—they advertised their services on the back of a local paper.

"We're prepared to offer you protection from Spence in return for any information you can get us on his new business activities." Carter dove right into the purpose of their meeting.

"You really think you can guarantee that?" Jessie asked pointedly.

"Do you have any real guarantee of that now?" His gaze fell to the bruises on her face.

"I see being irritating is a prerequisite for employment with St. Louis' Finest," Jessie muttered, glad for the interruption when the waitress brought their beer.

"Spence is in a vise right now; he's getting pressure from both sides. He's only going to get more volatile as the vise tightens," Gabe reasoned with her.

"What do you want from me?"

"Just tell us what you see. Any conversations you overhear. If you hear something, pass it along to Gabe. He'll be your handler."

"My handler, huh?" Jessie bit the inside of her lip to keep from laughing at that one. "I suppose if I don't do this, you're going to make my life miserable."

"Something like that," Carter agreed.

"I'll think about it."

"You'll think about it?"

"Isn't that what I just said?"

"You have twenty-four hours to 'think' about it," he relented. "Look, I promised my wife I'd be home at a decent hour... can you get her home, Gabe?"

"Sure thing, Captain."

"Listen, Jessie...you haven't heard anything about my wife, have you?" Carter turned back to ask after taking two steps away.

"Not a peep," Jessie promised, quite proud of her ability to keep a straight face. As soon as they were alone, she smacked Gabe soundly on the arm.

"What was that for?"

"You jerk. You used me."

"Honey, if my intent was to use you, I'd have gotten what I needed a lot sooner than this. I've been remarkably patient with you so far."

"Is that so?"

"Absolutely."

The pair seemed to be moving ever closer to each other, as if being pulled by an invisible force. Jessie's eyes greedily devoured his face. She wondered what his scruff would feel like against her skin.

"If you're my 'handler' that's one very big reason for us to stay clear of each other."

"Of course."

"I mean, really, what would be the point of us hooking up? It's not like it could go anywhere."

"To be perfectly honest, I can't think much beyond wondering if you taste as good as you look," he admitted. "Why couldn't we go anywhere?"

"Really? You have to ask that?" She sat back in her chair just in time for the waitress to place a heaping plate of nachos in front of them. Jessie knew Harmony would work her nearly to death the next morning if she heard about this indulgence, so she resolved not to mention it and helped herself to some food.

"Should I have ordered two plates?"

"You weren't seriously going to eat all of them, were you?" She didn't wait for an answer. "Wow, do these people know it's summer? It's freezing in here."

"Jessie my girl, whatchya' doing here?"

Jessie's heart nearly stopped when she recognized Dan standing in front of her, a big grin on his friendly face. "Danny, wow, you play here, too?"

"And here I was telling myself you came to see me."

"I didn't know this was your other gig... but I'm looking forward to hearing you."

"Join us, Dan? Jessie didn't leave many nachos, though. We'll have to order more." Gabe motioned for him to sit.

"Don't you give my girl trouble, Gabe."

"Yeah, don't give his girl trouble," Jessie made a face at him. Even though she worried Dan would accidentally get her in trouble back in Cherokee Street, it was nice to see him. And strangely, not a surprise that he knew Gabe.

In his soccer jersey and newsboy cap, the burly man fit right in the little Irish pub. By his friendly and unassuming nature, one might not realize how fascinating a story his was. He'd opened for Bon Jovi and Tom Petty back in the day and now seemed quite content to chat amicably with the prostitute and the police officer while waiting for the Cards game to end so his set could begin.

At O'Malley's, his sound was very Irish folk. Here, it was something altogether different. With a wink at Jessie, he began his set with a cover of Dire Straits' Romeo and Juliet. Jessie rolled her eyes and Gabe grinned smugly at her as Dan painted a picture she wasn't sure she was comfortable with.

Was Gabe just another one of her deals? What would happen when the novelty of being treated like a person wore off? And what if it didn't wear off before Gabe got over being a love-struck Romeo?

But her irritation could only last so long with Dan's all-encompassing voice wrapping around her, somehow managing to break through the chaos of sound to get inside her soul to soothe her troubled spirit. It was obvious he was in another place entirely and Jessie had the feeling that if she closed her eyes and let him, he'd take her there, too.

And then, just like that, the song was over and the din returned. Dan chomped his gum happily as he seemed to decide what to play next before weaving the spell all over again.

Jessie found it impossible to not be swept away by the music and the man so near to her. But she was also mindful of the bar's resident cop that kept walking through. The last thing she wanted was for it to get back to Captain Carter that Gabe was cozied up to someone like her. She also didn't need it getting back to Spence that she'd been seen with a cop.

"It's really stupid being here." She leaned in close to Gabe's ear.

"Probably," he agreed after a short pause. "If I take you back to my place, someone we know would probably see us. You want to go find somewhere in the suburbs?"

"I want to find somewhere far away from here. Just for a few days. I want to be just a woman with a man. Is there anywhere we could do that?" Jessie felt like a foolish little girl for admitting it, but the words were out before she could stop them.

"You know what? I can arrange that." He appeared thoughtful. "If you can get away for a few days, that is. We'll head out Tuesday afternoon."

"You don't have to do that." Jessie shook her head, still keenly embarrassed by her outburst.

"No, it's a great idea. I've wanted to toss you over my shoulder and run you away from here since the moment I met you. It just felt a little caveman, so I resisted the temptation."

"I appreciate that," she told him wryly. She wasn't really sure what to do once that was decided. She didn't want to go, but knew she shouldn't stay, either. Dan decided for her when his next song was a favorite Springsteen cover.

She leaned against the wall, her legs propped on Gabe's lap beneath the table. He absentmindedly traced lazy circles on her skin just above her cowgirl boots. The casual touch and the music were enough to make her forget all the reasons to not be sitting there.

She might not be able to name the jumble he had caused in her, but she did know that he filled her with the oddest desire to please him. And while she was quite convinced that she could never give him what he really wanted—she would never be free of Spence—she could give him one thing he wanted.

"Do me a favor?" She pulled him towards her as she leaned towards him.

"Anything." He smiled in a way that made her mind go blank for a moment. She blinked a few times before her thoughts came back.

"Tell Carter I'll do what he wants. Just as soon as we get back."

"Hey, that's not why I'm doing any of this—you know that, right?"

"Sure, I know that." She nodded, not entirely convinced herself.

"Damn it, Jessie." He wrapped his fingers through her hair and pulled her to him, his mouth hungrily claiming hers.

Maybe he couldn't convey whatever message he intended to with his kiss, but he did succeed in clearing her mind of anything other than him. When he finally pulled back, his eyes searching for something in hers, she half-heartedly shoved at him.

"That was really stupid. You'll get yourself pulled from my case."

"Argh." Gabe's gargled cry of frustration made Jessie smile. "You are going to be the death of me, woman."

"Take me home before it's the other way around." She playfully shoved at him again.

He grudgingly obliged. Jessie leaned over to kiss Dan's cheek goodbye as Gabe tossed a tip in the jar. Jessie clung to Gabe's side, her face buried in his shoulder in hopes no one would recognize her on the way out.

When they made it back to the car, she sunk low in the seat, determined to not ride back the way she'd come. They worked out the details for Tuesday afternoon and then talked about nothing really of consequence. She wanted to ask him to take her to their little diner for a greasy burger but thought that might seem too desperate. So she settled for a tender goodnight kiss at the Metrolink station by the Scottrade Center and the promise of stolen time away on the horizon.

Chapter Six

With plans to make and a bag to pack, the next few days went more quickly than Jessie imagined they would. She was disturbed to realize it was harder to shut off her mind when she worked since she'd met Gabe. It was an unfortunate side effect.

From her first encounter with Spence, Jessie had been finely tuning the art of detaching her mind from her body as needed. She could now go on autopilot completely on demand. Or rather, she could until meeting the scruffy cop with dark good looks and a dimple. Damn that dimple.

Once she made that unfortunate discovery, it was impossible to work. At the rate she was buying herself from Spence, she'd blow through her mattress money in no time. With that worry looming overhead, she knew the time had come to organize and count her savings.

After counting out twenty envelopes, each containing a thousand dollars, she felt a little better about her ability to avoid work for a while. She also decided not to bother with packing and to just ask Gabe to take her shopping on the way down. She wanted clothes that covered her body. She wanted to walk into a room and not be noticed.

There was nothing in her wardrobe now that didn't command male attention.

"Jess?" Harmony tapped at her door hesitantly.

"Just a second." Jessie shoved the last envelope back under her mattress and ran to grab the door.

"Are you okay?"

"Sure… why?"

"I don't know. You just seem a little off lately."

"I'm okay, really," Jessie assured her with a friendly smile. "Sorry if I've seemed weird or something."

"Have you heard anything from Gabe lately?"

"Not lately." Jessie shrugged, mentally adding that lately could mean in the past day or two. "Have you?"

"Nah, it's been weirdly quiet. I haven't seen any heat at all, actually. It makes me a little nervous."

"Huh. That's odd. Wonder where they went... maybe they're just better at hiding."

"Or they found an informant."

"Or that," Jessie nodded carefully.

"I worry about you, Jessie."

"Shouldn't that be the other way around? I'm the older, wiser friend, after all."

"Older, yes." Harmony stuck her tongue out at Jessie and dodged her playful swat.

"Seriously, though. Vance stopped me at the market. He's worried about you, too."

"Vance is a nervous wreck because Spence is making his job nearly impossible. It's tough to protect someone who keeps throwing themselves in front of a train."

"Yes, I know." Harmony gave her a very pointed look.

Jessie wasn't sure if she should be offended or flattered. She wasn't used to people caring one way or the other about her. It was almost like having an odd little family in Vance and Harmony. She impulsively gave Harmony a quick hug.

"I promise I won't play in traffic, Mom."

"Thank you. Now, can I treat you to Ho's for dinner?"

"Sure," Jessie agreed with a grin. Ho's might be a little out of their way, but the Chinese food was good and it made Jessie giggle to eat there.

Tuesday morning dawned clear and bright. An added bonus was the absence of the oppressively sticky humidity that usually clung to St. Louis air in late August. In its place was a warm summer breeze that promised fall would be right around the corner.

She curled up in her easy chair, carefully writing a note to Spence explaining that she'd been hired for an extended stay. She occasionally paused in thought, chewing on the end of her pen absentmindedly while trying to decide the best way to keep Spence from going berserk on her when she returned.

It finally dawned on her that there would be one sure-fire way to set his mind at ease. It just so happened it would also be a good way to keep better tabs on Spence as a police informant. Gabe wouldn't like it much, but there was no reason for him to know about it ahead of time—that would probably spoil their time together.

So she scribbled out the rest of her note, shoved some bills in the envelope as a down payment on her time, and dropped the envelope in Spence's bowl. She had a little time before she was supposed to meet Gabe, but she was getting restless in her apartment.

Harmony was at class, so Jessie scrawled out a quick note to her—a condensed version of her note to Spence—before beginning the process of zigzagging her way to the little coffee shop where she'd promised to meet Gabe. Maybe she was being overly cautious, but she felt better taking an indirect route.

The coffee shop was a trendy place in the county with a decent assortment of java and gelato. It was the time of day when the crowd was a mix of housewives taking a break from errands and business people meeting outside the office. Jessie couldn't have felt more out of place if she tried.

She ordered herself a smoothie and sat in the back corner, burying her nose in a copy of the River City Gazette—more to look less conspicuous than because she was dying to catch up on current events in her fair hamlet.

She'd regretted not wearing a watch and was debating wandering around the little strip mall to kill time when at last Gabe was standing before her with an amused grin on his face.

"What?" she eyed him warily.

"I've been watching you for five minutes and you haven't turned the page once. That must be a riveting article."

"Five minutes? Why didn't you say hi, you big dork."

"I was waiting for my coffee." He held up his cup as a defense. "Besides, I like watching you."

"Voyeur."

"You're all kinds of sassy today, aren't you?"

"Just uncomfortable," she admitted, gathering up the papers she'd scattered on the table. "Can we go now?"

"Are you excited?"

"Ask me again when we're on the road."

"Do you mind if we eat dinner early?" He held his hand out to Jessie, who gratefully accepted it and followed him to the door.

"You're in charge."

"Where's your bag?"

"I didn't bring one." Jessie hoped he wouldn't be too put out with her. "I was kind of thinking I could run in somewhere along the way to buy a few things."

"Um, sure." He seemed a little confused by her request, but was intuitive enough not to ask her reasoning.

She hadn't realized just how soon he meant when he'd asked if they could eat early. Jessie was glad she'd been too nervous for lunch, because it felt like they'd barely gotten on the road when he was exiting at a little town called Eureka and pulling into an old brown building labeled "Phil's Barbeque."

It was dark and fairly empty given the early hour. There was nothing exceptional about the place, causing Jessie to wonder why Gabe was so excited about bringing her here.

"Hi folks," a lanky man with bright blue eyes greeted them from the kitchen before his face lit up in recognition. "Hey Gabe. Long time no see, sir. How you been?"

Gabe smilingly responded and the two exchanged pleasantries, the other man leaving the kitchen to join them in the empty dining room. They took a seat towards the back and Gabe ordered them a couple of beers after introducing Jessie to the man, who turned out to be the owner.

Jessie wasn't sure she was in the mood for a beer until she took a sip of the large draft set in front of her and decided immediately it was the best she'd ever had. So was the fried chicken sandwich and french fries she had for dinner. She could practically feel the calories attaching themselves to her hips as she ate, but she didn't care. It was decadently amazing.

Between the enormous beer, the sheer number of calories

consumed, and the easy conversation, Jessie felt a little dazed by the time she stood stretching in the parking lot, waiting for Gabe to unlock her door.

She had no idea where he was taking her as he hopped back on Highway 44, but she didn't really care. The sun was shining and it was a perfect 82 degrees, so they took the top off the Jeep and turned the music up. Miles of blacktop flew by beneath, taking the couple further and further from all that stood between them.

Jessie leaned back in the seat, watching the lush green hills pass by. Warmth radiated from her neck where Gabe's free hand rested lightly when he could spare it. She'd begun to wonder if he'd forgotten her request to stop for clothes when he pulled into a large outlet mall.

"We used to get our school clothes here when I was a kid. My mom swore by the place. Sorry, it's all I could think of," he offered a little helplessly.

"No, it's perfect." She straightened and stretched the kinks out of her back.

Gabe was a saint, walking patiently through each store with her as she scoured sales racks. As soon as Jessie settled on her first purchase, she went to the restroom to change.

"What you had on was fine," Gabe pointed out to her when she emerged in a new outfit.

"People were staring at me."

"Honey, people would stare at you in a gunny sack. You're beautiful."

"Thank you." Jessie flushed, looking anywhere but at him.

She happened to disagree with him about the reason for the stares. She felt much less self-conscious now that she was wearing a plain gray t-shirt and a pair of denim capris. Three stores later, she had a sufficient wardrobe for the week, along with some tennis shoes and a leather bag to use as a suitcase. Gabe watched her with amusement as she bent over in the parking lot to transfer her clothes from the large plastic bags to her new satchel.

Two minutes after they climbed back in the car, he was pulling into a gas station, pronouncing it the last chance to use the bathroom or grab a fountain soda. Although Jessie took him up on both offers, she assumed he meant last chance until they reached their destination.

But when he took a back road instead of getting on the highway, Jessie wondered if maybe he'd meant it was literally the last chance in the foreseeable future. They wound through what was surely wild country. It was lush and beautiful; there was a certain rugged air to the place. Red and black cattle dotted most of the fields. They passed so many horses Jessie wondered if they were an acceptable mode of transportation in this part of the state.

It couldn't have been more different from her world. Funny, she hadn't thought Gabe looked out of place when she'd met him. But he seemed to fit here. There was an ease about him already.

"Where are we going?" she asked for the first time.

"Nope, sorry darlin'—it's a surprise."

She pouted a bit at that but let it go when it occurred to her that a trip like this had certain obligations that came with it. Ironically, that was suddenly making her nervous. It was idiotic, really. The ice cream man didn't get nervous if someone asked him for a scoop of ice cream off the clock. It was as simple as that, she told herself as she watched fields and woods slip past her window.

For the first time since she'd met Gabe, she tried to put her finger on the pull he had over her. She'd believed Harmony when her feelings had been declared a crush, but she hadn't really stopped to think about it. The truth was—he was more of a curiosity than anything. Sure, when he touched her she didn't want him to stop. There was something reassuring about him that made her feel warm… and valued.

But a normal woman in a normal relationship would at some point want to make love with the man in her life. The closer that inevitability came, the more it felt like just another deal for Jessie.

"What has you so worked up over there?"

She hadn't realized her expression was so transparent. Her brow furrowed as she tried to think of something to say. She finally gave up and settled on the truth.

"I've never done this before."

"What?"

"This," she emphasized the word, hoping she wouldn't have to spell it out for him.

"Gone for a ride down a country road?"

She sighed heavily. Surely he was toying with her. He hadn't seemed overly obtuse before.

"Stop it," she snapped. "I'm a little nervous, okay? I've never done this because I wanted to before... there. Are you happy now?"

"Whoa, whoa... what brought this on?" he pulled the Jeep off the road onto the grass, putting it into park and turning to face her.

"Are you just supposed to pull over like this? There's no shoulder."

"It's fine, Jess; don't change the subject."

"But I don't want to talk about it."

"You're right." He nodded in agreement. "Stewing over it makes so much more sense."

"You are such a jerk."

"There's my girl." He grinned, reaching out to tap the end of her nose playfully.

She shook her head and batted his hand away, her eyes seeking something to focus on that would alleviate her humiliation.

"Hey, look at me."

She stubbornly refused, her jaw jutting defiantly.

"We're not moving until you do."

Jessie could almost hear the clock ticking away the seconds as they sat there, each stubbornly refusing to budge. Finally, she turned to look at him, one eyebrow arched as if to say "this had better be good."

"I'm glad you told me, but Jessie that's not why I brought you down here."

"So it hasn't crossed your mind?"

"Well I didn't say that... but whether we do or we don't, I brought you here so we could be together with nothing standing between us. I just want to be near you. I want to hear you laugh and I want to know that you aren't looking over your shoulder or watching the clock. I want to lose myself in you."

"Oh."

"You don't believe me, do you?"

"No."

"Is there anything I can do?"

"Start driving again."

"And then you'll believe me?" He seemed doubtful.

"No, but I really am uncomfortable sitting on the side of the road like this."

"Fine." He sighed, putting the car into gear as he spoke. "I'm declaring this a sex-free trip then."

"Excuse me?"

"If that's what it takes."

"You're bluffing."

"Am not."

"Fine." Jessie folded her arms and regarded him coolly. "It's a sex-free trip."

"I'm glad we've got that worked out." He seemed to be convincing himself of that more than her. "Now we can enjoy ourselves."

Jessie couldn't contain the bubble of laughter that burst out. There was something very endearing about how unsettled he now seemed.

"What?"

"I don't know." She laughed even harder.

Gabe cut a few side-glances her way that said he wasn't amused before a grin tugged at the corner of his mouth. She giggled even harder and after a moment, his rich laughter joined hers. It washed over and through her, warming her from the top of her head to the tips of her toes and reminding her why she placed herself in this precarious position in the first place.

Her laughter stopped abruptly when she read the sign posted at the edge of the property he appeared to be turning onto.

Honey Branch Cave. Outdoor Weddings. Outdoor Picnics. Hosta Gardens. Hosta Sales.

"It sure is a long way to drive for a picnic," she teased nervously.

"I didn't bring a picnic… I'm sorry, should I have?"

"Are we buying hostas?" she asked hopefully.

"No, we're not buying hostas." He was smiling, obviously

enjoying her discomfort.

Her mind raced. It was ludicrous to think he'd brought her here to marry her. Did he think that would convince her to leave Spence? Was this some weird act of chivalry? She wanted to climb the door like a feral cat.

"You can relax. I didn't bring you here to spring a wedding on you, either."

"Oh thank God," she breathed a sigh of relief.

"That hurt."

Jessie didn't answer; she was too taken with their surroundings. At the end of the bumpy gravel road, they emerged in an empty parking lot surrounded by wooded gardens.

"It's beautiful." She breathed the words.

"You haven't seen the best part," he assured her as he turned the Jeep up a path Jessie wasn't entirely sure he was supposed to be driving on. "I think you'll like this."

He parked in front of an honest-to-God log cabin before hopping out to grab their bags. It was small with a sharply-angled tin roof, and it looked like it had been built at least a hundred years before. It had a covered porch with a swing hanging from it and a lone window on the front of the house.

With a boyish grin, he led her through the door. The interior was as tiny as it appeared from the outside. There was a bed to the left and a fireplace to the right and not much else.

"The kitchen back there is new. It was added on after the cabin was moved to this spot."

"The cabin was moved?" Jessie had never seen such a tiny kitchen. She was relieved to see running water, though.

"It used to stand by itself further back in the woods. You know, the last family to live here had 11 kids?"

"Did they stack them on top of each other?" Jessie couldn't envision 13 people sleeping in such a tiny space, let alone functioning.

"It was a very different way of life," he acknowledged.

"Wow. No television."

"Sorry, no T.V.," he agreed.

"I wish I'd known that before I agreed to this no sex thing."

Chapter Seven

J essie could tell by Gabe's expression he wasn't sure if he was supposed to laugh or not. She certainly wasn't going to help him figure it out. She buried her nose in the bouquet of wildflowers sitting on the kitchen counter.

"They're beautiful."

"I'm glad you like them." He seemed to want to cross the distance between them but instead leaned against the doorframe.

She wanted to go to him but smiled and folded her arms across her chest.

"Right." He rubbed the back of his neck with a rueful grin.

"This is a neat place." She looked for a way to break the awkward moment. "How'd you hear about it?"

"It's kind of a convoluted story." He either didn't know where to start or was hesitant to head into that territory.

Jessie realized her head was bobbing and she couldn't really say why. She had no idea what they were supposed to do next.

"Come on." He grabbed a flashlight and tossed it to Jessie.

"Stop throwing things at me." She held her arms up defensively, causing the flashlight to bounce off her and fall to the floor.

"Generally people catch things tossed at them."

"Do I look athletic?"

Gabe opened his mouth to answer but thought better of it. He shook his head and handed her his flashlight before retrieving the fallen one.

"Just stay close to me."

"Where are we going?"

"You'll see."

"Can we explore the gardens?"

"Later. I think you'll like this."

Jessie didn't argue, allowing Gabe to lead her out the cabin's side door, her hand safely ensconced in his.

"Oh, I almost forgot the pencil." He let go of her hand to dart back inside.

"I suppose you aren't going to tell me what that's for, either," she asked when he'd rejoined her.

"You'll see soon enough."

Just out of the cabin was a path leading down a hill to what looked like the mouth of a cave. Sun filtered through the treetops. The air was muggy—apparently this region of Missouri hadn't been granted the reprieve St. Louis had. Jessie had her doubts about hiking, but anything was better than the awkwardness of the cabin.

A rickety iron gate swung loosely on its hinges at the mouth of the cave. Now that she was so close, she was certain it was a cave; presumably the namesake of this place. It was easy to overlook if you didn't know it was there.

Though Jessie acknowledged the outdoorsy thing was not her forte, it seemed reasonable to her that if there was an iron gate barring entrance to a black hole in the center of the earth, maybe it was best to heed the advice.

Apparently this basic common sense was not as obvious as Jessie thought, because Gabe blithely stepped beyond the gate and threw the light switch on. The lever looked like something you'd see in a mad scientist's lab; only it was connected to clear round light bulbs strung up like Christmas lights along the cave ceiling.

The moment Jessie stepped out of the sun and into the realm of the cave, she was instantly bathed in cool air. It felt like standing in front of an open refrigerator door.

Gabe took her hand in his again, leading her across a wooden bridge to a narrow, gravel path. The light of the forest quickly faded behind them, leaving them completely dependent on the Christmas lights above and the flashlights Gabe had provided. Jessie was immensely grateful for the warmth of his hand.

The walls were bumpy, damp and draped with minerals. Gabe stopped to shine the light around the room and at the ceiling so Jessie could see how it made the calcite deposits glow bright white.

They left the first room and moved into a new area, this one with smooth walls. Just as Broadway Oyster Bar's benches had been covered with signatures and artwork, the walls of the cave had captured a montage of human history. Jessie peered more closely at the writing, taking the time to read over 150 years of signatures.

She wondered if it was even possible to read them all—they were everywhere. After a few minutes, they started walking again but this time more slowly as they read aloud to each other the names and dates that caught their interest.

"Is that spray paint?" Jessie pointed to a particularly large signature that ran across the top of the wall.

"It's residue from an old carbide lantern. People used to hold it up the cave wall and write with it."

Jessie tried to soak it all in. She could almost see the ghosts of all the lives that came through this place.

"This cave used to be a pretty popular spot," Gabe explained as they entered a large room. He stopped and looked around as if this spot held a memory or two for him as well.

"It's amazing."

"Teachers used to bring their classes here on field trips. It's been a date destination since the late 1800s. Jesse James used it as a hideout. During Prohibition, the owners brought a piano in here and turned this room into a local hot spot."

"They brought a piano where?"

"Here. This is the piano room… look, you can see what's left of the old piano up there."

"I think I can almost picture it." She smiled a little at that. Something fluttered close to her head and she threw herself at Gabe.

"That was an Eastern Pipistrelle." He smiled, wrapping his arms around her waist. "Missouri's smallest bat. You might see one or two males roosting alone in here, but we won't disrupt the big nest at the back of the cave."

"That sounds like a good plan." She was torn between trying to salvage her dignity and snuggling closer to Gabe. The heat of his embrace stood in stark contrast to the coolness of the cave. Everything in her wanted to tuck her head under his chin and just soak in the pleasure of his touch.

But that didn't seem conducive to a sex-free week, so she reluctantly pulled herself away and forged ahead. Offshoots promising other caverns to be explored dotted the way on either side of them. But they also looked small and dark and dirty and that was more dedication than Jessie felt at the moment.

The next room they came to was dominated by a large white cross set in a natural clay shelf on the right. It felt huge and imposing in the enclosed space. Jessie couldn't explain the emotions that washed over her at the sight of it, except maybe she'd spent a little too much time listening to the soundtrack of Jesus Christ Superstar. She couldn't resist reaching up to reverently touch the white wood, feeling silly even as she did.

"The KKK used to meet in this room. It's part of the cave's history most people aren't so proud of."

"So this is a Klan cross?" Jesse jumped back as if flames now lapped at the wood.

"Most likely," he admitted. "Sorry."

"How sad." She frowned at the cross, off-handedly wondering how one symbol could mean so many different things to so many different people.

"Is this the end of the cave?" Jessie pointed to what seemed to be a dead-end.

"For most. There's actually a shelf there that, if you were willing to crawl on your belly through the bats' nest, would loop you back around to a waterfall on the other end of the property."

"Good to know." She nodded, not sure what else to say.

"Look over here... this is the crown jewel of the cave."

"What's that?" She obligingly turned and followed the direction he was pointing. The inscription was simple, but it leapt out at her just the same. "Jesse James 1868" was carved into an overhang. She reached her fingers up warily to touch it. She knew little of the outlaw's life, but it was cool to think he'd once stood exactly where she did now.

"His actual signature is the big carbide one that sprawls over the entire overhang. A historian scrawled this in after she'd verified it."

Jessie stood back a little and shined her light on the area. The real signature was hard to make out—other than swirls of black carbide covered by dozens of other signatures.

"I like this place." Jessie wrapped her arms around herself for warmth, surveying the room they now stood in. "Thank you for bringing me here."

"Jesse James was always my hero," Gabe admitted. "This cave is one of my favorite places in this world. It's so... removed from it all."

"You know Jesse James was a bad guy, right? I mean, I wasn't exactly a straight-A student, but I do remember that much."

"I prefer to think of him as a victim of circumstance." Gabe moved to stand behind her, wrapping her up in his warmth as he spoke.

"How's that?" She asked absentmindedly, sinking back into him as she did.

"He was just a country boy with the misfortune of living in a border state during the Civil War."

"So you subscribe to the Robin Hood theory?" Jessie seemed to recall there was a great debate over whether James was a hero of his time or just a thug.

"No, he kept the money for himself. But I don't think he would have been an outlaw if his family farm hadn't been attacked by a Union militia when he was sixteen. They killed his brother, maimed his mama and beat Jesse. I think something inside him snapped that day."

"That's so young," Jessie murmured, thinking of the twists her own life had taken at a tender age.

"I don't know. I just always thought he was swept up in something bigger than himself and did the best he could to survive under the circumstances."

"I can identify with that." Jessie curled her arm around Gabe's, turning her head against his arm. A lifetime's worth of memories danced across her mind. They were layered with images of a man she didn't know, ripped from his boyhood into a life he didn't choose, spray-painting his name on a cave wall so someone might remember him when he was gone.

Jessie couldn't say why the need to connect with another human being overtook her just then. Maybe she needed to know that her chance wasn't gone. Maybe she wanted to know what it felt like to share something as intimate as a kiss with this man in this moment.

Whatever drove her, she found herself turning in his embrace. She looked up at him, her eyes trying to read his in the dim light. She leaned towards him, then away, her mind unsure of the choice her body seemed to have already made.

"Jessie." His voice was torn.

The torment in his voice, the expression on his face, each ragged breath... she knew right then that no one had ever seen her as clearly as he did. She'd been a nuisance, a burden on the state, a prize to be had and an object of desire. In this timeless instant, she was a woman. Nothing more, nothing less.

That was the thought burning on her brain when she wound her fingers through his hair and hungrily sought his mouth with her own. He met her kiss hesitantly at first, but she could feel the exact moment his last reservation was released.

There was nothing frantic in his touch. Instead, his kisses were deep and thorough, as if he was slowly drawing her into his soul and robbing her of all her senses. Or maybe it was a heightening of the senses she was experiencing. Maybe she was feeling everything so much that there was no buffer in between the feelings; they were blending together like a finger painting. Strong strokes of brilliant color overlapped each other, creating something altogether different and new.

As his mouth drove her slowly insane, his hands caressed and tormented and fanned the fire that was rapidly becoming an inferno. Never in her life had she wanted anything as badly as she now wanted more of him. Only him.

She ripped his t-shirt off, eager to feel more of his skin against her own. Her shirt landed beside his on the floor of gravel and clay. And then they were back in each other's arms, their bodies moving to a shared rhythm as they explored the expanse of newly discovered skin.

If rational thought tried to rear its ugly head, Jessie shoved it ruthlessly aside. She wanted no part of anything save this delicious vortex of feeling. Beads of sweat dotted their skin despite the cool air that enveloped them.

They shifted positions and Jessie found herself with her back to the cave wall, her legs wrapped around Gabe's waist and her arms wrapped around his neck, as if she could completely surround him with her love.

She wanted this to last forever. She didn't think she could survive one more moment of the sweet torment. She couldn't explain the tears that flowed freely.

When it was over, he covered her neck with kisses as he murmured her name again and again. And still she cried.

"I'm sorry," she apologized, wiping her eyes as she tried to sort out her clothes.

"I hope they're good tears." He kissed her temple before plucking his shirt up to study it with dismay.

"You know, there are a few technical difficulties with this whole cave thing," she acknowledged. Her own clothes were filthy. "And there's no shower, is there?"

"Nope. But never fear... we have something even better."

"I find it very difficult to believe that there is anything better than a shower at the moment."

"Come on, I'll show you." He reached his hand out to take hers. She followed, her mind a jumble as she tried to sort out what just happened and take in the cave on their way out.

"Hey, wait a second." She dug her heels in when something caught her eye in a corridor near the entrance. "Look—it's my initials. JJ 1885."

"Some people say that Jesse James engraved that too. Only he supposedly died in 1882."

"You say that like you don't believe he did."

"I have it on pretty good authority that there might be some validity to the claims that he staged his death."

"What authority is that?"

"Can we talk about it while we're getting cleaned up?"

"Good point." Jessie relented and followed him out of the cave. As they stepped out of the shadow of their otherworld, the sun and the humidity instantly greeted them. It had cooled a little while they were underground, but it was still markedly warmer than their bodies were used to at the moment.

The heat made the clay drying on their bodies and clothes feel that much more miserable. They stopped by the cabin for Gabe to snag a couple of robes, whose presence made Jessie think he had put quite a bit of thought into this week.

As she followed him down the path from the cabin, she took in the beauty of her surroundings. The hostas were amazing—fitting nicely into the woods around them. Stone pathways and waterfalls and a gazebo dotted the way, adding to the Eden-esque quality of this place.

They came to a stop in front of a pool unlike any Jessie had ever seen. Surrounded by stone, it was two large circles with a wooden bridge crossing the point where the circles intersected. The patio around it was a breathtaking garden in its own right. The water had an opaque quality that somehow enhanced the beauty of it all. It beckoned her to sink down into its warmth, washing the grime of the cave away.

"Are you sure it's okay for us to be doing this?"

"Absolutely." He flashed his dimple at her in a way that made her think the answer should really have been "Absolutely not."

Truth be told, she didn't care if she should be skinny dipping in this pool in the middle of the woods with him or not. All that really mattered was the fact that she was. It was glorious and she was free and there was no one watching the door of the cabin to be sure she returned by curfew.

With a wicked grin, she splashed him before diving under the water so he couldn't retaliate. He chuckled and dove after her. They played and splashed as the sun sank in the horizon.

"That's amazing." She paused to admire the sky. It was like none she'd ever seen before. The colors were brighter, the expanse bigger.

"You forget how beautiful it is when you're away. Then you come back and think 'how did I ever leave a sky like that?'"

"I'm not going to ruin the moment by asking you about your past." She pulled him to her, loving the feel of his slick wet skin against hers. "But I do still want to hear about Jesse James. You promised me."

He answered with a mischievous smile and a kiss. It was there, beneath the first stars of the evening with the woods thriving with life around them and the gentle warm water lapping at their skin, Jessie made love to a man for the second time in her life.

Memories of pain and degradation might have crept back into the corners of her mind if she had let them, but she guarded fiercely against anything other than Gabe and this place filling her senses. Nothing else existed. Not tonight.

Chapter Eight

So much for the no sex thing, eh?" Jessie observed as they devoured their microwaved dinner.

"Sorry about that." He stopped eating to look sheepish.

"Don't be. I was just teasing. I'm sorry," she quickly reassured him.

"No, I am. I don't want you to think I'm just talk. I really meant what I said… There's just something about you that makes me forget my best intentions."

"I'll take that as a compliment."

"It is."

"It's not like I thought it would be."

"How so?" He seemed mildly concerned.

"It's better. Not like… never mind."

"Aw, now, you can't do that to a man. Not like what?"

"Work," she finally finished weakly, afraid to meet his eye.

"That's a relief." There was a smile in his voice as he tipped her chin up with his finger. "Don't crawl back in your shell now. I can't say I want to dwell on your past, but we can't have much of a relationship if you're afraid to remind me who you really are."

"Is this a relationship?"

"An odd one, but yes… why, don't you think it is?"

"Harmony had to tell me I was attracted to you and not having a stroke. I'm not the person to ask in this situation."

"You thought you were having a stroke?" He chuckled. "I've never had that kind of effect on a woman."

Jessie blushed in response and concentrated on her food.

"Wasn't there someone before… well, before," he finished awkwardly.

"No fair. You know way more about me than I know about you.

You tell me something first."

"What is this, truth or dare?"

"If that's what it takes to pry some information out of you."

"That could be fun."

"Shut up and talk," Jessie snapped.

"That might be difficult."

"I hate you, Gabe Adams. You know that?"

"I love you too, Jessie girl." He said the words jokingly, but the moment they were out silence fell like an anvil. The only movement in the room was blinking for a full sixty seconds.

Jessie opened her mouth to say something in return, but had no clue what that should be, so she closed her mouth again.

"So you want to know something about me?" Gabe was the first to recover. "Let's see... I used to be in the army. I have no idea how I've managed to not be called up again in the past seven years. I'm guessing my Captain has pulled some strings because of the case we're working on."

"Army, huh?" Jessie could see that. She bet he was cute in his uniform.

"Yep."

"Ever been married?"

"Once."

"What happened?"

"She was a lot prettier on the outside than she was on the in. She and Riley Brunner are friends, actually."

"Ah. Ajax-girl... should I be worried? I've been so careful not to turn into a walking disease..."

"No." He chuckled ruefully. "You don't need to be worried."

"Sorry. Go on."

"I'm not sure if I want to go on."

"Don't pout," she admonished, moving to gather their dishes as she spoke.

"I'm not pouting."

"Don't worry—it's a very masculine pout. But it's still a pout."

"You're kind of a pain in the ass, you know that?"

"If you tell me her name, I'll find her and beat her up for you.

Someone probably should if she's dumb enough to let you go. Other than that, I don't know what to say. I don't like the thought of you belonging to someone else before me," she admitted.

He choked on his water.

"Don't be like that. That's different."

"How so?" He tilted his head and furrowed his brow in thought.

"I didn't choose to belong to anyone."

"Then how did you wind up in Spence's clutches?"

Jessie wasn't sure she wanted to delve into her sordid past. It would ruin their lovely night. She shrugged, trying to decide what best to say. "The state gives you the boot on your eighteenth birthday. I didn't have anywhere to go but the Eads Bridge. I ran into Spence outside a soup kitchen down on Washington. He offered me a place to stay. He was a good looking guy and seemed nice enough...."

Gabe's expression was dark. Jessie worried that she'd ruined their night, but she'd come this far so she took a deep breath and plunged ahead.

"You know, normally a virgin is worth big money on the street. So the fact that Spence took that for himself instead of taking the free money says a lot."

"So, there was no one in high school... "

"I told you I've never done this because I wanted to before."

"I guess I didn't believe you."

"I don't want to talk about Spence." A shudder ran down the length of Jessie's spine.

"You know what? I don't either." He stood and stretched.

"Tell me about your family." Jessie crawled under the covers of the bed, snuggling up with her pillow and looking expectantly at Gabe.

"I have one."

"Mom and Dad?"

"Mom passed away three years ago. Dad's still actively disapproving of my life choices."

"Brothers? Sisters?"

"One older sister. A little bossy, but she means well and would do anything for me."

Jessie wondered if his sister was the one who prepared the cabin for them. She might never tell Gabe this, but she wanted to meet his father and sister. She wished she was the kind of woman a man could take home to his family. She'd never cared about that kind of thing before.

"Hey, what's with the sad eyes?" He reached out to stroke her cheek.

"Not sad," she lied. "I like hearing about your family."

"You won't think that when you meet them," he promised. "They're a colossal pain."

"Meet them?" Her heart soared.

"Sure. But not this week. This week is ours."

Jessie didn't blame him for stalling. The fact that he had mentioned it at all meant something.

"What about you?"

"What about me?"

"Do you have parents?"

"I'm sure I did at some point." She shrugged nonchalantly. "I don't really remember them, though. Those first few years were a little hazy…. I mean, I kind of remember flashes of the house I lived in with my mother. Every now and then, I'll walk past someone who smells like she did. Roses. Well, that fake rose smell anyway."

"You don't remember her?"

"Not really. Just a dingy brown couch and rust colored shag carpeting in the house where we lived." Jessie reached back into the hidden crevices in her mind. "I do remember her hands. They were so delicate. I thought she was a fairy princess because her hands were so delicate."

"How old were you when you last saw her?"

"I was about five when she went away. A woman with a nice smile and a blue business suit came and took me to live with another family. There was always another family after that—or a group home."

Gabe paused, his gaze breaking away from hers. "Do you know what happened to her?"

"Someone told me that she died. I don't know how. I never

asked. I guess I figured it didn't matter so much how she got there."

"I'm so sorry." At that, he pulled her into his arms. Jessie closed her eyes and simply enjoyed the way it felt to have a pair of strong arms wrapped around her because they wanted to protect rather than possess her. "You really got the shaft in life, didn't you?"

"Worrying about what's fair seems like a waste of time. I try to roll with it and move on."

"While I agree with you, I'm still going to be angry on your behalf."

"Go for it." Jessie smiled a little. She liked someone being angry on her behalf.

"Why does that feel like a minor victory?"

"What?"

"You're going to let me care what happened to you." He grinned.

"I can't control what you care about." She tried to sound disinterested.

"Whatever. I'm winning you over."

"Why on earth would you want to?"

"Because you're the most beautiful, fascinating woman I've ever met. Because I'm a better person when I'm around you. And because you make me laugh."

"I like your laugh." Jessie chose not to remind him that she was the very definition of used goods.

"How did we get so serious all of a sudden?"

"It's your fault. You were trying to dodge telling me more about Jesse James."

"Oh, is that what happened?"

Jessie nodded primly.

"Then please allow me to atone for my sins." He nuzzled her neck, his fingers trailed down her ribs to the small of her waist.

"That's not what I meant," she protested half-heartedly. "I want to hear about Jesse James. Come on, you promised."

"Did I?" He straightened, a mischievous glint in his eye. "I wouldn't want to break a promise."

He rolled onto his back, tucking Jessie against his side as he decided where to begin. With a deep breath, he launched into the known history of one of America's most notorious outlaws. Even the basics facts, like that he was born in 1847 in Clay County, Missouri sounded better when they were delivered by his deep, rich voice.

She tossed one leg over his and absentmindedly traced lazy circles on his washboard stomach as she listened to him spin a tale of a confused and angry young boy, following his older brother into the ranks of Will Quantrill's raiders in the Civil War. Frank was the ruthless one; Jesse was the one that captured the imagination of dime novelists. Maybe because he seemed to regret hurting others. Maybe because he was young and good-looking.

He rattled off obscure facts and family trees long into the night. Occasionally the narrative would be broken up by playful banter or the random kiss. He never did get around to telling her his theories on James' staged death, and as she drifted off to sleep, she promised herself she'd remember to ask him in the morning.

Only the tender rays of dawn brought a lazy bought of lovemaking, not more discussions about a bygone bandit. When they were up and dressed, they took off to explore the gardens. Gabe remembered they never signed their names on the cave walls, so that was their next stop. Jessie signed her name under the initials assumed to belong to James. It just seemed fitting.

After another quick swim in the pool, they ate a lunch of cheese and crackers with a bottle of Missouri wine before whiling away the afternoon sprawled on the bed, talking about anything and everything.

She told him about Harmony being the smartest woman she'd ever met and about the friendship she'd formed with Vance over the years. Though more than five years her junior, he had lately assumed the role of her protector. They talked about Dan and what a good guy he was. Gabe told her about the guys at work: which ones were jerks and which ones were decent.

Under normal circumstances, Jessie would have been getting restless by the second night. As it was, there was still so much to learn about him. And there was always his laugh, which seemed to come much more readily in their current setting. She couldn't get enough of that laugh.

For someone who'd never spent more than the random school fieldtrip away from the city, she found her new surroundings both fascinating and peaceful. The sky at night was black velvet, something that could never be achieved with the lights from the city interfering. The stars sparkled merrily on their inky backdrop. On their second night in the cabin, they curled up in the porch swing and admired the stars as they continued to share anything that came to mind.

The next morning brought with it unwelcome reminders that their time at the cabin was finite. This would be their last full day together. They ate a breakfast of fresh fruit and took a meandering walk in the gardens before he took her on a longer trek to see the old mill. Of course, he knew the history of that, too. It was ever more obvious to Jessie he'd brought her to his home.

It was also evermore obvious to Jessie that she didn't want to go back to St. Louis. She liked strolling down a dirt road with her hand in his. But as the day crept on, it became harder to ignore the thought worming its way to the front of her mind. Gabe was going to be furious with her when he found out what she had asked Spence for.

There probably wasn't any way to make him understand why she felt the need to take care of this herself. He'd probably spout all kinds of reasons why she should let him rescue her. Maybe he'd be right—she was crazy.

But something deep in her bones longed to be the one that set her life straight. Like maybe if she could do this, then she'd really be the kind of woman he could love and she wouldn't be just a fascination.

But that wasn't something she could put into words, so it did her no good when she finally broke down and told Gabe what she planned to do. She fully expected him to yell, to argue his point. She wasn't prepared for the stony expression that instantly dropped over his face. He started to speak but the words couldn't seem to find their way beyond his throat. With a pained expression and a terse shake of the head, he stormed out of the cabin.

"Gabe," she called, taking off after him once she'd regained her wits. "Gabe, don't just walk out on me like that."

"No." He kept walking.

"Gabe! Stop!" Her voice left little room for disagreement.

"No." He shook his head as he stopped. "No. You aren't going to do this."

"Why not? You know it's the best way to find out what the hell is going on and end this thing."

"Because it's hard enough thinking about the reality of what you do, but not him, Jess. Not him."

On some level, Jessie understood that. Johns came and went. They got a few minutes of her life and then she never saw them again. Spence was different.

"I don't want to do this." She closed her eyes, unable to bear the expression on his face as he turned to her.

"Then don't." His voice was soft, pleading. "I'll hide you here. No one will find you."

"I can't live my entire life in a remote cave, babe. As long as I'm alive, he won't let me go."

"Then we'll fake your death. It's worked before. Jessie, please just don't go through with this."

"If everything works out like I hope, then I'll have what you need on him in no time. Then he'll be in jail and I'll be free. You know it's the fastest and easiest way to end this—if your judgment wasn't clouded, you'd see that."

"But if he realizes what you're up to, he'll kill you."

"And I'll still be free."

"Don't... don't say that." He rolled his head as if he could jar that thought loose by doing so. Jessie could hear the tears in his voice and it ripped out a piece of her soul to know she'd caused him pain.

"He won't catch me. I've been tap dancing around Spence for a lot of years. I'll be fine. And I'm sure Vance'll look out for me."

"I don't like this at all." His voice said he was bending though he still shook his head no.

"Please understand why I have to do this." She held her arms open to him.

"I can't stomach the thought of his hands on you."

"I won't let him touch me," she promised.

"How are you going to work that one?"

"I have no idea, but I'll think of something. I'll do anything to take that look off your face."

"I'll never forgive myself if something happens to you." He crossed the distance between them and scooped her into his arms. She kissed his eyes, his cheeks, his forehead before he caught her mouth with his own. There was a greed in his touch she hadn't felt before. To be fair, there was a certain amount of greed in her response.

They moved past their first real fight in the old-fashioned way, and spent the rest of the evening intertwined on the porch swing, wrapped in each other and a quilt. The conversation centered mostly on how they could incapacitate Spence enough he wouldn't be a threat to Jessie, but would still be able to lead them to the men Gabe had spent years trying to catch.

The later it was, the sillier the suggestions got. At one point Jessie might have suggested paying someone to throw a fastball at just the right spot, but tossed the idea aside because she thought it would be too small a target to hit from a distance.

It was her last night to sleep curled up at his side. She wanted to stay awake, to relish every breath he took, but sleep claimed her despite her intentions. The rays of sunlight that danced through their window in the morning seemed to taunt her.

She didn't want to go. Everything in her cried out to just run away. As they visited the cave one last time, she ran her fingers almost lovingly over the initials she'd decided with certainty were Jesse's.

"How'd he do it?"

"Fake his death? In the usual way. Paid a friend to pretend shoot him, buried some poor schmuck who looked enough like him to pass."

"He killed someone in his place?" Jessie didn't like that idea; it marred the romanticized version she had dancing through her head already.

"If I remember the story correctly, the guy beat the crap out of his wife and kids on a regular basis. Jesse anonymously gave them a decent sum of money in his place."

"So it worked out, then."

"For everyone but the schmuck, yes, it worked out quite well."

"You never told me how you know all of this."

"Local lore has it that Jesse moved to the Ozark Mountains and started a new life. He fell head-over-heels in love with the daughter of the family that owned this property at the time. Her daddy didn't trust the mysterious stranger that seemed to drop out of nowhere, so he refused to let them marry. So, she moved in with him."

"Why didn't she just marry him against her father's wishes?"

"Who knows? I guess she told herself she wasn't disobeying him that way." Gabe shrugged.

"There's a loophole if I ever saw one."

"Well, they had a daughter together. Her daddy was furious. He never did claim her after that. Never saw his granddaughter."

"That's so sad."

"Rumor has it Jesse and his new love were happy together. It's supposed to be a romantic story."

"Unless you're his first wife left to raise his kids with no money and the stigma of being an outlaw's wife."

"Yeah. Unless you're her."

Chapter Nine

The ride back went too quickly. Jessie could feel a weight settling over her more with each passing mile. She'd gone her whole life without any real connection to another human being. Now she didn't want to let her connection with Gabe go. It would be so hard being near him but not able to touch him, to laugh with him.

"Back to the fishbowl," she sighed, blinking back tears as they crossed the St. Louis County line. It wouldn't be long now until they parted ways.

"We'll find ways to communicate," he promised. "And I'll always be around. If you get into trouble or decide you want out, just say the word."

"I'll be okay. I just don't want to go is all."

"Then don't."

"Gabe, not again. Please?"

He pulled the Jeep into a Metrolink parking lot, shifting in his seat to face her once they were stopped. "I don't want to let you out of this car."

"You know I'm crazy about you... right?" She swallowed hard, considering her next words. "You... you're... you're really important to me."

"Wow, don't completely overwhelm me with your flowery words of love there, babe."

"Shut up. You are such a jerk."

"That's more like it." He grinned before growing serious. "You're pretty important to me, too. Please be careful."

There were a thousand things Jessie wanted to say to him. They swirled around inside her, straining to be free. None of them seemed quite able to string together into a coherent sentence that could work

its way past her defensive barriers, though. All that finally came out
was a flat "I'll be careful" as her hand sought the door handle. "See
you around."

"Damn it, Jessie," he growled, exploding from the car to cover
the distance between them. He pulled her to him, claiming her
mouth as his hands cupped her face. "Don't shut me out now."

Her eyes locked with his, saying all the things her voice could
not. She allowed her hands to follow a path of their own volition up
his arms to cup his face as he had hers, the scruff of his jaw standing
in stark contrast to the silken hair that brushed her fingertips. She
wanted to memorize each muscle along the way, each sensation she
experienced with him so close.

She gave him one last lingering kiss before stepping back.

"See you around."

He nodded, kissing the back of her hand before releasing her.
Jessie didn't look back—she didn't trust herself to move forward
again if she did. She caught a glimpse of him leaning against the Jeep
as the light rail pulled away from the station.

She'd left her bags in his Jeep intentionally. She didn't want to
explain where the clothes came from when she returned. Now that
the parting was behind her, returning to Spence loomed large on the
horizon.

He was waiting for her when she walked through the door of
her apartment. One look at Harmony's puffy eyes told Jessie she
wouldn't be happy with what was about to unfold. Despite Spence's
warning otherwise, Harmony immediately flew into Jessie's arms.

"I'm sorry," Jessie whispered into Harmony's ear. "I didn't mean
to make life harder for you."

"I'm going to miss you." Harmony started crying again.

"Does that mean your answer is yes?" Jessie looked to Spence in
time to see his head nod ever so slightly. Her stomach clenched with
nerves even as she breathed a sigh of relief. The thought hadn't
occurred to her before that moment that he could have said no.
"Thank you."

"You wanted this?" Harmony stared at her with a look of horror
and betrayal.

"I can't work the streets forever, baby girl. I'd like to move on while there's still something left of me."

"But Jessie…" Harmony's voice trailed off.

"I should probably go now. I'll see you at the gym tomorrow, okay?"

"Will you get up without me there?"

"I'll set an alarm," Jessie promised solemnly before turning her attention to Spence. "Just give me a second to gather a few things."

"We've already moved your things for you."

"Oh." Jessie paled a little. "Can I take one last look at my room?"

Spence motioned with his hand, granting her permission. She tried not to bolt to the room, nearly weeping with relief to see her bed had been left as it was. She had no idea how she'd get her money out from under the mattress now, but at least the bed was still there. She quickly crossed the room to run her hand under the mattress to reassure herself the envelopes were still there.

Only they weren't. Her heart flew to her throat; a dull roar filled her ears. She might have fainted right then and there but Spence's voice calling her from the other room brought her back to this moment.

She straightened and tried to look calm by the time she reappeared in the living room. With each step, the reality settled over her that she was getting ready to leave her home of 14 years. She would miss her little apartment and the vibrancy of Cherokee now that she'd be living in Spence's loft with him. Everything had happened so quickly, she hadn't had a chance to do all of the "one lasts" she'd planned to.

Spence was standing at the door waiting for her. Harmony had retreated to the kitchen, though Jessie could feel her hurt stare as Jessie took one last look around her home before accepting Spence's hand and following him down the stairs to the waiting Mercedes.

Her hand felt chilly in his; it held none of the warmth that radiated from Gabe's touch. He was long and lanky with Mediterranean coloring and cool green eyes. He always wore tailored suites. Most women who met him looked twice. A good portion of those quickly looked away when further scrutiny revealed that there was no soul behind those beautiful eyes.

Jessie had to admit to at least herself that she was more than a little scared. Like a lamb being led to slaughter, she followed him dutifully across the sidewalk to the waiting car.

Then everything happened so quickly it felt like Jessie stepped out of reality and into a dream. It wasn't until later, as she sat in the waiting room of the hospital covered in blood that she began to process the scene that had unfolded before her.

Like characters from a Tarantino movie, two men had boldly walked up to Spence in the middle of the street, one yanking him away from her while the other swung the baseball bat. The sound of bone cracking was unmistakable when the first swing connected with his shin. The second swing was the one that broke his nose and the reason for the blood that spattered all over Jessie.

Just as quickly as they arrived, they were gone. Vance chased them for a block before returning to help Spence. Together, he and Jessie shoved Spence into the Mercedes. Jessie ripped a strip of cloth from her shirt to stem the flow of blood from Spence's nose. She held his head in her lap and spoke in soothing tones as he groaned in pain.

The man made her stomach roil, but she didn't like seeing another human in pain. Had she heard about this after the fact, she would have snickered a little. Witnessing it firsthand was another story altogether.

When they pulled into the Alexian Brothers Hospital, Vance slammed the car into park and was there with lightning speed to help Jessie get Spence out of the car. Together, they got him in the doors. The blood made it look worse than it was, but helped get the attention of the emergency room staff. Spence was whisked away, leaving Vance and Jessie to face a glowering check-in attendant.

"I'm going to park the car. I'll be right back," Vance muttered and was gone, leaving Jessie alone in the face of the woman's disapproval.

She was halfway through the paperwork when Vance reappeared, relieving Jessie of the duty so she could go splash some cold water on her face. The bathroom mirror was not kind. If she hadn't been so shell shocked, she'd have been embarrassed to leave the bathroom. As it was, she just sort of wandered in a daze.

Until she found herself sitting in the waiting room, reliving that horrible instant over and over in her head and wondering if it was a result of Spence's dealings—or if it had been done to protect her.

The hospital called the police. It didn't take long for a couple of uniforms to show up to get their statement. Which, of course, was rehearsed and very noncommittal. Gabe was right on their heels, trying to look unconcerned as his eyes scoured Jessie for any sign of injury.

"Were you harmed, ma'am?" he finally interjected when it appeared no one else was going to ask.

"No, sir." She smiled a little. "They didn't touch me."

He seemed relieved at that. His entire reaction set Jessie's mind at ease that Spence wasn't suffering on her behalf. That is, until she caught the look that flickered between Gabe and Vance.

She didn't know if she was impressed, terrified or sickened by the efficiency with which they had rendered Spence unable to perform. By all accounts, it looked like a warning from the mob. If Jessie hadn't seen the look, she would have never known otherwise.

The guilt of knowing Spence had in fact been hurt so badly in the name of protecting her made it easier to pretend to dote on him on the ride home. Once his leg had been set and his nose taped, he'd been released into their care. The police weren't a problem for them, no doubt thanks to Gabe.

Together, Vance and Jessie got him up the stairs and into his room. Jessie cleaned him and helped him into his pajamas while Vance unloaded her things.

"I'm so glad I have you with me." Spence patted her hand affectionately once she'd tucked him into bed.

Jessie couldn't help but smile; the guy had enough pain medicine in him to tranquilize an elephant and it was making him loopy.

"I know you are," she told him. "Now get some sleep. It's been a long evening."

With Spence out, she refused to do anything else until she had a shower. The clothes she wore were tossed in the trash on her way by. She stood in the steamy water so long her skin turned pink, thinking about all that had happened and wondering what she was going to do with her entire life's savings gone.

"Jessie." Vance tapped at the door. "Are you okay in there?"

"Yeah, sure. Be right out." Jessie reluctantly turned off the shower and wrapped herself in a towel.

"I put your clothes in your room and I have a beer with your name on it out on the balcony."

"You're my hero." Jessie smiled, waiting for Vance to walk away before darting down the hall to the room she'd been given. She had no illusions that she'd been given her own room out of respect. She had her own room for the evenings Spence brought home diversions. The why didn't matter—she was just happy for what was.

She quickly dressed in cotton pajamas and scurried out to meet Vance on the balcony. He acknowledged her presence with his eyes then went back to watching the street below.

"I like what they've done with the Washington loft district," he commented.

"It is nice."

"You've had a busy day."

Jessie nodded at that. To think, she'd woken up this morning wrapped around Gabe in the middle of the woods. When she'd seen him this afternoon, they'd pretended not to know one another. And there was the whole mess with seeing her boss get his leg broken to keep him from feeling amorous, too.

"I don't suppose you have any idea why Spence was jumped today." She finally decided how to broach the subject.

"Looks like a rumor somehow got started about him possibly skimming cash off from his associates. That was a warning shot. You know, I heard it around anyway."

"Is he?"

Vance answered with a look that said she was stupid to ask that question. Stupid because the answer was obviously yes or stupid because it was obviously no?

"Thank you." She studied his profile. Sometimes it was hard to remember that he was only twenty-five. Maybe it was his sheer size, maybe just his calm demeanor.

"I don't like what you've got yourself mixed up in, but I'll do what I can to keep you from getting yourself killed."

"You probably know enough about everything to end all of this right now," Jessie blurted as soon as the thought occurred to her.

"But I don't think Gabe has dreamy-enough eyes to risk my life over it."

"I'm not risking my life over some guy's eyes," Jessie snapped. If she had to classify one thing about him worth risking her life over, it was probably his laugh. Although, he did have nice eyes; they tended to change from golden to warm brown depending on his mood.

"Sure." Vance looked over at Jessie with a disgusted snort.

"I'm not having this discussion with you right now."

"Look, just be careful. You've stayed with Spence for 14 years because you were scared of what he'd do to you if you left. That's nothing compared to the guys you're tangling with now."

"I'm not tangling with anybody. Not really."

"You just keep telling yourself that, sugar, and see how it works out for you."

"I need to be done, Vance. I just want to live before I die."

"Yeah, I know." His tone softened. "Look, I'd better go get some sleep while I can. Jason'll be outside the front door all night if you need anything. Try to have Spence up and coherent by four. He has guests coming for drinks."

"Drinks?"

"Don't worry; the staff will arrive in plenty of time to clean the place up."

Jessie merely nodded. She had never realized how different Spence's world was from her own. She wondered if it had always been that way, or if it was just one more byproduct of his new acquaintances.

It took her a while to fall asleep that night. She lay there long into the darkness, curled around her pillow as her mind ran wild. She missed Gabe so much the longing twisted itself around her insides. When sleep did finally stake its claim, her dreams were dark and turbulent.

While she did manage to wake up in time to meet Harmony as promised, Jessie felt like she could barely drag herself through the routine. What's worse, Jessie found herself unsure what to say to Harmony. Their easy camaraderie was gone and she didn't know how to fix that. Her friend seemed to defrost a bit towards the end of their time together, giving Jessie hope that time would heal the rift between them.

When she arrived back at the loft, Spence was calling for her from his room. Despite his complaints that his leg and face were throbbing, she denied him another dose of pain relief for fear he'd be passed out when his guests arrived. Instead, she concentrated on getting him ready despite the groping hands forever hindering her progress.

When she had him dressed and as presentable as he could be under the circumstances, she got him settled on the couch in front of the television and turned her attention to her own wardrobe. Her progress was interrupted by a knock at the door.

"Plan to do some light reading?" Vance questioned from her doorway. Jessie paused mid-mascara stroke to cut her eyes his way.

"What are you talking about?"

"A courier just delivered this." He held a worn book out.

"Oh. That." Jessie's mind scrambled for an explanation. One glance at the title told her who it was from. "I requested it from a used book store this morning while I was out. I didn't expect it to be delivered so quickly."

Vance merely arched an eyebrow as if he didn't believe a word she was saying, laying the book on the foot of her bed before striding out of the room. She forced herself to finish putting on her makeup before curling up in a corner chair with the book in her lap.

She lovingly ran her fingers along the leather binding, re-reading the title with a small smile. He'd sent her a book about the life and death of Jesse James. When she opened it, she instantly noticed the writing on the first page. "If found, return to 9722 Gravois Road, Apt 35D, St. Louis, MO 61154."

Jessie furrowed her brow. The ZIP code didn't seem right. The writing didn't fit, either. It looked too new and crisp for such worn paper. Gabe was trying to tell her something. Until she had more to go on, she contented herself to thumb through the comfortable pages.

She was feeling good about things by the time Vance announced their company had arrived. One look at the entourage in Spence's living room told her she'd been entirely wrong in her assumptions about who he was working with. Vance had been right—she was in way over her head.

Chapter Ten

S ometimes the world changes and although you know it, you forget to take that into account. This is the thought that ran through Jessie's brain as she registered the fact that the family Gabe was after was not Italian, but Bosnian.

She supposed it shouldn't matter. It wasn't as if the Italians were pussycats or anything. But they seemed to have a certain restraint to them the Bosnians weren't known for.

St. Louis hadn't been exactly an ethnically diverse town when she was growing up. She was happy that had changed. Her beloved Cherokee Street was often referred to as Little Mexico. And in the '90s, a flood of Bosnian refugees to South St. Louis brought new life to a dying town. Little Bosnia was a flourishing and vibrant community.

But with good often comes bad, and the organized crime syndicates born in the war-torn Eastern Bloc were hardened to say the least. Spence was a fool to have messed with them. She knew now why the police weren't concerned about catching Spence; they were just hoping he'd lead them to the boss before he got himself killed. It was a matter of when, not if.

And now they knew her face. She understood what Gabe was telling her with the book, why he'd been so insistent on whisking her away.

Warning bells sounded in her head as the leader of the group leveled his gaze on her. His broad head and close buzz cut gave him a pit bull look. The scar on his left eye made her think he'd once been in danger of losing it. Now the orb stood lifeless in its socket. The effect was chilling. She kept her expression bland and tried to be nothing more than an ornament at Spence's side.

"You have a new girl?" The man nodded towards Jessie. "I'd

have thought you'd be too busy with other concerns right now to be acquiring new toys. Even ones with legs like a thoroughbred."

"Jessie here has been one of my girls since the early days." Spence patted her as if she were indeed a horse. "Turns out she makes a pretty nurse, too."

Jessie wasn't sure how to respond to that, so she smiled and rose to refill drinks. Spence dismissed her as she set the decanter down, dashing her hopes of gleaning anything valuable from the visit. With one last glance at the three men in a desperate attempt to commit their faces to memory, she excused herself to her room where she jotted down any distinguishing characteristics she could remember on a tissue.

Even as she did so, she felt like a fool. The cops probably knew all of this. But she had no clue what she was supposed to be looking for. She had assumed she would know what to do. Now that the moment was here, that wasn't so much the case.

She knew when his guests were gone because he began calling her name. With a sigh, she set aside her Jesse James book and obediently went to see what he needed. His normally olive complexion appeared bleached; the fear was evident in his eyes. She reminded herself that he got himself into the situation; it wasn't her doing.

Still, it was more than for show when she stroked his cheek reassuringly. She pitied the man.

"It'll be okay." She knew her words were hollow.

"What do you know about it?"

She ignored the insinuation in his voice and went to get his pills off the bar, pouring him a slug of whiskey to wash them down.

"You could make it all better." The tone of his voice changed. Jessie knew by that tone it had occurred to him she'd been in his home a full twenty-four hours and they'd not had sex once. That was a wasted day in Spence's world.

"I could?" she replied in a sultry voice, straddling his lap as she spoke. "Whatever do you mean?"

He leaned towards her just as she leaned back.

"First, you'd better take your medicine." She held the bottle and the Jack Daniels up.

"What a good nurse." He smiled and obliged, in too much of a hurry to pay much heed to the number of pills she'd given him.

"Just give me a second to slip into something else. I think you'll like it." She slowly crawled off his lap, taunting him as she went. "You just lie back and rest while I'm gone."

She strolled saucily back to her room, closing the door behind her before curling up in her chair again with her book. Thirty minutes later, there was a light tap at her door. She opened it to find an amused expression on Vance's face.

"How much did you give him?"

"Enough." She smiled a little guiltily.

"Just make sure he's coherent again by noon on Wednesday. He's supposed to oversee a sale."

Jessie winced without thinking. She knew the goods exchanging hands would be a girl, probably around Harmony's age or younger.

"What makes me different from them?" she asked suddenly. "Why protect me and not them?"

"Would you rather I do neither?" he shot back.

"I guess I'd rather you do both."

"Some problems are too big to tackle. Hell, Jessie. You're more than I can handle as it is."

Jessie gave a half shrug, unsure what she could really say to that.

"Don't forget to feed him." Vance took Jessie's cue and dropped the subject.

"Of course not."

"And try not to make him OD. That would be a tough situation even for your cop boyfriend to help you out of."

"I'll remember that."

"I'll be back in the morning, okay?"

"Hey Vance." Jessie grabbed his arm as he turned to go.

"Yeah?"

"I don't suppose you can pave the way with Harmony for me?"

"I've been trying."

"Thanks."

"Anything else?"

"No. Sorry... thanks." She let go of his arm and stepped back awkwardly. Loneliness settled over her as she watched him go. Before she'd met Gabe, it hadn't really occurred to her to yearn for another's company—or at least, it hadn't for a long time.

She read a few more chapters of the Jesse James book, completely sucked into the story of his life. She amused herself for a while by cooking Spence dinner and finding new ways to slip him extra pain medicine. She went to bed early and beat Harmony to the gym the next morning, even with taking time to feed Spence some Vicodin-laced pancakes.

Harmony was slightly less frosty and Jessie decided to call that a win. Harmony even asked if Jessie wanted to meet her on the street for dinner.

It felt good to sit in the breezy back room of the Stable on Cherokee Street under the shadow of the old Lemp Brewery. Anheuser-Busch might be the lifeblood of St. Louis, but it was the old Lemp Brewery that held both mystery and charm. That's why Jessie liked it so much. Instead of a typical plain brick circa 1970 building like A-B, Lemp had an eerie beauty that was enhanced by its ornate stone carvings.

Jessie ignored the look Harmony gave her when she ordered a pizza. She was starving. All Spence kept in his refrigerator was tofu and other equally unappetizing and labor-intensive food. Her body needed a Bud Light and a carbonara pizza. She'd work extra hard in yoga the next day.

Other than the disapproval of food choice rolling off of Harmony in waves, things seemed better between them. Like maybe she'd forgiven Jessie for so quickly disappearing from her life.

"Vance says I'm getting a new roommate."

"Really?" Jessie frowned. She hadn't thought of that. "Do you know who?"

"They haven't said anything." She shook her head. "I guess I'll find out soon enough. She moves in next week."

"Maybe she won't be as lazy as me."

"You were hardly lazy."

"Will we still work out together?"

"As long as Spence will let you," Harmony quickly agreed.

"He's in no shape to disagree with much right now," Jessie

snickered. She didn't want to think much past the time when she ran out of those handy little pills.

Once the thought occurred to her that she could use all of his medicine too quickly, she began to ration it a little more carefully. Of course, she compensated by pouring larger glasses of Jack to chase them with.

Sometimes Spence would be coherent enough that she'd relay messages from other staff members and get instructions on household items to be completed in turn. Sometimes she'd sit at his side or give him a shoulder rub as she listened to his incoherent and rambling fears.

It was a very human side to Spence she'd never seen before. It made her hate him less and pity him more—even for just a little while.

At night, she curled up with her pillow and conjured up memories of Gabe. If she thought hard enough, she could almost feel him in the room with her.

Somehow the days rolled by and she managed to pass the time. She also managed to have Spence sobered and cleaned up by the time Vance appeared on Wednesday morning.

She considered it a lucky break when Spence demanded she ride with him to the sale. It seemed her new role in Spence's life was to be his ornament. An ornament he often forgot was there when he spoke to his business associates. Jessie wished Gabe would meet with her soon—both because she missed him and because she was worried she'd forget an important detail.

"I'll be happy when this day is over with," Spence pronounced crabbily once Vance and Jessie had him stuffed into the back seat of the Mercedes.

Jessie tried not to smirk. His head was probably killing him since she'd only given him a fraction of his usual dose that morning.

"We'll get you home as soon as we can," she promised.

"No, it's good to be out. I just want to get Aleksandar off my ass."

There wasn't really an answer to that so Jessie just nodded sympathetically.

The sleek black car looked out of place in the rundown neighborhood Vance drove them through. They pulled up in front of an abandoned warehouse. Jessie waited in the car with Spence while Vance disappeared inside. He returned a few moments later with a young girl tucked under his arm almost protectively. She was tall but thin enough to be considered waifish, with wispy blond hair and dull blue eyes that fixated on Jessie with hatred.

She squirmed under the weight of the girl's gaze. She knew it condemned her as a traitor to their gender. Jessie wanted to assure the girl she was one of the good guys. But a question tickled the back of her brain—would she be helping free this girl if not for Gabe? Or would she have continued looking the other way so long as there was food on her table and a roof over her head?

She felt dirty and small in that moment, with Spence's arm slung over her shoulder and his mouth constantly finding her shoulder, ear or neck. It took every ounce of willpower she had to not shrink from his touch. She struggled to resurrect the wall that had always been her haven in the past, but to no avail.

The ride to the posh end of town was a quiet one. Ladue was a suburb of St. Louis with old money and sprawling estates. The Mercedes pulled up to a wrought iron gate in front of a mansion that bordered on castle. It was the largest home Jessie had ever seen in her life. She couldn't imagine what it would be like to live in a place like that.

And a small part of her wondered how someone who so obviously had everything they could possibly need in life found it necessary to buy a young girl from a broken country. Maybe, just maybe, Jessie hadn't missed out on much by being poor.

"Aren't you coming?" Spence surprised her by impatiently barking.

"I'm sorry." She flushed, trying not to openly gawk as they stepped inside. She knew the marble floors under her feet were worth more than her entire life's earnings. Earnings that were gone, she reminded herself, so maybe there was something to be said for not keeping all your money under a mattress.

Still, there was a coolness to the mansion that she didn't like. It wasn't that the place was physically cold, but rather it lacked the warmth of a home. Everything was so white, so pristine. She couldn't fathom curling up on a couch to watch television here. The late-night popcorn fights she used to get into with Harmony would never happen in a place like this.

There was no joy. No laughter.

"Spence, it's good to see you again." A stocky man with salt-and-pepper hair joined them in the sitting room. His smile didn't reach his eyes as he shook hands with Spence. His lack of surprise over Spence's appearance told Jessie that word had traveled quickly.

"I think you'll be happy with your purchase Mr. Coleman. She's really quite exquisite. There's a bit of fire lurking under those eyes," Spence commented.

If he hadn't been talking about a human like she was a horse, Jessie might have felt sorry for him at the disdainful look he got from Mr. Coleman. As it was, Jessie wanted to grab the girl by the hand and run like hell out of this place, consequences be damned.

Jessie told herself that more good could be done in the long run if she bided her time and let Gabe handle things the right way. She wondered, though, if it was rational thought that kept her rooted to Spence's side... or fear.

Either way, she couldn't get that girl out of her mind as she settled Spence in for the night. The image of those eyes heaping accusations at her feet was seared into her brain. Once Spence was snoring soundly, Jessie changed into jeans and a t-shirt. She was still pulling her long blond hair into a ponytail as she told the guard at the door where she would be if he needed her.

O'Malley's Irish Pub was on the approved activity list, and for that, Jessie was eternally grateful. She needed the normalcy of hearing Danny's lilting Irish folk. It was a typical St. Louis building—dimly lit, with an exposed brick and wood interior. From the flags hanging inside and out to the support beam painted orange, white and green, the place left no doubt as to its Irish heritage. Jessie smiled at the fiddle hanging on the wall and the clock of three men standing in their underwear arm in arm that was affectionately known as "Three Drunk Micks." They made her feel like she'd come home.

"The prodigal daughter has returned," Danny declared jovially as he appeared from the crowd to hug Jessie.

"Good to see you." Jessie eagerly returned the hug. "Play me a happy song tonight."

"What's a pretty girl like you so sad about?" He smiled warmly before patting his pockets. "I almost forgot. I have something for you."

He pressed a key into her hands.

"What's this?"

"I was told you'll find it in the pages of a book. Our friends seemed to think you'd know what that meant."

"I think I do." She nodded slowly. "Thank you."

"No worries. You're just in time for the first set. Come on, I'll shove someone out of their seat."

"Hey Danny."

"Yes, love?"

"Could you tell our friend I need to talk to him?"

"That I can do." He nodded solemnly.

Jessie accepted the seat Danny cleared for her. The music began, wrapping itself around her as it always. She stared at the key in her hand, running the possibilities through her mind. It was the key to his Plymouth.

Chapter Eleven

J essie tried to let the music carry her away, but the image of the blond girl vied with the key for her attention. There wasn't much she could do about the girl until she spoke to Gabe. The key was most likely intended as her method of escape if things got bad. He'd probably stashed the Plymouth at the address in the book. She still hadn't figured out the phony ZIP code. Her best guess was that the numbers were a pass code of some sort.

She clutched the key in her hand, its presence making her feel more connected with Gabe. Instead of soothing her, being at O'Malley's only seemed to make her more restless. She missed Gabe. She didn't want to go back to her gilded cage. It all sucked and that was making her cranky.

She stood suddenly and marched over to the bar to order a shot of Tequila. That got the attention of a college kid next to her who ordered them another round.

"That is, if you think you can handle two shots." He smiled charmingly.

She gave him a crooked grin and licked her salted wrist before tossing the liquid fire down her throat. She arched her eyebrow as she sucked on the lime. He responded in kind even as the bartender poured another round.

Jessie wasn't sure how she got home. She vaguely recalled Vance showing up and pulling her away from a protesting crowd. The ride was a little fuzzy.

"I'm perfectly fiiiine," she protested when he slung her over his shoulder like a sack of potatoes.

"Uh-huh." He deftly unlocked the door.

"I'm so lucky to have you."

"I know." He dropped her unceremoniously on the bed.

"You're a good man... don't worry, I won't tell anybody." She put a finger over her lips to indicate it was their little secret.

"Get some sleep, Jessie."

"Can't sleep," she argued. "I'll see her eyes. She hated me. Harmony hates me, too. I bet Gabe hates me. Do you hate me? You don't, do you?"

"No one hates you, honey. Try to get some rest. It'll be better tomorrow."

"Why is my bed spinning?" She frowned after a moment of silence.

Vance's only response was his chuckle. It was the last memory Jessie had of the evening and it drifted in and out of her hazy brain as she tossed and turned.

Her alarm the next morning seemed particularly cruel. Still, she did its bidding and stumbled from her bed to rake a brush through her hair and splash some water on her face before dressing for yoga. She'd nearly made it to the door when she remembered deodorant and backtracked.

She tossed some toast at Spence on her way out the door, too hung over to care if it made him angry.

"You know I'll be out of this cast eventually, right?" he called after her. She waved without turning around in response. She'd deal with him later.

Jessie was grateful to Vance for setting her alarm, but would have appreciated a little more time to get there. As it was, she skidded into class halfway through the first sun salutation. She tossed her sunglasses beside her mat with the tennis shoes she kicked off, rushing through the first two poses to catch up with the group.

She barely noticed the disapproving arch to Harmony's eyebrow. She was too preoccupied with the rich laughter coming from the far corner of the room. Her heart hammered in her chest; she recognized that laugh. It had been nearly a week since she'd seen Gabe. Man, he looked good.

"Mr. Adams, when I said you could observe, I assumed it meant you wouldn't disturb the participants," the seventy-year-old woman who led class admonished. Jessie ducked her head to hide her smile.

She knew the petite little hippy just might be the one human on this earth that could bring Gabe to his knees.

"Maybe Mr. Adams would like to participate. There's a mat open next to me," Jessie offered helpfully.

"Don't think I didn't notice your tardiness." She turned her disapproval to Jessie.

"Sorry."

Gabe made a face at Jessie and she made one back.

"Alright then. Mr. Adams, Jessie will show you what to do as we go along."

Jessie nearly clapped with glee. Watching Gabe attempt yoga was one of the few activities that could coax her out of her hangover-induced crankiness.

"You sure you're up to this?" he murmured with a grin as he kicked his shoes into a pile with hers. "Looks like you had a rough night."

"I can handle it… can you?"

"It'll be a breeze." He rolled his head, stretching his neck.

"Uh-huh." She moved to stand behind him, aligning his body for the first pose as the class began their second salute to the sun. For one entire round, she moved in concert with his body, hers over his as she taught him each pose. The deep breathing she was doing had little to do with yoga and a whole lot to do with his proximity.

For a few delicious moments, they were the only two people in the room—at least, as far as Jessie was concerned anyway.

It was over before Jessie was ready, but she grudgingly moved back to her mat to perform the next sequence beside Gabe. She was torn between enjoying his struggles and losing herself to her own routine. Nothing cleared her mind quite like yoga.

When the instructor pulled him back into a proper downward dog, Jessie decided wholeheartedly to just enjoy the show.

"Oh yeah, I can feel the difference there," he was saying in a strained voice.

At one point, the woman shook her head in disgust and instructed Jessie to help him again. "Don't be so easy on him this time."

"I will be merciless," Jessie solemnly promised, breaking her own warrior pose to help Gabe align his.

"I miss you," he breathed in her ear as she leaned in to him. She paused, her eyes brushing his. How could she possibly tell him how much she missed him too? He nodded, the small smile that tugged at his mouth telling her he understood.

"I need to talk to you."

"That's why I'm here."

"I didn't expect Danny to see you so soon."

"He was worried about you." His lip twitched. Jessie rolled her eyes and repositioned his hips for him.

"I'm pretty sure I won that contest," Jessie informed him in a whisper.

"I'd hate to see the other guy."

"I hate you."

"I love you, too."

"You guys are going to get in trouble," Harmony admonished.

"Sorry." Jessie bit her lip guiltily.

"Can we get out of here?" he implored.

"Come on." She scooped up their shoes.

"Don't forget these." He grabbed her glasses.

Jessie wanted to touch him. It was crazy how much. Instead, she slid her tennis shoes back on and plucked her sunglasses from his hand.

"Did you get the key?" he asked as they ducked into a private corner of the gym.

"Yeah. Thanks. What do you know about some guy named Coleman? Lives in Ladue."

"Is he a customer or a player?"

"Customer."

"Doesn't ring a bell. I'll look into him. Do you have any more than that on him?"

Jessie gave him the address and a description after glancing around nervously. "Gabe, we delivered a girl there yesterday. Promise me you'll get her back."

"I can't promise."

"Yes, you can. I know you can get her back."

"It's more complicated than that."

"No, it's not. Either you go get her or I will. I need to know she'll be okay."

"Why?"

"She looked at me like I was the one that did that to her...because I stood by and let them."

"I still can't promise anyone will do anything about this one girl. Not if it'll risk the rest of the operation."

"But she matters. Right?"

"To you and to me, sure."

"What aren't you telling me?" Jessie frowned. Something in his answer triggered warning bells in her mind.

"I'd rather talk to you alone... somewhere where we can really talk. Do you think you could meet me on the roof of Spence's building tomorrow night at nine?"

"You're scaring me."

"It'll be okay. That I will promise." He kissed her forehead.

Jessie wanted to chastise him for making promises he couldn't keep, but she needed to believe this one too badly to do that.

"Is there anything else?" He brought the conversation back.

"I can't believe I didn't tell you this first." Jessie was irritated with herself. "They're keeping the girls in a warehouse off Vandeventer."

"You're sure?"

Jessie nodded, reciting the address she'd committed to memory. "It's where we picked up the girl anyway."

"I'll send someone to check it out. Thanks."

"I have no idea what I'm doing here."

"You're doing a great job."

"I don't think you'd tell me if I wasn't."

Gabe smiled guiltily and shrugged. "Are you okay?"

Jessie nodded.

"Not sure I believe you, darlin'."

"It's stupid."

"What?" Concern etched his brow.

"I mean, I'm enjoying not having to work the streets anymore—

don't get me wrong... but I'm lonely. I want to go home."

"You can walk away from this," he reminded her.

"No, I can't. Not now. I have to do what I can to protect these girls."

"Be careful."

"Are you guys just about done?" Harmony appeared at the door. "You're drawing attention, you know."

"Thanks." Gabe scowled but acknowledged that furtive glances were being cast their way by the curious yoga class.

"Tomorrow at nine?" Jessie couldn't help reaching up to brush his cheek with her fingertips.

"It's a date." He caught her hand and kissed her palm.

With a small smile at him, she followed Harmony onto the street. The hateful sun mocked her and she hid behind her sunglasses again.

"I can't believe you fell for a cop." Harmony shook her head in disgust. "You used to be so practical."

"I know." Jessie didn't bother denying it. "Grab a cup of coffee with me?"

"Can't. I have class."

"Okay." Jessie felt deflated. The day loomed long ahead of her. "Have fun."

"See you tomorrow morning, okay?"

She was happy to have been forgiven by Harmony, but it wasn't really doing her much good at the moment. It seemed there was nothing to do but head back to Spence's with two days to kill.

He was awake on the couch when she returned, a terse look on his face.

"You know I should kick you out on your ass for the way you treated me this morning."

"I do." She sighed and sank on the couch next to him. Everything in his body language said he was safe enough at the moment.

"Vance told me about your little binge last night." A smile tugged the corner of his mouth. It was the first true smile Jessie could remember seeing on him; there was no trace of mocking in it.

"I rose to the challenge. That's all."

"Did you win?"

"Wiped the floor with them." Jessie didn't know if that was necessarily true, but it sounded good.

"Thatta girl."

"You want to play cards?" Jessie suggested after an awkward silence.

"Poker?"

"How about Rummy?" She offered instead, knowing the only version of poker in Spence's world involved stripping.

"Sure. Why not?"

Jessie rooted through the bar until she found some playing cards. She curled up in the oversized chair across from Spence as she shuffled the deck.

"Your nose looks better," Jessie commented.

"Thanks. It hurts like hell today."

"I forgot your pain medicine, sorry. You want me to get it?"

"Nah. It'll just put me to sleep again. I like sitting upright for a while."

"Let me know if you change your mind." She began dealing the cards.

"You're different lately," he observed, eyeballing her from above his hand.

"Maybe you've just never really seen me before." She studied the cards in her own hand.

"I know you better than you think," he argued. "I know you work out obsessively to counteract your huge appetite because you worry about keeping up with the younger girls."

"Ouch."

"I know you spend every Wednesday night at O'Malley's because of Danny. I personally think he's some sort of a father figure to you."

"Is that so?" She wondered why she was suddenly on the couch of Dr. Spence.

"I know Vance moonlights as your protector. I used to worry he had a crush on you, but now I think you two have some weird brother/sister thing going on."

"I could see that." Jessie gave in and played along.

"I know you like Bud Light, wine from a box and Blues—both the music and the team."

"Impressive," Jessie acknowledged. She had to admit she was surprised at his depth of knowledge. "Rummy."

"That's crap. Deal again."

"Sore loser." She gathered the cards to shuffle.

"I also know that you hate me."

She silently slid the cards towards him to cut the deck.

"I've never thought that was fair of you. I took you in and gave you a roof over your head and you hate me for it."

Jessie arched an eyebrow. She had a different view of things, but opening up a discussion along those lines wouldn't do her much good.

"We've had a good run, you and me...haven't we?" His pale green eyes met hers with startling honesty. She wasn't sure how to respond.

"You're in it pretty deep, aren't you, Spence?"

He opened his mouth to protest and instead tapped the deck for Jessie to deal. She wasn't sure what else there was to say. How do you ask someone why they aren't getting off the Titanic?

For as long as she'd known him, if Spence was in arm's reach he was trying to get his hands on her. The fact that he was coherent and hadn't propositioned her once was unsettling because it meant he had something weighing heavy on his mind. He seemed to know he was a dead man walking. She kept circling back to the same question—why didn't he leave? Why did he still hand girls over to monsters if he knew it was doing nothing to save his hide?

For that matter, why hadn't she left when Gabe first suggested it weeks ago? Because deep down you know—there's nowhere to hide. A tiger by the tail is better than one lurking in the bushes.

So the retired prostitute-turned-informant and the dejected pimp whiled away the better part of two days playing Rummy and eating takeout.

If Harmony noticed Jessie's detached behavior at the gym, she was nice enough not to mention it. Jessie felt a bit like she was having an out-of-body experience as she struggled to reconcile the tyrant who'd ruled her for so long with the broken man sitting at home waiting to die. As much as she had hated the one, she pitied the other.

"You free for lunch?" Harmony asked as they wandered back down Cherokee after their workout.

"Actually, yeah. I could go for some lunch. How about tacos?"

"I'll see if Vance can join us."

"Is he allowed to?" Jessie remembered the night not so long ago when Vance had furtively slipped up to her room to warn her Gabe was a cop.

"He seems to breaking all the rules lately," Harmony answered cryptically.

"Hey, I'll be right back." Jessie's mind changed gears when she caught a glimpse of Danny walking into the Cherokee Market. She jogged to catch up with him.

"Hey, there's a girl. How's your head?" He winked at her.

"Just fine, thank you." She made a face at him. "In all seriousness... thanks for everything."

Dan waved off her thanks but accepted her quick hug with a smile. She met Harmony at La Vallesana just as Vance appeared from one of the flats down the street. The women waited for him before going in to order.

It was a good day to sit under the big blue umbrellas eating the most authentic Mexican food the Midwest had to offer. The oppression of summer was a memory and the crisp fall air had yet to arrive, in between stood meteorological perfection.

Still, sadness tugged at Jessie's heart. There was a hint of goodbye in the air. She wondered what her friends would do if something happened to Spence, where they would go. Which was a little funny, because she had no real idea what she would do when the moment came... not beyond getting herself to the address written in the front of her book, anyway. It wouldn't be the first time she found herself on the streets and penniless. She'd find a way to survive now, too.

She wasn't surprised to find Spence where she left him on the couch. He stopped vacantly flipping through channels when she walked in.

"Want to play more Rummy?"

"Why not?" She grabbed the cards as she kicked off her shoes and curled up in her chair. She had a few hours to kill before she needed to get ready for her date with Gabe.

She declared a truce at seven to fix them some dinner. Despite their odd little rapport, she didn't think twice about drugging his share of the food. There was a limit to her magnanimous feelings towards Spence, and it was somewhere on this side of him interfering with her precious time with Gabe.

Once she had him squared away for the evening, Jessie hurried to her room to dress. She didn't even try to look nonchalant about her appearance, pulling her favorite outfit out of the closet and tossing it on the bed before jumping in the shower. Twenty minutes to nine, she stood in front of a full-length mirror twisting and turning to gauge every angle. Wispy blond hair framed a baby doll face. A splash of honey colored her skin, thanks to the time she'd spent outside with Gabe the week before. She liked the way the color made her eyes look even bluer.

The dress was one she seldom wore. It was bought on impulse and had spent many years languishing in her closet. Her life rarely called for long, flowing skirts—even if they were almost translucent. Its halter-style top and fitted waist made her feel girly... pretty. She didn't bother with shoes. With her luck, they'd only fall off as she scaled the ladder to the roof.

"Where are you headed?" Jason sat up a little straighter when Jessie emerged from the apartment.

"For a walk. I'm tired of watching Spence sleep."

"It's not Wednesday. I don't think I'm supposed to let you leave."

"I'm not leaving... I'll be in the building. Promise." In, on... what's the difference? Jessie mentally amended.

"You look awful pretty to be going for a walk," he hesitated.

"Why thank you." She leaned over and kissed his cheek, choosing to distract rather than answer the question. "See you in a bit."

He nodded warily but let her leave. Once she was out of sight, her pace quickened. She was early; maybe Gabe would be too. Time together was too rare of a commodity to waste.

"You're early." His velvet voice greeted her the moment she stepped onto the roof. "And you're ravishing."

Jessie answered by launching herself at him. He caught her with a chuckle before claiming her mouth with a hunger that rivaled her own. His fingers wove through her hair, his hands cupping her head. She wanted to touch and taste and feel all of him.

"We should talk." He reluctantly ended the kiss and rested his forehead on hers.

Her heart seemed to stop beating as she waited for what came next; the tone of his voice terrified her.

"Jessie, I'm leaving."

The words hung in the air between them. Her pulse now pounded ferociously in her ears.

"Leaving to go where?" She took a step back.

"Afghanistan. I've been called up."

She took a few steadying breaths while her mind raced. "When?"

"I leave in the morning."

"No!" Pain and rage flowed through her and poured themselves into that one word. "No."

"Trust me; I've tried everything I can think of to postpone this until after the case. They've done it before; I don't know why they didn't this time."

"Is it because of me? Did someone find out about us?"

"I doubt it. I think Uncle Sam is just getting desperate for numbers."

There were a thousand questions Jessie wanted to ask. Only one surfaced. "What does that mean for us?"

"I'm doing everything I can to make sure you're taken care of...can't say I trust Brunner to look out for you," he snarled.

"That's not what I meant—I can take care of myself."

"Are we really back at this again?"

"I'm sorry if I happen to be more worried about you being target practice for some zealot halfway across the world and yes, I know

it's selfish, but I'm going to miss you. This past week has been hell."
Her gestures became more agitated as she spoke. "And now you're
going away for God knows how long. I mean, these wars are never
going to end. Tell them I don't want you to go."

"That doesn't sound very patriotic." He gathered her in his
arms. "I'm going to miss you too, you know."

"Will I even hear from you while you're gone?"

"I've taken care of that." He pulled a cell phone out of his pocket
and handed it to her. "I will call you every chance I get—at least
once a week. I will find you when I get back."

"You did promise me everything would be alright," she
reminded him.

"That I did... have I mentioned how amazing you look tonight?"

"Are you trying to flatter your way out of trouble?"

"Maybe a little."

"You should have told me sooner."

"In retrospect, yeah, I really should have. I think I'd convinced
myself Carter would be able to put it off again."

"You had to at least suspect he couldn't or you wouldn't have
sent me the key."

"I sent you the key because I can't watch you every second of the
day even when I'm in St. Louis."

"Can I see you off tomorrow?"

"I'm not sure that's a good idea. Now that you're living with
Spence, you're being watched as closely as he is."

"He knows he's in trouble." Her mind changed tracks.

"That doesn't surprise me," he answered wryly as he led her to a
cushioned chaise lounge someone had set up. He sat down and
pulled her onto his lap, where she gladly curled up.

"It's been an odd few days," she frowned, unsure how to explain
it.

"Has he hurt you?" Gabe tensed.

"No, quite the opposite actually. He's being very... human."

"Oh. Huh. That's good, I guess."

"You guess? I have to say I much prefer it. Although now I'm
wrestling with guilt."

"Guilt? Really? Do you not remember the bruises he gave you?"

Gabe's irritation was evident.

"Yes, I remember the bruises." She spat the words out. "You know what? This is not the way I want to spend our last night together."

"Don't try to change the subject."

"Why not? This one is stupid."

"Stupid? Or just uncomfortable?"

"You suck, you know that? You big, fat jerk." Jessie scrambled off his lap.

"Why? Because I don't like the thought of you feeling sorry for the man who has abused you for 14 years?"

"Excuse the hell out of me for having a heart," she snarled.

"I have a heart."

"Sure you do, and a whore walked all over it so now you're taking that out on me. Is that why you chased me? Was I a whore you could get back at?"

"You're not a whore!"

"You're right, I am retired now."

"Stop it," he growled.

"No, you brought this up. I said I felt sorry for someone and now suddenly you're worried I'll be giving him freebies while you're gone... that's it, right?"

"Stop it." He grabbed her by the arms, causing her eyes to snap with fire.

"Or what?" she dared him.

"Damn it, Jessie. When will you get it through your thick skull that I love you so much it makes me stupid?"

The retort died in her throat. His eyes were anguished and she knew her lash out had hurt him. She sighed heavily. "I don't know why you make me so crazy."

A slow smile crossed his face as he lowered his head to brush her lips with his own. The kiss turned slow and torturous. It brought with it a smoldering fire that wound its way through her. She arched into him, a whimper escaping her throat. Something about the sound snapped his restraint. His passion unleashed hers and she greedily sought more of him. Always more of him.

It was dizzying. It was delicious. She couldn't help but cry as he held her to his chest, stroking her back as they lay on the oversized lounge, their skin warmed by the others' touch and cooled by the breeze that danced about them.

She wanted to proclaim that she'd love him as long as there was breath in her body but didn't know how to without sounding like a fool. How did she even know it was love? She had no point of reference. There was nothing in her past to indicate she was even capable of loving. Not that long ago Harmony had to tell her what a crush felt like.

"A twenty for your thoughts."

"The price has gone up that much, huh?"

"I figured I had to compete with other sources of revenue."

"You are such a jerk. And I make way more than that. Made, actually."

"You haven't answered the question."

"Nothing to say. My brain was completely empty just then."

"That can't be true. I bet you were at least thinking about what a great lover I am."

"Wow. If the cop/soldier gigs don't work out, you really should consider being a psychic. Truly astounding."

"Aw, now you're just being hateful."

"Yeah, I am." She smiled, tracing lazy circles up and down his side. "I'm being hateful because I don't want you to leave."

"I don't want to go, either. But I'll be back before you know it."

She wished she could believe him.

Chapter Twelve

Mother Nature was kind enough to cater to Jessie's mood the next morning. A gray, cold drizzle had settled over the city. She went through the motions of making Spence's breakfast and listening to his random thoughts on life as they played another round of Rummy.

The drizzle turned into a steady rain and Jessie excused herself to go lie down. She noticed a flashing red light on the cell phone when she pulled her book out of the drawer by her bed. Tears burned her eyes as she listened to the message from Gabe three times before grudgingly erasing it. She didn't want someone stumbling across his assurances that all would be well or his reminder that he loved her.

She curled up with the phone, letting the rain and the memories lull her to sleep. Her subconscious was given room to play, and in her dreams Gabe's rich laughter still rumbled. His voice stroked her weary spirit. His hands were there to comfort and arouse.

Commotion erupted in the loft, causing Jessie to shoot up from the bed. Vance burst into her room, his expression dire.

"What did you do?"

"I don't know what you're talking about." She struggled to clear her head of the nap-induced fog.

"Coleman was arrested today; three girls were removed from his property. The warehouse was raided. Aleksandar is on the warpath. He thinks he has a mole."

"And the first place he's looking is at the guy that was skimming cash? Does he really think Spence is that stupid?"

"Oh he doesn't think Spence is the mole—he thinks Spence is the one dumb enough to let a pretty woman get the best of him."

"Oh." She absorbed that information. "You should leave.

Distance yourself from me."

"I'm not going anywhere. There's no time even if I wanted to—I'm surprised I beat them here."

"What did you think would happen?" She held his eyes for a moment. "Spence was dead anyway. Don't put this at my feet."

"What's at your feet?" Spence leaned heavily against her doorframe.

"Aleksandar's boys are on their way over. They think Jessie is working with the cops," Vance answered.

"Are you?" Spence's voice was low and calm.

Jessie instinctively put the bed in between them as her gaze met his.

"I see." He took a deep breath. "I really should have seen that one coming."

"What you're doing isn't right. Those girls... they aren't property. They're people."

"No, they're Aleksandar's property. Just like you're my property."

"You've been so close to human this week, I almost forgot." Her jaw jutted defiantly.

"Where is he?" Vance interrupted, demanding Jessie's attention. "Does he have a way to extract you?"

"He's in Afghanistan... well, on his way."

Vance muttered a terse expletive under his breath. "So he let you do his dirty work and left you to face the fallout?"

"It's not like that."

"Who's he?" Spence frowned.

"What is it like?" Vance demanded. "How the hell am I supposed to get you out of here?"

"I'll get myself out."

"You did this for some guy?" Color flooded Spence's face and he trembled with rage. He made a lunge for Jessie, falling short of his goal. The phone clattered to the floor as he landed on the bed. His attention turned from Jessie to the cell. "This is from him, isn't it?"

She made a grab for it but he beat her there, shoving her away as he scooped up the prize.

"Give that to me." She held her hand out, wishing it didn't

tremble as she did so.

"Maybe you're right—I don't know you. I underestimated how cold you could be."

"Or how far you could push me." She refused to back down. "I don't belong to you Spence. I don't belong to any man."

With a wounded howl of rage, Spence hurled the phone with all of the force he could muster. It exploded against the wall as the front door burst open. Aleksandar strode through the door, a grim smile spreading across his face when his one good eye landed on Jessie. With a nod, the three of them were surrounded and escorted to the SUV waiting in front of the building.

"I knew you were trouble. I told myself that when I first saw you on Spence's arm—you know that?" Aleksandar never took his eyes off of Jessie. "I considered keeping you after Spence was dispensed of."

"What's the saying about borrowing trouble?" Jessie arched an eyebrow.

"The fiery ones are the most fun to break."

"Get a saddle out and I will feed you your own…"

"Jessie…" Vance cut her off.

"Sadly, we won't get to see how that would have worked out—it sounds fun, really. But if I let you live after today, well then I've just sent the message that I'm weak. I can't let people think that, can I?"

"It's worth a shot." Jessie shrugged. Spence stared at her as if she'd grown a second head. Vance now seemed resigned to the fact that Jessie's mouth was sealing their fate.

"You would have been fun." Aleksandar stroked her cheek with one long finger.

"Still could be," Jessie offered in her most sultry voice.

"Valiant attempt, Jessie, but I don't think so." His attention turned to Vance for the first time. "Now, to be honest, I'm still figuring you out."

"How so?"

"I can't decide if you would be an asset or as much trouble as the girl."

Vance's expression remained impassive.

"Wait until I've tended to these two; I'd like to speak with you before making a decision."

"Take all the time you need," Vance replied calmly.

"Good to know I surrounded myself with such loyalty," Spence pouted.

"This from the man who was cheating me?" Aleksandar observed. "I took a chance on you because I was assured of your talents. I see now that was a mistake."

Spence stared out the window, watching the raindrops snake trails across the glass. Jessie felt strangely hollow as the city she loved passed by. She expected to feel fear or sadness as the SUV crossed the bridge into Illinois and headed north. Instead, there was a piece of her that felt almost relieved the battle was over. She was so very tired.

Out-of-body experiences were becoming strangely normal for Jessie these days. That's how it seemed as she and Spence were loaded onto a 20-foot boat and lined up along the railing. Jessie looked down at the dark, churning water and knew she should be afraid, but it didn't seem real. She couldn't begrudge Vance for standing with their captors. He'd never made any bones about his intention to stay alive at any cost. He certainly hadn't asked for any of this.

There was no sun to sink in the horizon, but gray skies turned to black, signaling the arrival of night. Jessie closed her eyes, focusing on the wind and the stinging rain pelting her face. If this was to be her last sensation, she wanted to experience it fully.

She knew the Mississippi would ravage their bodies and if they should turn up, they'd become a message to anyone else who might want to go against Aleksandar.

"I'm not mad at you anymore," Spence interrupted her thoughts.

"You're not mad at me?" Jessie's eyes flew open. "Really? Because if I remember correctly, you're the one that got involved with these people first. Everything that's happened since then points straight back to your initial decision."

"Truce?" he suggested with an odd little smile.

Jessie couldn't help half a smile of her own. She took a breath to tell him she accepted his truce when the sound of gunfire exploded in her ear. A shocked expression was forever etched on Spence's face as he toppled over the railing.

Just like that, he was gone. Jessie didn't have time to process the picture of the mighty Mississippi gobbling up the offering. She blinked once, took a deep breath, and dove in just as the second shot rang out.

She thought she heard Vance shout, but the boat, the rain and the sound of several tons of dirt being carried downstream all resounded in her ears. Were those more shots?

There was so much dirt in the big brown water, she could taste the metallic grit. The boat didn't even slow down. She allowed herself a split second to catch her bearings; the river clawed at her legs, pulling her towards its hidden secrets.

Her earlier apathy disappeared as a voice somewhere inside of her shouted "swim." She obeyed.

Using every one of her carefully honed muscles, she began to fight the river. She was disoriented and exhausted, but she continued to slice through the rapidly moving current. All of her life she'd heard warnings about this Mississippi—those who went in didn't come out—she now ruthlessly shoved the memories of those warnings aside.

She did not know how long she swam. Her sole focus was propelling herself towards the shoreline she knew would be there. Fears of man-sized alligator gar lurking below with their wicked teeth toyed with her. Did they eat flesh? She couldn't remember. She did remember seeing one in a tank once and that was enough to urge her onward.

The constant tug of the current wore at her. Sometime after her muscles began screaming in protest, they went a fuzzy kind of numb. When at last she crawled up on a muddy riverbank, she was too exhausted to worry about things like water moccasin holes. She did not know where she was, but it was solid ground and for the moment that would have to be good enough.

It was dark—dark enough she knew she was still a ways off from the city. For the first time in her life, she was alone in the woods, undoubtedly in one of several parks that dotted the riverfront north of St. Louis. Tremors wracked her body from the exertion and the cold. She wedged herself in between a grove of trees to block the wind and allowed the darkness to overcome her.

She awoke disoriented and unable to focus on much beyond how incredibly tired her body was. Light filtered through the trees. Somewhere in the distance, she could hear a family bickering. The mother thought they were lost. The father swore they were not. A teenager bemoaned the idiocy of her parents. A younger child apparently picked some poison ivy as a souvenir. The clichéd scene made Jessie smile. Then it made her wonder if she was lying in poison ivy.

Once she ascertained that she was not in a bed of itch-inducing plants, she leaned against the tree and closed her eyes. She knew she needed to get to the Plymouth, but the question was how. It was on the south side of the city and she was pretty far north. She was also covered in Mississippi grime without a penny to her name.

It was hard deciding much; with her eyes closed, visions of Spence's demise plagued her. Her eyes flew back open, brimming with tears. Had she and Gabe done that to him or had he done it to himself? Did she have blood on her hands?

But the girl was free. A lot of girls were free now. That had to count for something. She wished Gabe were there. Had he known about the raid and left her to face it alone? She didn't think so.

But now was not the time to sit and wonder about things that were really neither here nor there. Now, she had to figure out how to get to an address in Affton on the south side of St. Louis.

With that goal fixed in her mind, she stood and attempted to dust herself off before realizing with a wry smile that the effort was futile. She fought the underbrush until she stumbled onto a path, eliciting a startled scream from the mother of the bickering family.

"Sorry folks." Jessie held up her hands in a gesture of surrender. "Didn't mean to scare you."

"Are you alright?" The man studied her with a frown.

"Fine, thank you." Jessie tried to smile reassuringly.

"What are you doing out here?"

"What are you doing out here?" she tossed back.

"Communing with God," the teenager answered with a derisive

sneer directed at her mother.

"Sounds fun... I guess you could say I was out here for a baptism," Jessie responded. She certainly was dead to her old life. The analogy amused her.

"A baptism? In the Mississippi?"

"Sure. Rebirth can happen all kinds of crazy ways, right?"

"Right," the mother spoke for the first time, an odd expression on her face. "Do you need a ride somewhere?"

"Carey." The husband looked at her in shock. "We have to be at my parents' soon."

"No worries. I wouldn't want to dirty your car anyway."

"No, I want to give you a ride... please?" the mother insisted. Jessie wondered what caused the sudden sense of camaraderie between herself and this woman.

"I need to get south of the city," she hesitantly conceded—it did solve a problem for her. "Anywhere south of River Des Peres would be amazing."

The husband opened his mouth to protest but was silenced by a glare from his wife who told her they'd be delighted. Jessie couldn't be sure, but it sounded like the woman followed up by asking her husband under her breath if he listened to the sermons he preached.

She didn't like putting them out, but her options were rather limited at the moment. Together they found their way out of the woods and back to the family's green Honda Pilot. Jessie sat in the back with the kids, who stared at her as if she were an alien.

"Why are you so dirty?" the boy asked.

"Don't you ever play in the mud?"

"Mom wouldn't like it," he sighed mournfully.

"One day you'll be grown and then you can play in the mud, too."

"Cool."

"Really?" The teenage girl did not look amused.

"Where should we drop you off?" their father interrupted.

"Anywhere is fine. I really can't thank you enough."

"Seriously, where do you need to go?"

"Affton. Gravois Road... but you don't have to go that far,

really."

"It's no big deal." This time it was the husband assuring her. Whatever the wife said must have hit home.

It was an awkward ride, but she couldn't complain. They dropped her off in a Dairy Queen parking lot at the corner of Gravois and Mackenzie. She waved goodbye to the family in the green Honda Pilot, gave the Dairy Queen a longing look, and started walking. Crossing Gravois was the hardest part. Once she made it to the other side alive, she was pleased to realize how close to the address she was.

The Public Storage facility was tucked back from the road. She entered the 5-digit code at the gate and it slowly lifted. Her guess about the odd ZIP code had been right. The first building of storage sheds she found were labeled A. She kept walking towards the back of the lot, passing two other buildings before she came to a set of carports labeled D. And there in lot number 35 was the Plymouth.

To Jessie, the big car was a welcome friend. As she slid behind the wheel for the first time, the weight of the past 24-hours crashed over her. Images of Spence, the look on his face. The blood. And then he was gone. Her shoulder throbbed and she realized with a start that a bullet had nicked her. How had she missed that?

Tears came then. Her entire body trembled with sorrow and shock. She allowed herself the luxury of tears for a moment, then pulled herself together and put the key in the ignition. The big engine roared to life; there was something very assuring in its deep, rumbling growl.

She needed to keep moving away from St. Louis; that much was certain. Fortunately, she had an entire tank of gas before she had to worry about where the next tank would come from.

She drove in silence, with nothing but Gabe's lingering scent to keep her company. Jessie didn't mind so much. She needed time to process.

Without any real clue where she should go, Jessie realized she'd made her way to Highway 44 west—the road she'd taken with Gabe. Before her, rolling hills that had been vibrant green just weeks ago were now muted in tone, as if they were taking a deep breath before bursting into the song of fall. Though she'd never seen it, she was certain these hills would be alive with color soon.

She toyed with the idea of stopping in Eureka. The picturesque little town held special meaning to her now. Practical took precedence over sentimental and she pushed on.

By the time she pulled into the rest stop just out of St. Louis, Jessie was feeling the full effects of no food and extreme physical exertion. She rooted through the car, looking for anything that might help her. The glove box held a map and registration papers. The back seat furnished the hat she'd worn that night at Nick's. While finding it brought some measure of comfort, it did little to feed her growling belly.

Her last hope was the trunk, and it offered up the mother lode. The clothes she'd bought on their trip were neatly packed in suitcases, along with a few sweaters and t-shirts that appeared to be Gabe's. She held them to her nose, savoring the masculine scent that clung to them.

Tucked into the side of the suitcase was a large manila envelope. She grabbed it and a change of clothes, then headed for the bathroom before her bladder gave way.

Jessie felt like a new person after washing some of the grime off in the restroom sink. A bath would have been heaven, but the quick rinse and new clothes did wonders. She took her old clothes with her, afraid to leave a trail just in case she was being followed.

Back in the car, she finally opened the large envelope. In it was a credit card in the name of J. Howard. Jessie smiled. Thanks to the book Gabe had given her, she knew that moniker. Howard was the assumed name Jesse James was living under at the time of his supposed death.

Along with the credit card was a bankcard, checkbook and a note that read, "Vance found your savings when he moved your things. Hope you don't mind, I opened a bank account with it. Everything you need should be in here. Love you."

Jessie wanted to weep with relief. Instead, she fired the old car to life and headed to the nearest fast food restaurant. Once her belly was full, she pushed herself to go another 100 miles before checking into a Holiday Inn just off the highway. After lugging her suitcase to her room, she indulged in a long bath before ordering a pizza to be delivered.

She fell asleep in front of the television before the sun had even set, and woke up with barely enough time to get ready before checkout. After a breakfast of cold pizza, she went to grab the map out of the glove box. Sometime in the night, her next step had become clear.

With no easy way to contact Gabe, she decided to head towards the small town they'd passed on their way to the cave. It seemed like a good place to hide and it would buy her time to track down his unit.

Chapter Thirteen

Jessie was happy to learn that she was relatively close to Ava, her end destination. The town was cute; it even had an actual town square. After a few hours of wandering, she found the lone apartment building. It was a large square with two floors of apartments on all sides. She called the number on the sign and made arrangements to tour an apartment the next day. In the meantime, she checked into the Super 8 motel and went in search of food.

"I'm sorry Ms. Howard. We can't seem to find much of a credit history on you."

Twenty-four hours after she'd gone in search of food, Jessie found herself standing in the middle of a decent but dark little apartment listening to a kindly older man tell her why she didn't qualify for the apartment.

"I understand," she nodded. Apparently there was a limit to what Gabe could accomplish on such short notice. "How much did you say this apartment is?"

"It's two-fifty."

"Per month?" she choked.

"Yes."

"Are you sure?"

"Yes..." He was starting to get irritated.

"Well, how about if I pay you for the first year up front?"

"Excuse me?"

"How else can I establish credit?" She smiled prettily at him.

"That's not normally how we do it," he hedged.

"Please?"

"You got cash?"

"Why don't I write you a check and I won't move in until it clears the bank. How's that?"

"Welcome home." He smiled broadly at her and extended his hand.

And home it was. After a few more nights at the Super 8, Jessie dove headlong into furniture shopping. It didn't take much to fill her small apartment, but when she was done, everything was set up just right. She chose warm colors when decorating to complement the dark brown carpets. The end result was incredibly cozy.

The weeks blended one into the next. The crisp air and ever-changing trees reminded Jessie of the passage of time. She was grateful for that, and would have been numb without them.

Once the shock of that fateful day had begun to subside, Jessie realized she was lonely. She missed Gabe, Harmony and Vance. She wondered how they were doing.

And she wished she had someone to tell on the day she first noticed her cycle was weeks past due. With little fanfare, she'd gone down to the general store and bought a test. It didn't seem possible that it came back positive, but it did.

An odd mixture of happy and nervous fluttered through her as she tried to process the information. She and Gabe were going to be parents. Would he be happy? She hoped so. Either way, it was something she'd thought beyond her grasp and yet, here it was.

The apartment suddenly seemed too small, too empty. Even if she had no one to tell, she wanted to at least be in the company of other people. She slid on her jacket and locked up her apartment—more out of habit than necessity.

She drove the Plymouth the short distance to the square and parked it in front of a little diner she'd been meaning to try. Ma's seemed like an appropriate place to celebrate. The restaurant was full but somber, making Jessie think she'd inadvertently walked in on something she shouldn't have.

"I'll be right with you," the waitress called out as Jessie slid onto a stool at the counter.

She helped herself to a menu and was ready to order by the time the harried waitress appeared.

"Sorry for the wait, sugar. We're bustin' at the seams tonight since the news about Ma's son got around."

"I'm sorry; I'm new in town…" She furrowed her brow.

"He died—over in Afghanistan. Just got redeployed... barely off the plane and was hit with a roadside bomb. Poor soul." The waitress took a moment to cross herself before getting the glass of milk Jessie ordered.

The burger lost some of its appeal after hearing the fate of Ma's son. It occurred to Jessie that she'd been so immersed in her own trauma, she hadn't put much thought into the fact that Gabe was in very real danger. She missed him, but the question had always been when he came home—not if.

When she'd choked down enough food to be polite, she paid her tab and wandered out onto the street. Not sure how best to start her search, she piled back into the Plymouth and just started driving. When she passed the Douglas County Library, she did a u-turn.

Once she was sitting in front of the Internet browser, she didn't know what to do next.

"What are you looking for, honey?" the friendly librarian called out when she saw the look on Jessie's face.

"A friend. I guess I'm not sure where to start."

"Google." The woman smiled. "Everything's on Google."

"Good point." Jessie flashed her a winning smile before following the advice. As she began to type, the search engine began suggesting searches. A morbid curiosity took over Jessie, and she selected the second choice supplied by Google: Afghanistan troop deaths. Another click and she was on the government's website for casualties in the Afghan war. One more and she was staring at a list of names.

And there was one name that stood out from all the rest. Gabriel Adams, Sergeant First Class, hostile - IED attack.

Pain slammed her in the chest. In frantic denial, she scrolled across the line, hoping that it was another Gabe. Not hers. Let some other woman deal with this injustice. Claws dug into her heart and twisted and she knew that she couldn't foist this misery off on someone else—it would be hers.

"Thank you," she mumbled at the concerned librarian before stumbling across the parking lot to her car... his car. Somehow she made it home without causing a wreck. It took her three tries, but she finally managed to unlock the door. She kicked it closed behind her before falling to the toilet, where she lost her lunch.

When she was pretty sure she could move again, she crawled over to her bed and burrowed under the covers. And there she stayed for the better part of two months.

The baby made her ravenously hungry despite her mood, so she ventured out to stock the refrigerator when necessary. Other than that, she allowed herself the right to simply exist as she grieved.

Vance and Harmony drifted in and out of her thoughts, but the pervading memory was that of Gabe. And then there came a day when she realized that her thickening waist no longer fit comfortably in her clothes and she must either go naked or venture out into the world for more than groceries.

She grudgingly showered, noting for the first time that her blonde hair was rapidly fading to its natural golden brown. That brought a little smile to her face—she hadn't seen her own hair color in a long time.

"Wow—how long was I out?" Jessie muttered to herself when she felt the nip in the wind. The trees had completely shed their leaves. Jessie wasn't sure what day it was; although she was fairly certain it was November.

To her consternation, the Wal-Mart parking lot was empty, as was the town square. Jessie frowned, wondering what she was missing. She parked the Plymouth on the square and got out to walk. She was tired of her apartment and the brisk air felt good.

A movement in Ma's Diner caught her eye; it seemed to be the one place in town that was open.

"Afternoon," an older gentleman with graying hair and square glasses greeted Jessie when she stepped inside.

"Hello." She smiled tentatively, looking around the empty diner. "Where is everyone?"

"Not many people out and about on Thanksgiving," he responded kindly.

"Thanksgiving... really?"

"You sound about like me." He smiled and set a menu in front of her. "Can I get you something to drink?"

"Coffee... no, wait... hot chocolate."

"You sure?"

"I want coffee, but it's bad for the baby," she sighed. She really could use the coffee.

"Congratulations, then." He handed her a steaming mug of cocoa. "So, what brings you to Ma's on Thanksgiving?"

"I guess I lost track of time. I've been a bit of a recluse lately."

"I know the feeling. I was supposed to have Thanksgiving dinner with my daughter and her family, but I couldn't do it. Bless her soul; she's just so... determined to be cheerful."

"Don't have much use for cheerful, either," Jessie commiserated. "My name's Jessie, by the way."

"Milo." He shook her outstretched hand. "But most folks call me Ma."

"Interesting," Jessie mused. Now she understood why he wasn't in the mood for giving thanks. He'd lost his son recently.

"You been in town long?"

"A few months."

"Surprised I haven't seen you around. Small town."

"Like I said, I've been a bit of a hermit."

"You the girl that paid for your rent up front?"

"Word does travel."

"Most folks think you're on the run from the law."

"You can set their minds at ease—I'm just mourning a love lost. Eventually I'll get around to starting a new life, I guess." Jessie didn't see the need for telling him she'd be on the run from something much worse than the law if they knew she was alive. Come to think of it, the law could be looking for her, too, and she just didn't know it.

"I'll be sure to pass the word along," he nodded. "And I'm sorry to hear."

"Was the outlaw story more interesting?" she teased, unwilling to think about Gabe.

"We have our fair share of good outlaw stories." He smiled.

"So I've heard." A sad smile played upon her lips.

"You know Jesse James settled here after he faked his death."

"I saw the initials at Honeybranch."

"Did you, now? Not many people get into Honeybranch these days."

"I think his life is fascinating. I wonder what happened to the daughter."

"Same thing that happens to most women in these parts—she married a local boy and had a passel of kids," he chuckled. "You certainly have done your homework on local lore."

"The stories are what drew me here."

"Any idea what you're going to do now that you are?"

"None whatsoever," she frowned. "I am sick of being in my apartment. I know that much."

"You could always work here. Beth's been after me to hire some help for a while now."

"Really?" Jessie sat up a little straighter. The idea had appeal— she liked this man. There was something comforting in his kind chuckle.

"Sure," he smiled. "How about Saturday and Sunday mornings and a couple of afternoons through the week?"

"That would be nice," she agreed enthusiastically. It would be good to be around people again. After all, what good was her new freedom if all she did was hide in a dark little apartment?

"Why don't you come in this weekend to bus tables and learn the ropes? Say, five Saturday morning?"

Jessie nearly choked. "Huh. Could be interesting. Not sure I've ever seen that particular time of day. Not on purpose anyway."

With another chuckle, Milo poured himself a cup of coffee and sat down next to Jessie at the counter. They whiled away the next few hours talking about anything and nothing in particular. At some point, Milo produced a deck of cards.

"Do you play Rummy?" he asked.

"Five-card draw?" she countered, visions of those last days with Spence flickered in her mind.

Milo nodded his approval and started shuffling the deck. Eventually she called a halt to the game to order dinner before heading home.

"You know what? I had a good day today," she informed the Plymouth as she turned the ignition. "I think we've made our first friend."

Maybe there was something wrong with a person who would talk to a car, but it was the closest she could come to talking to Gabe. Who knows, maybe he heard her, wherever he was.

She flipped on the television to fill the apartment with sound and fell asleep on the couch, her fingers toying with the brim of Gabe's cowboy hat.

The next morning she battled the Christmas shoppers because she needed clothes to wear. It didn't bother her to be the only person in the store with no one to buy presents for, but she was aware of it. She'd bought Harmony a fancy leather portfolio the year before because it seemed like a good gift for a smart person. That was the first gift she'd given anyone since she was five, so it wasn't exactly a hard habit to break.

She also bought herself an alarm clock while she was at the store. The new clock proved its mettle when it roused her at four o'clock in the morning the next day. She was inordinately proud of herself for showing up at Ma's before he did.

"You the new girl?"

"That's me." Jessie recognized the waitress from her first venture into the little diner. She offered a hand. "Jessie."

"Good to meet you, Jessie. I'm Beth."

Jessie followed Beth inside, glad to be in out of the nippy morning. She did her best to be helpful, but felt mostly useless as the proficient waitress went about her morning routine.

"Morning, ladies," Milo called as he entered.

Both women said their hellos, Jessie a little more enthusiastically than Beth.

"I suppose I'll be expected to decorate for Christmas, now," Milo grumbled, noting that his neighbors had apparently decked their establishments out overnight. "Do you know anything about decorating for Christmas?" He looked at Jessie expectantly.

"Red and green, right?"

"I don't believe you two." Beth tsked her disapproval. "Decorating for Christmas is supposed to be fun."

"I'm sure I can figure it out," Jessie assured him, ignoring Beth's admonishment.

"After the morning rush, you mind sticking around to help decorate?"

"Gladly." Jessie really was glad for an excuse to stay longer.

"Would you ladies like some breakfast?" Milo offered.

"You've never fed me breakfast before," Beth huffed.

"I'm offering you some breakfast now," he scowled. "Do you want it or not?"

"I ate oatmeal before I came in," she grumbled.

"No thank you." Jessie was afraid to accept his offer under the weight of Beth's glare.

"Suit yourself, then," he sighed. "Guess we'd better open up shop."

The customers trickled in at first, but the place was soon bustling with activity. Jessie worked hard to keep up with the constant stream of dirty dishes. She was exhausted and thoroughly disgusted by the time the breakfast rush abated, but she felt strangely exhilarated. When Milo smiled approvingly at her, she flushed with pride.

Milo gave her some cash and instructions to get what she needed to "Christmas the place up." Jessie wondered where his Christmas decorations were from the previous year, but didn't ask.

The diner got a little pop of business around lunch, but it was more of a slow, steady stream of people than the madhouse of morning. By one o'clock, the place was pretty calm again and Milo was nosing through the bags Jessie had brought back from the store while she filled out the employment paperwork he'd given her. She tried to be discreet about checking her fake ID for things she should know. Gabe had stuck with the truth when possible – things like her first name and birthday – but the social was manufactured and she had no clue what it was.

"I thought you decided not to decorate for Christmas anymore last year when you threw everything out," Beth reminded him as she sat and sipped on a Coca-Cola.

"I did, but you've been nagging me since Halloween. I couldn't take another month of it."

The gentle ribbing continued as the three of them sorted through the decorations. The women began hanging garland while Milo got them all a bowl of chili for a late lunch. Beth took off afterwards, but Jessie stuck around to help Milo put the finishing touches on the décor.

She handed the mistletoe up to Milo, who perched precariously on a stool to hammer a nail above the door. She couldn't help but smile at the thought of Gabe walking through that door, pulling her into a rakish kiss under the mistletoe. That seemed like something he would have done.

"You miss your man?" Milo read the look on her face.

"Very much." Her throat constricted instantly at the emotion. "How are you doing?"

"That boy was a pain in the ass. Never did what he was told. But I miss him. He was a good man. Always helping people, you know?"

"I do," she nodded.

"You must be tired." He paused to consider her. "I didn't work you too hard today, did I?"

"Are you saying I'm fragile?" She arched an eyebrow and pinned him with her gaze.

"Wouldn't dream of it." He held his hands up in surrender. "But the second shift'll be coming in soon. You might as well head home."

"Oh. Okay. Tomorrow morning, then?"

"Bright and early." He patted her shoulder affectionately.

Jessie gathered her things from the back, sliding her coat on as she walked out the door. The cold smacked her in the face as soon as she stepped into the biting wind. Missouri winters could be unforgiving affairs.

She sat in the Plymouth for a few minutes, holding her hands in front of the heater periodically to test for warmth before tucking her arms back around herself. Eventually she deemed it warm enough to drive and headed over to Wal-Mart. It was her second time in the store in as many days, but this time she was here to wander the Christmas aisles.

It had occurred to her as she hung garland that like it or not, the world was going to continue to turn without Gabe in it. She had to make a life for herself if she was going to be any kind of a mother.

There seemed no better place to start than by decorating her apartment for Christmas.

She took her time in picking out just the right garland and ornaments. It brought back memories of stringing popcorn garland last year with Harmony. The two women had stayed up late into the night, eating as much popcorn as they strung and listening to Christmas music. On a whim, Jessie tossed a Christmas CD in her cart after a packet of gold ornaments.

When she'd filled her cart with Christmas cheer, she stopped by the baby aisle to stare at the little sleepers. It still didn't seem real. She ran her fingers over a fuzzy, yellow-and-white sleeper with ducks on it. It was so tiny. After a brief debate, she put that in her cart too.

Once she had everything unloaded, Jessie contented herself to putter around her apartment, sipping apple cider and decking out her home. Her favorite decoration was the Santa statue by the door. It was kitschy, but cute. Kind of like a garden gnome. She realized halfway through putting together the Christmas tree that she'd begun to talk to her stomach. It made her feel less alone. By the time she sank into bed that night, she was so tired her legs felt like putty, but she was also happier than she'd been in a long while.

Waking up at four o'clock in the morning was slightly more difficult on day two. Still, she managed to be there and functional shortly after Beth arrived to unlock the door. She'd settled into a steady rhythm before the breakfast rush was in full swing. At a quarter to ten, the general din stopped suddenly with the entrance of an attractive brunette in her mid-forties. There was something in her air to be reckoned with as she marched through the diner to the kitchen, heads turning in her wake.

Jessie hesitated to follow the woman into the kitchen, but the desperate need for clean spoons drove her through the doors. Besides, the large open windows on the kitchen meant they had little privacy anyway.

"Jessie, would you order your father around like a child?" Milo demanded as Jessie tried to be invisible.

"I never knew my father." She shrugged.

"You're no help. Tell you what, why don't you go to church with my daughter—she's determined to save a soul."

"Gotta get these spoons to Beth." Jessie darted back out the door before she could be corralled into anything. She had nothing against church per se, but it would be embarrassing if she were struck down for crossing the threshold.

"Jessie—coffee mugs," Beth called as soon as the spoons were in place.

Jessie took a deep breath and dove back into the kitchen just as the woman was informing Milo, "You can't be mad at God forever."

"I'm not mad really." Milo buttered some toast. "More like lodging a formal complaint."

"Well, while you're lodging your complaint, your grandchildren are missing you." The woman crossed her arms as Jessie ducked back out the door.

"Plates," Beth called out no sooner than the mugs were set down.

"How did you people survive before I came along?" Jessie muttered, venturing back into the kitchen for plates.

"Will you at least come to dinner?"

"Alright, alright. Dinner."

Jessie scurried back out of the kitchen, grateful when the woman left. Milo was surly after that, so Jessie avoided him carefully.

"Grandchildren miss me… not likely," he informed the French toast as he flipped it. "I bet she has to pay them to stick around for dinner tonight."

Chapter Fourteen

J essie melted into the couch as soon as she got home. Every piece of her hurt, but the day had passed so quickly it was worth it. Customers at the diner were beginning to chat with her as she bussed tables. For the first time in her life, she felt like the average person could see her. She was no longer an invisible member of society.

She wondered if Jesse James ever worried about his new neighbors finding out his past. More and more, she thought about what life had been like for the granddaughter who was never acknowledged. She wondered what kind of person could throw away a kid like that. Really, the more pressing question was whether or not a throwaway kid could make good in the end.

"No one's ever going to toss you aside," she told the bump in her stomach. Maybe it was the desire to make good on that promise that prompted her to look up the nearest family clinic. The book she'd checked out from the library told her she was in her second trimester now and well past the time for scheduling her first prenatal checkup.

She found herself inexplicably nervous when the time for the exam actually arrived, and equally relieved when it was over with and they had both been pronounced healthy. Armed with a printout of her newly-scheduled doctor's appointments, she realized just how glad she was to have a job now. Even at a subsidized clinic, having a baby uninsured was bound to be expensive. She wondered if there would be anything left when it was all said and done, but there was no sense worrying about that at this stage in the game.

Time flew by since Milo always seemed to have an excuse for her to be at the diner when he was. She enjoyed his odd mix of cranky and kind, taking great pleasure in teasing him as much as he did her. It wasn't long until the two were fast friends.

So it really shouldn't have surprised Jessie the day she walked into work to find the diner decorated with streamers and balloons. "Happy Birthday Jessie" adorned a banner across the far wall.

"Surprise!" a dozen people called when she opened the door. Tears sprang to her eyes and she did a quick u-turn back onto the sidewalk where she gulped in the cold air.

"Jessie." Worry etched Milo's face as he joined her outside. "What's wrong?"

"I've never had a birthday party before," she admitted, flames spreading across her face.

"Oh." He seemed surprised by that. "Not sure if we can live up to the pressure of being your first party, but why don't you come give us a try?"

She let him tuck her hand in the crook of his arm, following him shyly back into the little restaurant. Jessie almost bolted when an enthusiastic cheer went up as they reentered the room, but Milo tightened his grip until she relaxed.

"I never figured you for being such a frightened little bird." He winked.

"Is that the cranky old man equivalent of calling me a chicken?"

"Something like that."

"Fine, I'll go enjoy myself."

"Thatta girl."

"And Milo...thank you."

She made the rounds, chatting with the people she had come to call her friends over the past few weeks.

"Jessie get over here; I've got someone I want you to meet." Milo flagged Jessie down.

She excused herself from a conversation with the man who owned the hardware store and made her way to where Milo stood with a couple about the same age as she and Gabe. The man was the epitome of cowboy; his pregnant wife looked up at him with such adoration it was almost more than Jessie could bear to watch.

"It's so good to meet you, Jessie. I'm Hailey and this is Ethan." The woman greeted Jessie with genuine warmth.

"Pleased to meet you, ma'am." Ethan tipped his head.

"They own Tumbleweed Ranch down the way," Milo explained as if Jessie should know what that meant.

They settled into an easy conversation. She liked them immediately but couldn't help the twinge of jealously their happiness brought. She was a little relieved when Beth interrupted their chat to cut the cake.

All in all, it was the best birthday party Jessie could have asked for and she spent most of the afternoon laughing.

"You guys did not have to get me gifts; this party is more than enough," she protested when they started handing prettily-wrapped packages her way.

"Nonsense." Beth smiled. "It's just a little something."

That little something turned out to be everything from a towel set to knick-knacks to baby furniture. Jessie was flushed with gratitude by the time the pile was opened.

"Thank you." She hugged a sheepish Milo by the neck.

"Hey Ma, the phone's for you," Beth called.

"Take a message," he scowled.

"I think you'll want to take this one." Her smile was knowing.

The entire diner seemed to pick up on Beth's tone, and a hush fell over the previously boisterous crowd.

It was hard for Jessie to hear what Milo was saying, but he was nodding and there were tears in his eyes. When he hung up the phone, he turned to the crowd, a grin unlike any other across his face.

"He's alive. My boy's alive. He'll be home by next week."

The crowd converged on Milo, but Jessie could only sink into the nearest chair. From the bubbles of conversation floating around her, she gathered that Milo's son had been badly burned and had suffered multiple broken bones, but was in fact alive and on his way home.

"I'm so happy for you." Jessie managed that much before retreating to the safety of the Plymouth. She held back the tears until she was home, curled up in bed with Gabe's hat. Then she sobbed for all of the brutal unfairness in the world.

Later that night, she stood on her front porch wrapped in Gabe's sweater and staring at the most beautiful stars she'd ever seen.

"What did I do to piss you off so bad?" she murmured at the heavens. "Tell me and I'll fix it."

The stars twinkled merrily in response.

"Are you even up there? If so... consider this my formal complaint being lodged." The stars didn't answer and her nose was going numb. Deflated and broken, Jessie went to bed.

After a morning of aimlessly puttering around her apartment, she was too annoyed with herself to muddle through the afternoon in the same way so she bundled up and got in the Plymouth, headed anywhere but there. She filled up her tank on the way out of town and just drove.

At some point, the scenery became familiar and she knew she was close to their cave. Acting on instinct, she found herself bumping along a welcome gravel road. She parked the car in front of the log cabin and got out hesitantly.

"Hello?"

Silence was her only answer. She called out again before deciding she was most likely alone. The cave was securely locked and she wasn't about to get arrested for breaking in. She didn't even try the door to the cabin, contenting herself to settle in on the front porch swing.

The crisp air and gentle rustling of the woods soothed her troubled spirit. She let her mind wander. Had Jesse James done anything with the second chance he'd been given? Had he done good in this world once his slate was clean?

As she soaked in her surroundings, the pieces began to fall together. And then, with startling clarity, she knew what she must do with her own clean slate. The how escaped her, but knowing the what was enough to fill her with a new sense of hope.

She wrapped her arms around herself and walked back to the Plymouth, thinking it was sad to see such a beautiful place sit empty and alone. She wondered what happened for it to be abandoned.

All through the evening, she went through the motions of a typical day, but her mind was abuzz with the possibilities of her newfound purpose. The next day she arrived at work early, eager to talk to Milo. Maybe he'd have some ideas.

She could tell he was worried about her, and it took several reassurances for him to stop asking if she was okay. It was almost as if he felt guilty for leaving her to mourn alone. Eventually, he seemed confident enough of her mental stability that he let himself be excited about his son's return.

A dreary drizzle of snow had settled in, which made for a slow afternoon at the diner. She was making them lunch, implementing the skills learned in her recent cooking lessons, when she broached the subject on her mind with Milo.

"So, I've been thinking about what to do... now... next."

"Other than have a healthy baby and learn to be a short order cook, you mean?"

"Yeah. Besides that."

"Okay..."

"I want to help the throwaway kids out there."

"All of them?"

"As many as I can," she answered. "Hey, do you want brown or white gravy on your mashed potatoes?"

"Brown. So how do you plan to do this, exactly?"

"Not sure. I'm thinking I want to set up sort of a halfway house for kids coming out of the foster system. A place to stay while they get their feet under them, mentors to show them how to do it."

"Doesn't the state have that kind of stuff already?" He accepted the plate Jessie handed him through the kitchen window. "Jessie girl, that looks amazing."

"Thanks." She blushed. "And no, they don't. They send kids packing on their 18th birthday with nothing and nowhere to go... at least, they used to. I doubt that's changed."

"You seem to have some firsthand knowledge." Milo regarded her.

"A bit." She blushed deeper as she wiped her hands on her apron. "Do you want a dinner roll?"

"Sure."

Jessie passed the dinner roll and her own plate through the window before coming around to the counter to get herself a glass of milk.

"Jessie my girl, you are shaping up to be a fine cook. This looks delicious."

"Thanks," Jessie beamed at him. The bell on the front door merrily jingled as she rounded the corner and she tried not to groan. A customer meant her efforts would be cold by the time she could enjoy them. She looked up and her smile vanished. The blood drained from her face. He looked as surprised as she, but recovered more quickly and strode to cover the distance between them as she hit the floor in a dead faint.

Chapter Fifteen

When her eyes fluttered open, she wondered if she'd been transported into some sort of a dream. If it hadn't been for the steady throb in the back of her head, she'd have been certain of it.

How else could she now be cradled in Gabe's arms, his anxious face only inches from hers? What other explanation could there be for the hand that cupped her face or the thumb that stroked her cheek?

Unable to speak, Jessie reached her fingers up to touch his face, fully expecting them to go right through a mirage. Only they didn't, and the face was different. Still beautiful, but hardened by a network of scars working their way down the right side from his temple to his neck. His warm chocolate eyes seemed so worried—about her. Didn't he know he was the one that was dead?

"Jessie, Jessie." Milo's face appeared above Gabe's. "Are you okay? Do you think the baby's okay?"

"Baby?" Gabe choked on the word, his eyes flying from hers to her stomach and back again.

Suddenly, somehow, the spell between them was broken. He straightened, his body language altogether changing.

"Can you stand?" Milo was reaching for her as Gabe was almost shoving her off of him.

"I'm fine, I'm fine. Just a little embarrassed." She flushed and batted away their hands once she was on her feet. She looked expectantly at Gabe, but his face was cold. "You know what, though, maybe I should go home and lie down. Just to be safe. I'm so sorry Milo."

"No, it's my fault. I've been working you too hard. Gabe, drive Jessie home. I don't want her trying to go herself."

"Are you sure?" He seemed hesitant to leave.

"Of course, we've got plenty of time to catch up. Come on back when you get her settled," Milo insisted before hugging Gabe in the most impulsive action Jessie'd ever seen from him. "Praise God for second chances; we can talk when you get back son."

The truth crashed over Jessie at once and she felt so stupid for not seeing it sooner. Ma—Milo Adams. No wonder she liked him so much; he was Gabe's father.

"I'll call you later," she promised as she kissed Milo's cheek on the way out the back door.

"Where am I taking you?"

"The apartments on 8th." Jessie wanted to scream. She wanted to cry. Why was he being so distant? Why wasn't this a good reunion? "What did I miss here?"

"I doubt you miss much." He slammed the door to the Plymouth.

"What's that supposed to mean?"

"Is he going to be there?"

"He who?"

"That's rich. How long after I was gone before you two started procreating? Did you even wait that long?"

"Shut up, you bastard." She spat the words, furious at the tears that sprang to her eyes. Stupid hormones.

"I guess I know why you never returned my calls. I didn't want to believe it when they said the two of you ran off together."

"Who's they? Who did I run off with? Wait…you think this is Spence's baby? That he's here?" It dawned on Jessie where his mind had gone. She closed her eyes in a bid for patience.

"Tell me he's not." Gabe's voice was hard. He put the car into park and turned to face her.

"If I have to tell you—if there is a doubt in your mind—then you don't deserve me and you damn sure don't deserve this baby." With that, she got out and marched to her apartment, only to realize that he still had her keys. She turned to get them and bumped into a solid wall of chest.

"The baby's mine?" His voice was broken.

"Give me my keys, you big fat jerk."

"I love you, too." His forehead came to rest on hers.

"Get off of me." She shoved at him, wishing she wouldn't start crying so easily. She snatched her keys from his hand and turned to unlock her door, but his arms were around her, pulling her back before she could even get the key out of the lock.

"No, Jessie, I went completely out of my mind when I went to find you and you were gone. Everyone said you took off with Spence. You hadn't answered any of my calls. Please, listen to me."

"No. See, from my point of view, you left me for dead. I barely got away alive and then spent months mourning you because some stupid website told me you were gone forever. I've been scared and alone and you don't get to be mean to me now, Gabriel McAlister Adams." Her voice rose steadily as she spoke.

He answered her with a kiss. It was more than hungry; it was filled with months' worth of fear and uncertainty and longing. It was a thousand I'm sorrys and ten thousand I love yous. They stumbled back through the door together, barely kicking it closed before the clothes started falling.

She wanted to devour him, each and every inch of him. Jessie lost track of the kisses and caresses and all sense of time; she needed to rememorize the curve of every muscle. She hadn't done a good enough job of that before. She'd taken him for granted and the memories had faded too quickly. Now they flared back to life, fueled by the heat of his presence.

She closed her eyes and wept freely as he trailed feathery kisses along her neck, his hands running along the bends of her body.

And when they moved together, it was in perfect concert. He gathered her in his arms and held her close. Jessie wrapped her legs around him, sure she could never be close enough. How she loved this man.

They were still wrapped in each other's arms when the phone started ringing.

"Bet that's Milo." Jessie reached for the offending sound.

"I'll talk to him. Oh, he's going to be pissed at me."

"Then let me talk to him. He likes me."

"Very funny, thanks." Gabe made a face at her as he answered the phone.

Jessie couldn't help but feel bad for Gabe as she listened to a very different conversation than the kind she had with Milo. It was obvious that once Milo was assured that Jessie was indeed fine, he wasn't too happy with his son for not adequately answering his questions.

"We should probably get dressed," Gabe sighed when he hung up the phone. "He's coming over."

Jessie let out a shriek and moved as quickly as her new bulk would allow her to. It wasn't a long trip from the diner.

"That's my sweater." He seemed pleased by the fact that she'd donned something of his.

"It is." She smiled and ruffled his hair before moving to brush her own.

"I like the dark blonde."

"I'm glad."

"Is the baby a girl or a boy?" He ran his fingers through his own hair before bending over to place his hands on her stomach.

"I don't know yet." She smacked his hands away. "And you need to put clothes on."

She darted to the living room to start rounding clothes up from the floor, tossing them into the bedroom.

"Dang it, where's my bra?"

"Not sure." He shrugged and gave her a rakish grin. "I was a little preoccupied at the time."

"That helps." She scowled at him.

"Well, it's the truth."

"How are you not dressed yet?" She put her hands on her hips and regarded him with exasperation. Although she had to grudgingly admit that she liked the way he looked in jeans and nothing else. She licked her lips unconsciously and he playfully arched an eyebrow.

"Think we can fit another round in?"

"You're such a jerk."

"You were the one looking at me like I'm lunch."

"I never did get lunch because of you." Her mind switched

gears. "And put a shirt on."

A knock at the door silenced his reply and served as incentive for him to finally slide a white t-shirt on if nothing else. Jessie smirked before opening the door to a frowning Milo.

"What aren't you two telling me?"

"Milo...meet your grandchild." She took his hand and put it on her stomach. The look on his face made Gabe laugh before he could catch himself. He quickly sobered at the new look on Milo's face.

"Why didn't you tell me?" He looked at Jessie with wounded eyes.

"I didn't know. Not until Gabe walked into your diner. Then it fell into place."

"Gabe?" Milo looked to his son.

"Why don't you come in, Dad?"

"Oh, and you guys left these outside." Milo pulled the keys out of the doorknob and held them up.

"Thanks." Jessie sheepishly reclaimed them, noticing her bra on the Santa statue's head after she closed the door behind Milo.

"Why didn't you two say something at the diner?" he persisted.

"It was a lot to process at once," Gabe began, breaking off when he noticed Jessie trying to position herself between Milo and the bra. He pressed his lips together and swallowed the laughter before continuing. "I left for the war before Jessie even knew about the baby."

"This still doesn't make sense. Why didn't you call her when you did me?"

"I tried." He paused, considering his next words. "We'd lost touch."

"Lost touch? You're not married?"

"Not for his lack of trying," Jessie assured Milo, if for no other reason than to get Gabe out of hot water. "Now why don't you two go see what you can find me for lunch? I need to lie on the couch for a bit."

Jessie grabbed the bra and stuffed it behind the couch as soon as Milo was in the kitchen.

"You have no good groceries. You'd starve if it wasn't for me, you know that, young lady?"

"Then it's good I have you," she retorted. "And I do okay. There's decent fast food here for such a small town."

"Fast food. Humph. That's so bad for you."

"But I hate to cook."

"You're a good cook."

"That's different. I don't exactly have the same setup here."

"I have stepped into the Twilight Zone, haven't I?" Gabe looked from one to the other, reaching for Jessie as she joined the men in the kitchen.

"You should go lay down," Milo ordered.

"But I don't want to let her go," Gabe argued. "I thought I'd lost her forever."

Milo stopped rooting for food to study the pair. A small smile tugged at his mouth.

"I don't think I want to know the whole story. I like seeing you in love, Gabe. It suits you."

"I don't think I can tell you the whole story, Milo. But I was living a life you wouldn't approve of when Gabe found me. I was a prisoner in a world most don't understand." She snuggled deeper into Gabe's embrace, hugging his arms to her as she did. "Gabe saved me. And I saved him. And together we saved a whole lot of innocent girls from the same prison. And now I'm dead to that world—I live here."

Milo nodded. Silence hung in the air for a moment before he took a deep breath. "I'm going to the diner to make us some food. Try not to lose any more women's undergarments before I get back."

"I make no promises," Gabe chuckled. Jessie elbowed him in the ribs.

"I got your message after you left," Jessie told him once they were alone. "I listened to it three times before curling up with the phone and dreaming of you."

The look on Gabe's face said he needed to hear that. He tugged her back to the bedroom, this time to spread out on top of the bed in a lazy embrace while they talked.

"I didn't know what to think when you didn't answer the phone," he admitted.

"Vance woke me up that day. Said the raid had gone down already and that Aleksandar was coming for me. Spence found the phone and broke it...we were fighting when the men came. They loaded us into an SUV and drove us to a boat ramp north of St. Louis—in Illinois."

"Wait a second... the raid wasn't supposed to happen for two more days. They were supposed to extract you first."

"Guess that didn't seem too important once you were gone," she shrugged. "But I'm happy to know you thought I wasn't in danger. Vance was so pissed at you... said you let me do the dirty work and left me to pay the price."

"Where was Vance when the Bosnians showed up?" Gabe retorted.

"He was with us. But Aleksandar wasn't sure what to do with him. He saw potential in Vance. You know they shot him, Gabe. Spence. They lined us up and shot him. He'd just apologized and then he was gone. They tried to shoot me, too, but I jumped in the water."

"The Mississippi?"

"It seemed better than a bullet in the brain. Turns out it was."

His arms tightened around her and she couldn't be sure, but he seemed to be crying.

"I'm so sorry, baby. I'm so, so sorry."

"I missed you." She reached up to sink her fingers in his hair. She wanted to tell him it was all okay, but it wasn't yet. She still hadn't entirely processed that trauma. "So what about you? Why were you dead?"

"Clerical error."

"What really happened?"

"I'm telling you—a clerical error. I was injured. I have a few souvenirs to show for it." He ran a finger down the side of his face. "I didn't know what had happened at first or I would have called Dad sooner."

"You're not getting off that easy."

"Yeah, well, my story wasn't nearly as harrowing yours, and we have something more important to discuss at the moment."

"Really? What's that?"

"My dad will be back any time now and he will have one question burning on his brain—when's the wedding?"

"Who's wedding?"

"Ours."

"Tell me you're joking."

"Ouch."

"Seriously." Jessie sat up and folded her arms, glaring at him. "We barely know each other."

"We know each other at least a little." He gestured at her stomach.

"But that's not enough."

"Enough for what?" he snapped in exasperation.

"Enough to keep you from getting bored with me. You know who my best customers were? Other women's husbands." She felt cheap and embarrassed at the admission, but she'd always been thankful that no matter what she was, she wasn't the woman on the other end.

"Your faith in us is astounding."

"Two hours ago you were certain this was another man's baby. Your faith in us is astounding."

"Okay, look at this a different way. How are you going to pay for having a baby?"

"Cash."

"And you'll be completely penniless when it's all said and done."

"Are you suggesting I give birth someplace other than a hospital?" Jessie retorted.

"I'm suggesting you marry me and let me add you to my insurance plan."

"So in essence, you'd be paying me…"

"Good Lord, you can be stubborn woman." He ran his fingers through his hair in exasperation. "Isn't there anything else you'd rather do with that money? Is it so horrible to give us a chance?"

Jessie couldn't help but think of her halfway house for foster kids. The money sitting in her bank account would go a long way towards making that a reality.

"You're thinking about it," he grinned. "I can almost see the wheels turning."

"You are such a jerk."

"I love you, too. Marry me and maybe someday I can convince you to love me back."

"You stupid man. Have you even looked around this apartment?"

"What's that supposed to mean?"

She walked into the living room to retrieve the hat she'd clung to in his absence and held it up for him to see. "I've slept with this more nights than not. I actually wore a spot on the brim rubbing my thumb along it. I talk to your car like it's you. I get some pretty incredulous looks over that one. Let's see... your clothes are everywhere because if I'm not wearing them, I'm smelling them. Hell, the fact that I'm in Ava, Missouri should count for something."

"What are you trying to say, sugar?"

Jessie knew he was toying with her, trying to coax the words from her. She narrowed her eyes and considered calling him a jerk. Instead, she reached out to set the hat on his head and smiled. "You scare me."

"Because..."

"I love you," she conceded.

"Ah...she said it!" He rejoiced, coming off the bed to playfully twirl her around before pulling her into a bear hug. "Come on. You can totally divorce me and take everything I own if you get sick of me."

"I'll think about it."

"Better think fast," Gabe informed her when there was a knock at the door.

Jessie rolled her eyes and shoved him away so she could let Milo in.

"Hello Jessie-girl." Milo gave her a peck on the cheek as he passed by. "I brought roast beef and mashed potatoes. Hope that's okay."

"It's perfect. Can we get anything for you?"

"Maybe Gabe could grab the drinks out of the car. I made you a shake."

"Thank you." Jessie blinked back tears, cursing the hormones for her lack of control. "You didn't have to do that."

"Nonsense. It's a celebration. I brought beverages of a different kind for me and Gabe."

"Ah. Well, then I accept the milkshake with much thanks."

It was obvious that Gabe was enjoying this newfound truce with his father. The two men chatted about town gossip and Jessie found that more often than not, she had something to contribute. She had truly become a part of this place.

"So, have you two talked at all about marriage? You know Elizabeth will be fit to be tied." Milo leaned back in his chair, resting his folded hands on his full belly.

"Jessie here has some concerns about getting married just because of the baby... she thinks I'll get bored with her," Gabe tattled.

"The girl knows her mind. Don't go trying to get me to force her into a shotgun wedding," Milo reprimanded his son, whose face fell. "You'll have to win her over all on your own. And you're telling your sister. I'm already in trouble with her."

Jessie gave him a smug look before clearing away the dinner dishes. The party moved from the kitchen to the living room and was still going strong when Jessie fell asleep on Gabe's shoulder.

Chapter Sixteen

T he next few days were surreal. With Christmas so close, Jessie suddenly found herself in the odd predicament of having many gifts she felt compelled to buy and little time to do it. Even more frustrating was her complete lack of experience in picking out presents for people.

She and Gabe made a day of driving into Springfield to shop together for many of their friends and family, which took much of the burden off of her. But it did nothing to help her where he was concerned. And the fact that she couldn't think of one thing to buy him for Christmas only served to solidify her certainty that marriage was out of the question. She tried watching him closely as they shopped, hoping to gain some insight into what a man like him might enjoy. Unfortunately, he seemed to be the least materialistic person on the planet.

As if making up for lost time, they were together every waking moment. Gabe worked her shifts at the diner with her, although he was still on a disability leave from the STLPD, so it was unofficial assistance.

They talked constantly at first, filling each other in on every detail the other had missed. It meant the world to Jessie when he finally shared more than the basic facts about his time in Afghanistan, when he opened up about things like fear and pain and watching friends die at his side. She couldn't fully understand the horrors he'd seen, but her heart broke for him all the same. Sometimes he'd get a haunted look in his eyes that made her want to wrap him in her arms and soothe it all away.

Despite all he'd been through, even with the scars he would always carry and the bones that still protested the damage done, he was lucky to be alive and they both knew it. Not everyone in his unit had been so fortunate. Jessie felt both guilty for having wished that pain on another woman and grateful for the miracle of having Gabe home.

The more they talked, the more they began to piece together what had really happened in those few dark days. The more they pieced together, the more questions they had.

According to Dan, no one had seen Vance in over a month. Harmony had disappeared as well, though most people assumed she'd moved back in with her parents. Jessie toyed with the idea of checking; she felt like she owed Harmony at least that much.

Gabe called Carter for an update on the arrests made during the raid. There was some concern Coleman would walk away from the whole mess. His attorney seemed to be doing a good job of fast-talking his way out of the girls found captive. The Feds had gotten involved and were now trying to put together a money trail connecting Coleman to illegal activity.

Gabe tried to feel out the details of the raid, but didn't have much luck. All he really found out was that the Bosnians who hadn't been arrested had gone underground—Aleksandar included. And he got confirmation that both Spence and Jessie were presumed dead.

"Well, that's one piece of good news," he sighed when he hung up the phone, rubbing his forehead as if it would stimulate thought.

"What's that?"

"You're free to move on with life."

"I can't just walk away." She shook her head.

"Why not? It's been months since the raid. What can you even do at this point? What if they arrested you—what would happen to the baby?"

"Arrest me for what? Not dying when they wanted me to?"

"I don't know, but I wouldn't put it past them. Brunner hates you."

"He's probably the one that made the decision to move ahead with the raid."

"Yeah. And Carter's not telling me because word's gotten around that I pulled him off you the last time he tried to shut your mouth."

"I was pretty glad you did, by the way."

"You're welcome." He grinned at the memory. "I didn't know a person could get that red in the face and not have a coronary."

"You don't think there's anything else going on there, do you?"

"Like what?"

"I don't know. What if Brunner rushed things to protect Aleksandar? Wouldn't be the first time an officer was bought."

"Just because you don't like the guy." Gabe scowled but stopped short at the look Jessie gave him. "Sorry. You're right—it's a possibility. I'll keep nosing around."

"Are you planning on staying with the department?"

"I'm not sure, really."

"Oh." It hadn't occurred to Jessie that he could be going back to St. Louis once his leave was up. As much as she loved her old home, she wasn't ready to leave this place.

"What do you think I should do?" Gabe asked, thoroughly surprising Jessie.

"I like it here. I want to raise my baby in a place like this. Her roots are here."

"Her?"

"Either it's a girl or I apologize now for any gender confusion I might cause." She held her hands up.

"Okay." He nodded, considering. "I'll talk to Bobby after the holidays. Maybe they have room at the sheriff's department down here."

"What? You don't want to help run the diner?"

"I have no desire to be Ma Jr." He smiled and kissed her forehead. "And I think he's grooming you for that honor."

"Hardly." She regarded him skeptically. "I bus tables and wash dishes."

"I know my dad. He's training you."

"You'd really stay here because I want to?"

"It would be much harder to convince you to marry me if I lived four hours away."

"Stubborn man," she teased, but something inside warmed at his words. His persistence was endearing, but more than that, it was the first time in her life she'd been able to choose something as basic as where to live. The apartment didn't count; she'd stumbled into that. This was a conscious choice and it felt good.

It was hard finding time without Gabe around to seek advice on his Christmas present. He was staying with his father—a measure of decorum insisted on by his sister. Jessie was certain he gave in so easily as a way of toying with her. She missed him when he was gone, but he was always there bright and early the next morning. Sometimes he'd slide into bed with her before she was even awake.

Those were the mornings it was especially difficult to get out from under the covers. But this morning, Gabe was running late and Jessie seized the opportunity to seek help from one of Gabe's friends. The drive to Tumbleweed Ranch was a short one, made slightly longer by the u-turn Jessie had to make after zipping right past it.

Having never been there before, she was completely blown away by the rugged beauty of the place. She'd never been much into animals, more from lack of exposure than anything, but even she had to admit there was something magical about this ranch. She parked the Plymouth next to Ethan's old red truck and climbed out. A pack of dogs came barreling towards her and she quickly hopped back in.

They surrounded the car, howling merrily as their tails wagged greeting. Jessie eyed them suspiciously, wondering if they were trying to lure her into the open with a friendly demeanor. A big black and red speckled hound stood on his back legs, his paws on her window as nose sniffed around, leaving streaks she didn't want to identify on the glass. His ears were each twice the size of his big, slobbery face. A whistle sliced through the air and those ears came forward, his face wrinkling in concentration. Another whistle and his head whipped around; he clambered down from the car and merrily lumbered over to Ethan, the rest of his band of merry misfits following.

"Sorry about the welcoming committee." Ethan grinned, opening the door for her. "They love visitors."

"Ah." Jessie eyed them warily. The speckled dog meandered back over to say hello and she tentatively held a hand out for him to sniff; that seemed like the right way to greet a dog. She'd seen it once on television anyway.

"Don't worry, Blue is a big-ole baby," Ethan assured her. "Rover there is a bit shyer. We think he was being used for dogfights before he came our way. But he's friendly once he gets to know you. The rest of this pack came with the place. We let them stay when we bought it—didn't seem right to turn them out just because their owner got out of farming."

"Ah." Jessie said again. "They're very cute."

"Not a dog person?" He grinned. He had a very easy and contagious smile.

"Just not much experience."

"They'll grow on you. Hailey'd have a hundred if she could."

Jessie wasn't sure how to respond to that. She couldn't fathom the drool and fur that would come along with one hundred dogs.

"Hailey's not here right now," he told her apologetically. "She... had to run into town for a bit."

"That's okay; I came to see you, actually. I hope it's not a bad time."

"Not at all. I was just heading to the stables to turn the horses out. Walk with me?"

"Sure." Jessie was curious to see the horses she'd heard so much about. One thing she'd learned early on was that Ava prided itself in being the home of the Missouri Fox Trotter. And here, a stone's throw from the Missouri Fox Trotter Association and arena, Tumbleweed Ranch was home to more than a hundred Mustangs. It would have been considered sacrilege if anyone else had tried it. But being mad at Ethan and Hailey would have been like kicking a kitten; no sane person could do it.

"Most of the horses are free range. They're in the southwest pasture this week. The ones in here are either our riding horses, or the ones being trained," Ethan was explaining as he threw open the stable doors to let sunlight stream in.

"The government pays you to house wild Mustangs—isn't that what I heard?"

"Yep. And then we train them when they're adopted. We also contract with the BLM—Bureau of Land Management—to purchase twenty or so every year that we train and sell. Although, we try to do groundwork on as many of them as possible... it just makes things easier."

"Groundwork?"

"We teach them their manners."

"Oh. He's pretty."

"That's Tumbleweed. He's a special boy—aren't you?" Ethan ran his hand along the horse's face while the animal mouthed at his coat in a friendly greeting. It was an unusually colored animal.

Jessie wasn't sure what color to call him. Tan seemed the closest, but he was almost gray in a certain light. A brown horse nickered impatiently from the stall next to him.

"Alright, Mac, I'm coming..."

"Can I do something to help?" Jessie offered, not sure what she could possibly do.

"Sure." Ethan deftly slid a halter over the brown horse's head before opening the stall. He led the horse out and handed the end of the lead rope to Jessie. "Walk him that way. I'll be right there with Tumbleweed."

Jessie deeply regretted offering to help, but took the rope handed to her and walked in the direction told. The animal followed her docilely, for which she was eternally grateful. Before this moment, she had only seen horses on television or from a distance. Neither had given her a true feel for the power they contained. She couldn't imagine purposely crawling on the back of one of these beasts.

"I didn't know horses got this furry," she admitted, tentatively reaching out to touch Mac's neck as they stood waiting for Ethan and Tumbleweed.

"Some don't because their owners keep them blanketed or in heated stalls. Some people shave them. We let ours get their winter coats. We try to let them just be horses, you know?"

"I like it."

"Hailey says they look like teddy bears."

Jessie smiled, sinking her fingers into the thick fur. The horse was solid muscle underneath. "I like him."

"Mac and I go way back. He's my boy."

Jessie watched with interest as he released the two horses into a nearby paddock. They made a beeline for the hay. Ethan closed the gate and hung the halters on a nearby hook before going to retrieve more horses. Jessie followed, this time leading a gray mare while he led a black mare to a separate paddock. She felt like quite the pro by the time he closed the second gate.

"So, I'm sure you didn't come all the way out here this time of day to help me turn out horses." Ethan leaned against the gate he'd closed, turning his attention fully to Jessie.

"I need help. I have no idea what to get Gabe for Christmas."

"Cutting it a little close, aren't you?"

"I thought he was dead a week ago and haven't been able to shake him since. I'm surprised I got away this morning, to be honest."

"He's with Hailey picking out your gift," Ethan admitted with a chuckle.

"That explains it."

"He is a tough one to buy for." Ethan considered carefully. "How much do you want to spend?"

"How much should I spend?"

"I can't answer that one for you, but I need to know what ballpark I'm shooting for, Jess."

"Given the situation, if it's the right gift, I'll spend what I need to. I really want it to be something special."

"This is going to sound incredibly self-serving, but you could always get him a horse." Ethan shrugged.

"A horse?"

"He used to be my partner, before he got it in his head to move to the city. I've got a big bay out back that I know he'd love. If you guys are serious about staying here, I think he'd enjoy having a horse again."

"A horse," Jessie considered it. It was certainly a big gift. It wouldn't go unnoticed or be easily forgotten. "How much and what's your return policy?"

"The adoption fee is $125 because I haven't even started training him yet...and if he hates the gift, I'll buy him back."

"Aren't horses supposed to be expensive?"

"They are—to feed. You can board him here as long as you need, though."

"You really think he'd like it?"

"Like I said, maybe it's self-serving... but I really think training this horse would be good for him right now. He's got a lot bumping around in his brain."

"He wouldn't do something like this for himself," Jessie agreed. "He never stops to think about himself."

"Do you want to see the horse? Maybe that'll help."

"Yeah." Jessie straightened. "I would like to see him."

"Come on, then." Ethan motioned for her to follow him. She was surprised when he opened the door to his truck but climbed in.

"I don't want you to go to too much trouble."

"No trouble. It's just a bit of a long hike and I don't think I should put you on the back of a horse at the moment."

Jessie nodded, taking in the surroundings as they drove further into the property, stopping occasionally for Ethan to open and close gates. A few minutes later, they stopped in a clearing near a meandering, half-frozen creek. A herd of horses stood packed together near a mountain of hay. Their heads popped up at the sound of the truck, watching the intruders with wary curiosity.

Ethan sat in the window of his truck and let out a sharp whistle. The horses started and a large reddish animal came to the front of the group. His legs, mane and tail were black, and it looked like he had little white socks just over his hooves on three out of four legs. His long mane and tail were caught up in the wind, making him look like something straight out of the old west.

Jessie knew absolutely nothing about horses, but he was the most beautiful animal she'd ever seen. He matched Gabe: somehow elegant and rugged at once.

"I'll do it," she decided in an instant.

"Don't worry; if I'm wrong, Hailey'll have my hide."

"I'm not worried. He's so pretty—Gabe has to love him." Jessie couldn't help but laugh at Ethan's reassurance.

"I'll bring him up to one of the paddocks before you guys come over for dinner tomorrow night."

"Perfect. Thank you!" Jessie impulsively hugged Ethan's neck.

When they got back to the house, Ethan made Jessie a cup of hot apple cider while she filled out the adoption paperwork for the horse.

The dog known as Blue started making a noise that was a mix between a bark and a howl and Ethan scrambled to gather the paperwork.

"Hailey's home. Blue always bawls like that when she's back. We'd better hide this in case she brought Gabe with her."

A moment later, Gabe was walking through the front door with Hailey. Jessie couldn't help grinning at the secret she shared with Ethan. Gabe was sporting a similar smile, and Jessie took that to mean he was happy with his own outing.

"Funny meeting you here," he teased, leaning over to kiss Jessie good morning before greeting Ethan with a clap on the back.

Ethan insisted on making breakfast for everyone. The others sat around the kitchen table, sipping their hot drinks and debating whether or not Mary Atchison was secretly dating Bobby the Sheriff.

Hailey's teenage son wandered down the stairs at the smell of bacon. Rumpled and half-awake, he gave a small wave before pouring himself a glass of orange juice and stumbling to the living room to turn on the television.

He seemed like a good kid, which was a credit to Hailey. She'd raised him alone after her first husband had decided marriage might include work. Jessie wondered how difficult it had been for Hailey to trust Ethan on the heels of that.

After breakfast, Gabe stuck around to help Ethan with his chores. Just as he'd transformed on their first trip together, Gabe seemed to relax as he performed the physical labor. It made Jessie all the more sure of their decision to stay. Not that going back to St. Louis had ever been a choice for Jessie. She was pretty sure if she ever showed her face their again, she'd be dead shortly after.

Chapter Seventeen

Christmas morning was a beautiful thing. The day dawned crisp and cold, a fine layer of white dust covering a gray-toned world. It might not have been the fort-building snows of childhood, but any white on Christmas morning was better than none at all.

Her tree twinkled merrily with red and white lights, casting a happy glow on the presents wrapped in silver. Jessie put some water on the stove to make some apple cider before hurrying to freshen up before Gabe arrived.

By the time he let himself in the front door, she was sitting serenely by the tree in flannel pajamas, watching the lights and drinking her cider.

"Merry Christmas!" Her face lit up at the sight of him. He was ridiculously handsome. Jessie wondered how a flannel shirt and jeans could make anyone look so completely edible. She sat the mug of cider on the coffee table and held her arms out expectantly.

"I've never seen anything so beautiful in my life." He accepted the offering and scooped her into his arms. "Merry Christmas, baby… and baby."

"The second baby says hi back."

"I wish I could feel her kick." He placed his hands on Jessie's stomach with wonder.

"You will soon enough, I'm sure."

"Are you certain everything is okay? You don't look nearly as pregnant as my sister did."

"Everything's fine. We're just built differently. And I wouldn't tell your sister that if I were you," she advised.

"Do you want to exchange gifts?" He switched gears, suddenly as excited as a small child.

"I hadn't planned on doing that until tonight."

"Please?"

"But yours isn't here." She started to panic.

"Did you forget to get me a present? It's okay; I still love you."

"Very funny. It wouldn't fit here so Ethan's keeping it for me."

"It wouldn't fit?"

"I guess technically it would have, but that just seemed awkward," she toyed with him.

"Now I'm curious. Give me a hint?"

"Nope. But you can give me my present if you want."

"No fair. Maybe I should make you wait, too."

"If you want."

"Aren't you the slightest bit curious?"

"Whenever is fine," she assured him nonchalantly. In truth, she was dying of curiosity.

"Well, if you're going to beg, I guess you can open it now." He grabbed a small box from under the Christmas tree and handed it to her, sitting lightly on the edge of the coffee table to watch her open it.

Jessie eyed him warily, unnerved by the size of the box. Surely he wouldn't ruin the day by pushing marriage again. She carefully unwrapped the package to reveal a small velvet box. Her heart hammered in her throat. She cracked the box open and tears sprang to her eyes.

"Do you like it?" he asked anxiously when she didn't comment.

"It's beautiful." She kissed him lightly on the edge of the mouth. The necklace was beautiful, and incredibly sweet.

Yet for some reason she couldn't define, she was disappointed it wasn't a ring.

"It's your birthstone," he offered, reaching for the box.

"I know." She smiled. "It's amazing... and too much."

"The color reminded me of your eyes." He held the necklace up, the icy blue topaz and diamonds sparkled merrily as they reflected the twinkling Christmas lights.

"I love white gold." She reached up to touch the delicate chain. "Can you put it on me?"

She lifted her hair for him to fasten the pendant around her neck, smiling when he used the opportunity to kiss the back of her neck.

"Thank you so much, I love it," she promised, sinking her fingers in his hair to pull him in for a kiss.

"I'm not sure I believe you." He frowned. "There's something you aren't telling me."

Jessie questioned the sanity of falling in love with a man trained to know when he was being lied to.

"What do you want for breakfast?" she redirected the conversation.

"Not yet. You have one more present."

"No, I already can't compete."

"Good thing it's not a competition. I think you'll like this one." His face lit up again and he retrieved another box from under the tree. This was one was larger but flat. Curiosity piqued, Jessie accepted the box from him and quickly unwrapped it.

She had to read the paper three times before she processed what it was telling her, and even then she looked up at him incredulously, not sure she believed it.

"I don't understand."

"It's not as big of a deal as you might think."

"Is this for real?"

Gabe nodded, obviously pleased at her reaction.

"But how? Why?"

"None of us ever really had any use for it. It seemed too much for any one person. I talked to Dad and Elizabeth; they both thought it was a great idea. So we had the paperwork drawn up. Although, you owe us each a dollar. For some reason, it's better to put it down as a sale than a gift."

"Honeybranch is mine?"

"We thought it seemed like the perfect place to start your halfway house for foster children. With a little work, we can turn it back into a working ranch. The kids can live and work there while they figure out their next steps."

Jessie couldn't begin to process it all. She took a deep breath to say something and instead burst into tears. Gabe's expression was one of shock and he did the only thing there was to do; he wrapped her in his arms.

The flood of emotion embarrassed her, which made her cry even harder. She didn't know how to begin telling him what was wrong—or rather, what was right.

"I guess you've figured it out by now, but my family is the product of Jesse James's second life. The bitter old goat probably rolled over in his grave when the legitimate line of his family died out and the family estate passed to the hands of the bastard branch."

Jessie laughed at that, wiping her eyes as she did. "But why would you give it to me?"

"I'd give you my whole life if you'd let me. This way, it's no strings attached. If you give me the boot, the land is still yours."

"I get that you're nuts, but why would your sister and father do that?"

"Neither of them have any real use for the land but none of us can bring ourselves to sell the place. They like the idea of using it to help kids in need."

"Wait a second… if you own the place, why haven't you been staying there?"

Gabe shrugged, standing up to grab her mug off the coffee table. "Do you need a refill?"

"I'd love an answer to my question."

"When you opened the necklace a look flickered across your face… what was it?"

"More apple cider would be lovely."

"That's what I thought," he snickered. "Do you want an omelet while I'm at it?"

"Sure." Jessie leaned back on the couch, toying absentmindedly with the pendant while she flipped through the deed papers for her new property. "I don't think I've ever even seen 285 acres, let alone thought about owning that much. Actually, I've never really owned anything before."

"If you want to go explore later, let me know. I can give you the grand tour. There's a main house there, too. I know your rent is paid up here, but you could move to the house if you wanted. Of course, I'd feel better if you had a dog or something."

"A dog?" Jessie couldn't help the small shudder as she thought of Blue.

"Yeah, you know… walks on four legs, wags its tail at you when you come home, barks at intruders… a dog."

"I'll have to think about that one."

"You don't like dogs?" He stopped mid-motion to stare incredulously at her. "Who doesn't like dogs?"

"Rethinking our relationship now?"

"You really don't like dogs?"

"They're very cute… from a distance."

"You've just not been properly acclimated, that's all. First chance we get, let's get you a dog."

"I'd prefer not."

"Maybe we'll just look at some; then you can decide."

"Sure. I'll look," she promised, if only to move the conversation along. She didn't want to spend Christmas morning arguing over the merits of having a dog. Maybe getting a horse would satisfy his sudden need for a four-legged creature.

The rest of the morning was a cozy one, though Jessie occasionally had to consciously set aside stray thoughts that would creep into her brain and threaten her contentment. Memories of Vance and Harmony haunted her. Was Harmony having a good Christmas with her family? Was she safe and warm and happy?

Then there were the doubts that would break through—was a whore with no college education really the best and most competent person to run a charity? Why was Gabe so certain she would leave him? Did she look that crazy? And Jessie didn't even want to think about becoming a mother. Sure, she talked to her stomach and might occasionally stop to look at the baby things that were accumulating in the spare room, but she didn't dwell on what came after pregnancy.

Whenever doubts or memories would creep in, Gabe inevitably chased them away with a mischievous grin. His timing was so flawless, Jessie began to suspect that he'd learned her tells.

Still, there was a part of her that recognized the fact that she was living in a fairy tale. If she didn't tie up the loose ends of her reality, they would eventually shatter her illusions.

She didn't have too much time to deliberate on it, though, because their tranquil morning turned into rushing around in preparation for the afternoon rounds. They had promised Gabe's family they would eat lunch with them, and the closer it got, the less Jessie felt like eating. She found his sister utterly terrifying.

"How on earth did you ever convince her to help you set up the cabin for our stay?" Jessie asked Gabe as they drove to the four-bedroom ranch house sitting on three acres at the edge of town.

"Could you say no to this face?" He gave her his most pleading expression.

Jessie laughed. Even if he was teasing, it was the truth. The man was incredibly difficult to deny. Knowing that Elizabeth was susceptible to his charm gave Jessie hope that they had more in common than appeared on the surface.

Elizabeth's husband, Jay, was an affable guy with a receding hairline and expanding belly. The hairline he kept covered by a baseball cap. The belly occasionally peeked out from beneath the t-shirt he wore under his flannel. Elizabeth never failed to tug the shirt down if she noticed this grievance.

Jessie liked Jay instantly and it seemed the feeling was mutual. Elizabeth still terrified her. Her cold disapproval hung in the air between them, though both women tried to be polite.

Jessie had to hide a grin when she overheard Elizabeth reading her two teenagers the riot act because they hadn't warmly greeted their grandfather and uncle. Milo's assessment had been correct—those kids could care less about being around their family. After stiff hugs, they plopped down on the couch, earbuds in and noses buried in handheld games.

"I can't thank you both enough for what you did," Jessie started when she had Milo and Elizabeth in the same room.

"I like your idea for helping kids; glad I could help." Milo beamed at her.

"I'm glad to be rid of that hunk of land. I was sick of paying taxes on the stupid thing." Elizabeth frowned.

Jessie gave up after that. She made herself as unobtrusive as possible, half watching *It's a Wonderful Life*, and half listening to Gabe talk sports with Jay and Milo.

Opening presents was a subdued affair. Milo liked the personalized apron Jessie picked out for him. Elizabeth seemed pleased with her religious plaque. Jay seemed appreciative of the new flannel shirt that looked remarkably like the one he was wearing.

After eating as little as possible of a dried out turkey, she followed Gabe and Jay out to the kennels behind the house so Jay could show off the latest litter of Bloodhound puppies. Jessie could tell by the look on Gabe's face that it was only a matter of time before he was foisting one of those slobbering, muddy beasts off on her.

She tried not to show any interest in any particular dog, lest he get any bright ideas. One puppy seemed to have a different inclination, and was determined to clamber after her no matter how often she discreetly dodged it.

"I think you have a friend." Gabe didn't miss the interchange between Jessie and the black and tan fur ball.

"His paws are bigger than his brain." Jessie frowned and sidestepped the dog again.

"Aw... how can you say that about him?" Gabe scooped the puppy into his arms, slipping into baby-speak as he and the animal looked imploringly at her. A mountain of skin fell over the puppy's eyes and a bubble of laughter escaped before Jessie could catch it. "Ha! I knew you thought he was cute."

"Funny looking and cute are two different things. And please tell me you aren't planning on talking like that to our child. You'll stunt its growth."

"She's a cold, hard woman," Gabe told the puppy, which licked his nose in response.

"I'm going to say goodbye to Milo." Jessie shook her head, leaving him and the dog to their own devices.

Jessie was beyond caring if she was being rude; she said a cursory goodbye to Elizabeth and a warm one to Milo before going to wait in the car for Gabe. The teenagers had long since dematerialized. She rolled down the window to shout Merry Christmas at Jay as he passed by. He grinned and blew her a kiss.

"Your sister is certainly a warm and fuzzy kind of person,"

Jessie observed as they pulled away from the tidy little house.

"Yeah, she takes her position as matriarch pretty seriously."

"Can you assure her I have no designs on her place in the world?"

Gabe simply grinned and Jessie let it drop, although she secretly thought it might be fun to watch Elizabeth and Aleksandar square off in a cage match.

The bright spot for the visit was that it cured years of feeling as if she'd missed out on something special by not having family to celebrate with on Christmas day. She'd never realized how brutal the process was.

She and Gabe took a short nap together before heading over to Tumbleweed Ranch for dinner. Jessie was actually looking forward to the third celebration of the day.

The atmosphere in the Johnston household was entirely different than at Elizabeth's. A fire crackled in the hearth and laughter spilled out, reaching their ears on the walkway outside.

"Hey, there they are," Milo called out from the living room as Ethan ushered them into his home.

"Are you following us old man?" Jessie couldn't help laughing at the change in his demeanor.

"Only the party, my dear."

"Which, of course, is us," Gabe countered.

"Says the man who was napping 20 minutes ago," Jessie teased.

"I wasn't the only one," he reminded her as he sat a load of presents down under the tree before taking the stack from her hands as well.

"Careful, I haven't given you your gift yet. I could always return it."

"You could always give it to me now." He gave her his most beseeching look.

"Jessie, Gabe!" Hailey practically glowed as she greeted her guests. There were hugs all around before Jessie was swept into the kitchen by Hailey while the men stretched out in the living room.

"How on earth did you put all of this together?" Jessie marveled as she helped Hailey set the meal out on the table.

"I married a man who can cook."

"Ethan made this?"

"Most of it. Before I married him, my idea of a hot breakfast was sticking a Pop Tart in the toaster."

"I knew I liked you." Jessie smiled appreciatively. "How did you and Ethan meet?"

"He hired me to be the barn manager before this was Tumbleweed Ranch. How about you and Gabe? How did you meet?"

"You were the barn manager?" Jessie asked out of both a genuine curiosity and a desire to dodge the question.

"Yeah. I had no real experience with horses, but the business sense Ethan was looking for. And I was desperate enough for a job down here that he could afford me. Are you avoiding my question?"

"Little bit," she admitted, before making a split-second decision that would change the course of their friendship for better or worse.

Chapter Eighteen

As much as Jessie was enjoying this happy little bubble she seemed to have landed in, the reality was that no one here, other than Gabe, truly knew her. While she was certain anonymity was keeping her alive, it also created the nagging fear that if these people knew her true self, they would reject her.

"Gabe was supposed to arrest me to get to my pimp, but couldn't quite bring himself to," she found herself saying.

To Hailey's credit, she paused for only a beat before nodding her head as if Jessie's statement contained nothing out of the ordinary.

"He, Spence, had started working for the Bosnian mafia. I wound up being an informant. Kind of an odd beginning, I know."

"No, it's very Romeo and Juliet... star-crossed lovers and whatnot."

Jessie smiled at a memory. "That always was our song... Romeo and Juliet. A mutual friend sang it for us once and it kind of stuck."

"See? Not so unusual after all," Hailey assured her before letting out a snort of a laugh. "What does Elizabeth think about that?'

"Oh wow." Jessie couldn't help laughing, too. "She has no clue. I sincerely hope she never does."

"Can't say that I blame you."

"Actually, you're the first person I've told. Gabe even changed my last name. He's worried about who would come looking for me if word got around where I was."

"You poor thing." Hailey frowned.

"Are you sure you never worked the streets?" Jessie studied her.

"Why's that?"

"Most people wouldn't be this nonchalant about the bomb I just dropped."

"True," Hailey admitted. "I actually have not worked the streets.

That's probably the one job I didn't do... although it would have been fun to see my family's reaction if I had. I do tend to be a little unconventional by most people's standards. And really, who am I to judge?"

Jessie smiled; she found Hailey utterly refreshing.

"Will it drive you crazy if I ask a thousand questions, though? I bet your life was fascinating."

"That's not the word I would use, but questions don't bother me. One condition, though."

"What's that?"

"Will you teach me to ride a horse? After our babies are born, I mean."

"Gladly." Hailey beamed at her.

"This world is so foreign to me. I want to be at ease—like Gabe."

"What about Gabe?" He poked his head into the kitchen as if on cue.

"We were just talking about big, furry dorks."

"You sweet-talker, you." He kissed the top of her head and swiped a dinner roll in one fluid motion.

"Are you going to steal food or help?" Hailey arched an eyebrow and pointed to the ham. "The carving knife is in the cupboard by the sink."

"Ethan, your wife's putting me to work," Gabe protested loudly, obeying nonetheless.

"Don't look at me." Ethan appeared in the doorway. "I was going to ask you to take a look at one of my geldings later. I need your two-cents."

"No such thing as a free meal these days," Gabe teased.

"Cool, food's ready." Aaron followed his nose into the kitchen. Unlike the teenagers in Gabe's family, Hailey's son seemed quite content in the company of adults. Jessie wondered if that was a product of being an only child.

Dinner was fun, even if Jessie had no clue what they were talking about most of the time. She'd never met people so crazy about horses, and had never realized how little she knew on the subject.

Eventually Gabe brought the conversation around to Honeybranch cave and Jessie's plans for it, intentionally drawing her into the discourse. Ethan and Hailey excitedly started rattling off ideas for turning the place into a working ranch, drawing from their experience when deciding how to manage their own place. Jessie again found her head reeling and wondered if she'd bitten off more than she could chew.

Later, the men cleared the dishes while the women lingered at the table, chatting about their day thus far. Jessie was encouraged to learn that Hailey dreaded Christmas afternoons with Ethan's family. It was good to know she wasn't alone there.

"His mom still hasn't forgiven me for taking her baby away."

"How old was Ethan when you got married?"

"Thirty-eight," Hailey snickered. "Did you like your necklace?"

"Very much." Jessie smiled, her fingers moving to trace the pendant.

"You know the blue topaz is a symbol of love and fidelity?"

"It's my birthstone."

"Yes, but Gabe was really excited about the double meaning there. He was like a kid at, well, Christmas."

Jessie found that knowledge comforting. He'd found a way to promise faithfulness without pushing her on the marriage issue. It was crazy how good he was.

"He's not a normal man, is he?"

"Nope. He and Ethan are both too good to be true."

"Was it hard for you? Trusting Ethan, I mean."

"Really hard. I almost blew it with him," Hailey admitted. "I was so sure he'd get sick of me and take off. I didn't want to put Aaron and me through that again."

"What made you change your mind?"

"My son. He's always been smarter than me. He pointed out that there was 100% chance of being miserable if I didn't give it a shot."

"Smart kid."

"I have no idea where he got it from." Hailey shook her head.

"Can Gabe go take a look at that horse with us now, Ethan?" Aaron finished loading the dishwasher and looked up expectantly.

"I'll go with you." Jessie stood up, followed by Hailey. Gabe eyed them each, wary of their angelic expressions.

Ethan turned on the floodlights on their way to the stables. From a distance, Jessie could see the horse pacing in the paddock. His fluid movements made him seem to float. Jessie was so intent on watching the horse, she nearly came out of her skin when something bumped her from behind.

"Blue, stop that," Hailey admonished the dog as he came alongside them, tongue lolling out. "Sorry. He seems to really like you."

Gabe's laughter rang out in the night, and Jessie just shook her head.

"So… what do you think of him?" Jessie slid beside Gabe once they'd come to a stop along the fence line.

"He's amazing."

"Sorry he's not wrapped."

"This is my gift?"

Jessie nodded, trying to read the expression on his face.

"It's been a lot of years since I've had one of these."

"I can always help if you've forgotten how it's done," Ethan offered.

"I think I can manage," Gabe assured him dryly.

"Do you like him?"

"I'm in shock. He's perfect… I thought you didn't like four-legged creatures."

"You're not planning on bringing him in my house, are you?"

"No."

"Then we're good."

After a few minutes of admiring the horse, everyone else wandered back to the house, leaving Gabe and Jessie alone.

"Do you really like him?"

"I really like him," Gabe promised, pulling her into a hug. "But not nearly as much as I like you. Are you happy here, with me?"

Jessie nodded, unsure if she could voice all of the feelings that tumbled around inside.

"What aren't you telling me?"

"I'm scared."

"You don't have anything to be afraid of."

"You can't promise that." She shook her head. "And I can't shake the feeling that it's not over."

"I won't let anything happen to you." He tipped her face up so he could look into her eyes.

"You know something." She studied his face closely. "You talked to someone in St. Louis. There's something you aren't telling me."

"I didn't want to worry you on Christmas," he hedged.

"What?"

"Let's not do this now. Tomorrow."

"Not tomorrow." Jessie pushed away from him, her eyes snapping with anger. "This is my life we're talking about here. I thought you wanted to be my husband, not my next pimp."

"Excuse me?"

"Spence would have treated me like my wee little female brain was too weak to handle something. He would have decided what was best for me without my input. How is this different?"

"Don't compare me to him." Gabe's voice was low and hard.

"Don't keep things from me," she countered, her own voice laced with steel.

"What do you want to know? Three Bosnians have turned up in the river. It looks like someone is methodically killing everyone we were trying to arrest. Coleman was released on bail and disappeared the next day—they're searching the rivers now."

"Vance." Jessie paled.

"Vance is fine," he assured her.

"No. It's Vance, working from within to settle things his own way. You need to tell him I'm alive."

"If word gets out that you're alive, Aleksandar will find you."

"If it doesn't, Vance is going to wind up in prison for the rest of his life and it'll be my fault."

"Jessie, if he did this, it's already too late. I can't let him just walk away."

"But he did it for me." She was so frustrated she wanted to stamp her foot.

"Let's walk away from the paddock, we're upsetting the horse."

"So?" Jessie demanded, not particularly caring about the horse at the moment. "You would arrest Vance? Really?"

"I don't want to spook a wild horse, Jess. They have memories like elephants. And if Vance committed murder, then yes—I would arrest him."

"Do you know how to get a hold of him?" Jessie followed Gabe away from the fence, wrapping her arms around herself for warmth as they walked.

"What makes you think I would tell you if I did?"

"Because it's my decision to make."

"The baby is half mine. If you're going to get yourself killed, at least wait until the baby is born."

"Nice. Look, all I want to do is get word to Vance that I'm okay. He's my friend, Gabe. He protected me; I owe the same to him."

"I don't know how to reach him." Gabe held his hands up in surrender.

Jessie let the subject drop and the pair walked back to the house in silence. He was probably wishing he'd stayed single. She was figuring out how she could get all the way to St. Louis without him following her.

If the distance between them was noticed, everyone was polite enough to not mention it. Her enjoyment of the evening was significantly dampened with so much weighing on her mind, and for the first time, she used the pregnancy as an excuse to head home early.

She expected Gabe to head to his father's house after dropping her off. Instead, he stretched out on her bed.

"To what do I owe the honor?" She couldn't keep the sarcasm from creeping into her voice.

"I don't trust you to stay put."

"So I'm under house arrest?"

"Wouldn't dream of it. But you do have a constant companion for the foreseeable future."

Jessie stood rooted to her spot, seething with rage and unsure what to do with it. She grabbed the closest thing to her hand and hurled it at him.

"Have you lost your mind?" He flew out of the bed after the snowman figurine bounced off his thigh. She answered by pinging a ball of socks off his forehead.

"You jerk. Maybe I don't want to be protected. Maybe I like danger. You can't just show up and say 'Oh, I'm alive' and make yourself my ruler. It doesn't work that way." She threw a shoe at him to emphasize her point.

"Damn it, Jessie, stop throwing things at me." He caught the shoe and hurled it to the ground.

"Maybe I like throwing things." She chucked another shoe at him.

"You drive me completely insane." He batted the shoe away like a fly, closing the distance between them.

"I'm tired of being bossed around. I'm sick to death of being babysat. I got along just fine without you so why don't you go?"

"Are you forgetting how you got here…who made sure you had a car and money and clothes?"

"You owed me that much. You got me into this mess." She glared at him, her face inches from his.

"Oh, I got you in to this? Really? Is that the story these days?"

"I never would have agreed to be an informant if I hadn't wanted to please you. I wouldn't have seen what was happening. I'd be in my apartment with my friend completely oblivious to all of this."

"You'd be happier knowing Coleman still had those girls locked in his basement?"

"That's not fair." She felt the fight draining out of her.

"But it's the truth."

"Yeah, well. The truth sucks… and it doesn't give you the right to become my new lord and master." She shook him off and stormed from the room. She couldn't quite tell if she was mad at him or the situation, but he was an easier target. Besides, being angry with him would make it easier to do what was necessary to slip away.

Nothing he'd said changed the fact that she had to find Vance; she had to try to convince him to leave St. Louis and never look back.

Chapter Nineteen

It was another two weeks before Jessie's chance came. Gabe delivered her to work then headed to Ethan's to start training his horse. The diner was busy, so she waited until after the breakfast rush to feign a dizzy spell. Milo insisted on driving her home before the lunch rush hit.

Jessie felt a little guilty for lying to him and for leaving him shorthanded during the afternoon. But she didn't have much time to lose before Gabe discovered her missing, and she needed enough of a head start to find Vance, Harmony or Dan before Gabe dragged her kicking and screaming back to the Ozarks.

She jotted a quick note that said simply "I'm okay" and tacked it to the refrigerator door before snagging the spare key to the Plymouth. Thankfully, she'd had the presence of mind to hide it in her makeup bag after his declaration that he would stop her from returning to St. Louis by any means necessary.

Leaving the note probably cost her some of her lead-time; if she hadn't, he might have wasted an hour or so looking for her. But she couldn't bring herself to be that cruel to him, no matter how maddening he was.

She dressed in jeans and one of Gabe's flannel shirts. It was large enough on her she looked formless rather than pregnant. The added layer of a winter coat further disguised her current condition. If she did run across the wrong person, she didn't want the pregnancy to be used against her or Gabe.

The drive felt like it would never end—partially because she had to stop every hour to pee, partially because she was making herself crazy with second guesses and what ifs.

Unsure of where else to start, Jessie began her search at the Washington University campus. If Harmony hadn't gone home, Jessie didn't want to startle her parents. Finding Harmony at school seemed her safest bet. While she had little hope of seeing Harmony there in the evening, Jessie wanted to get a feel for the campus layout. That and the safest place to track Dan down would be at Nick's after nine o'clock, so she had some time to kill.

After a fruitless tour of the Wash U parking lot, Jessie made a pass through Little Bosnia. It seemed the most likely place to find Vance and she was fairly certain no one there would recognize the Plymouth. She wasn't sure what she'd do if she found Vance since showing her face on those streets would be too dangerous even by her standards.

It was a moot point anyway and she found herself eating a late dinner at the Denny's on Hampton while she waited to go to Nick's. She'd purchased a Go phone for the sole purpose of having a number to give Dan should he say he had a way of contacting Vance. It was the second cell phone she'd ever owned and she hoped it fared better than her first.

She tried deep breathing to sooth her jumbled nerves on the short drive from Denny's to the Irish pub. It didn't surprise her to see Gabe standing outside the bar, chatting easily to the uniformed officer at the door. Still, her stomach tightened just a bit.

He recognized his car instantly. She parked in the lot across the street and watched him wrap up his conversation. She didn't budge as he crossed the road or even after he leaned against the car and folded his arms across his chest. They stayed like that for a moment, regarding each other silently and deciding what to say next.

Jessie finally took a deep breath and slid out of the car, leaning against the door in a pose similar to his. They still didn't speak, but it was progress.

"You really are determined to do this, aren't you?" There was reluctant resignation on his face.

"If you won't let me go talk to Dan, I'll grab a late dinner in Little Bosnia."

"You're determined to kill me, aren't you?"

"Can we go inside now? I'm cold."

"Stay close to me, okay?"

"Anyone we know inside?"

"No, but this is a pretty popular spot. I don't want to take any chances. Hey Jessie…"

"Yeah?"

He kissed her thoroughly, sparking a new kind of fire in her veins.

"It's been way too long since I've done that." His breath still mingled with hers. "Are you sure you want to do this?"

"I have to."

"Then let's get it over with." He took her hand in his and they crossed the street together.

The hockey game was still on, so Dan hadn't started playing yet. He was standing at the bar chatting with the bartender while he waited. Jessie grabbed them a table while Gabe went to get Dan's attention.   Jessie watched the two men greet each other warmly. Gabe seemed to be telling Dan something as they walked towards her. Jessie assumed from the look on Dan's face he was being prepped to see a ghost.

"Jessie-girl, as I live and breathe. You're a sight for sore eyes, darlin'."

"I've missed you, Danny." Nostalgia washed over her at the sight of her old friend.

"Are you doing okay? How's life treating you these days?"

"I'm good. How about you?"

"Same as ever." He looked from Jessie to Gabe and back again. "So you two ran off together? I didn't believe it when the rumors started flowing about you and Spence."

"There are a couple of different stories out there," Jessie told him. "Some people think I'm with Spence and others think I'm dead. It's best that everyone believes whatever story is already in their head, you know?"

"He got you in a big old mess, didn't he?"

"Yeah, well, things are okay now."

"Good, good. But I'm guessing you didn't just come to reminisce." Danny pinned her with his gaze.

Gabe smiled, but let Jessie do the talking.

"I need to get word to Vance. Last I heard he was working for the Bosnians. It's kind of important. I can't just stroll past Bevo Mill calling his name...I was hoping you would know how to get in touch with him."

"I haven't seen Vance but once or twice since you left and he doesn't stop to visit with anyone from Cherokee anymore."

"Is there anyone who could get a message to him? Do you know where Harmony is?"

"Harmony moved on, too. I heard she's still in school. Some people say she's living at home, others say she's on campus. Others say she left St. Louis altogether."

"If I give you my number, can you get it to Vance if you see him?"

"Sure," he promised, accepting the slip of paper she handed him. "Are you guys sticking around for the set?"

"Wouldn't miss it." She smiled, leaning over the table to give him a quick kiss on the cheek.

As always, Danny's music wrapped itself around Jessie, completely saturating her senses. Gabe pulled her to him and she gladly curled against his side. With a grin and a twinkle in his eyes, Danny played their song for them and for a moment, all the world felt right.

When Jessie could hardly keep her eyes open, they waved goodbye to Dan. It took some convincing for Gabe to let her drive the Plymouth; he was certain she'd fall asleep at the wheel. Eventually he caved and she followed him to a Drury Inn outside of the city limits. Jessie wasted no time before crawling under the covers once they were checked in.

Gabe showered then stretched out on the bed beside her to watch television. It seemed so natural to use his chest as a pillow, one arm and one leg thrown over him as she slept. He was so incredibly solid. Did taking comfort in that make her weak, or simply human?

Jessie wasn't sure what woke her, but the moonlight streaming through the window assured her it was still the middle of the night. The television was off and Gabe's breathing was even. She raised her head to find him awake and watching her.

"Can't sleep?" She propped herself up on an elbow.

"I like watching you sleep."

Jessie didn't know what to say to that. It unnerved her how completely he exposed his feelings to her.

"What?"

"You." She smiled, kissing his stomach before looking back up at him. "You seemed so dark and mysterious when we first met. Turns out you're just a big softy."

"That sounds manly."

"Sorry."

"Are you ever going to stop running from us?"

"I'm here now, aren't I?" She rested her cheek on his chest, unwilling to look at him.

"Only because I caught you," he reminded her. "You'll find some reason to slip out of my grasp again tomorrow."

"I love you Gabe. I really do," she promised. "I'm just not ready to belong to anyone right now."

"How am I supposed to take that?" The pain was raw in his voice.

"I belonged to the state; then I belonged to Spence. I've never just been Jessie. Hell, I don't even know who she is. If I marry you, then I don't get to figure that out before I become your wife and that's who I am. I don't want to be a frustrated soccer mom wishing her life away."

"And that's the only future you see with me?"

"That's what marriage to anybody means to me. I've yet to see anything to convince me otherwise."

"Good to know." His chuckle was derisive.

"Why don't we talk about this when we get home? Let's concentrate on finding Harmony or Vance for now."

"And here I thought you'd be willing to go home tomorrow," he teased, lightening the mood.

"Fat chance." She laughed. "We are going back to school in the morning."

"You think she knows where to find him?"

"I'd be really surprised if not. Looking back, those two were always together. I think there was something going on with them and I was so wrapped up in you I just didn't notice."

"I could see that." He thought about her words for a minute. "Have you thought about the possibility that she's involved in whatever Vance is? Maybe she's not as innocent as she appears."

"I refuse to believe that." Jessie shook her head. "She's too smart for that. I'll never forgive myself if she threw away a bright future over this mess. Please tell me you won't arrest her if she did."

"Would you stop asking me to break the law?"

"Sorry."

"My entire adult life has been focused on upholding the law, justice. When love failed me, when humanity failed me, I had justice. Please don't ask me to walk away from that."

"Law and justice aren't always the same thing," Jessie pointed out quietly. "But you're right. It's not fair of me to ask that of you."

"We really are an oddly matched pair, aren't we?"

"I'd like to think the differences complement each other." Jessie shrugged lightly.

"I know they do." He maneuvered their position so he could kiss her. There was such sorrow in his kiss. She knew her hesitancy to marry was hurting him. She didn't know how to bridge that gap between them.

Words could never convey everything he made her feel. Words could not heal the wounds she'd given and they wouldn't bind him to her. So she let her touch speak what words could not as she loved him the best way she knew how.

Chapter Twenty

J essie pulled herself out of bed long before she was ready. Of course, Gabe had already brought their suitcases up and gone off again in search of food. She was proud to be showered and dressed by the time he returned.

A large flannel shirt and jeans were the wardrobe for the day again. She felt fat and frumpy in her new garb, but it was ridiculously comfortable. Gabe didn't seem to mind the new look. He swept her into a long good morning kiss before setting a baseball cap on her head to complete the ensemble.

After a muffin and a glass of orange juice, they set off for the Wash U campus. This time they parked the red Jeep and strolled around the campus, enjoying the crisp winter day and hoping to luck into stumbling across some clue as to Harmony's whereabouts.

"I'm not sure if being here makes me feel smarter or dumber." Jessie, in fact, felt very old wandering amongst so many fresh-faced youth. "Oh wow…"

"What?"

"I know that guy." Jessie ducked her head against Gabe's arm.

"Do I want to know?"

"Probably not," she admitted. "Is he gone yet?"

"Actually, he's still standing there talking to a student." Gabe seemed to be warring with amusement and irritation. "Hey, there she is."

He took off in the other direction, leaving her exposed. Before she could think to take off after him, her eyes met the professor's. She could see him reaching back into his memory, trying to place the face. A smile tugged the corners of her mouth—how could she forget the erstwhile Shakespeare? Not many people showed up in 16th century costumes. He'd taken himself very seriously. She'd struggled not to giggle.

She was once again struggling not to laugh as she darted to catch up to Gabe. She muttered an apology at his look of irritation, quickly turning her attention to catching up with Harmony.

Jessie was tempted to call out to her, but something in her friend's demeanor kept her from it. Harmony was walking with purpose and was headed away from the main campus. Gabe seemed inclined to agree with Jessie, and the pair quietly followed Harmony. They pulled back when she stopped at the Metrolink platform, turning towards the kiosk to buy tickets so Harmony wouldn't see them when she nervously scanned the area.

When the sleek rail train pulled into the station, they boarded two doors down from her. To Jessie, it felt odd to be stalking her old roommate. But she couldn't escape the warning bells tingling in the back of her brain that Harmony was acting like a person with something to hide.

And there was also the fact that after Jessie had let them think she was dead, her friends might not welcome the sight of her. She looked up at Gabe, trying to read his expression. He glanced down and gave her a reassuring wink.

Harmony got off the train at the riverfront; Jessie and Gabe followed as she boarded the Casino Queen. The place was fairly quiet, although the permanent haze of smoke still clung to the air from the night before. The mechanical song of the slot machines could be heard in the distance.

"There's our guy," Gabe murmured to Jessie. "And there he goes. He saw me."

Gabe sped up, trying to cut Vance off at the pass. Jessie tried to keep up but was easily outdistanced by Gabe's long legs and lack of baby bulk. It was obvious Vance hadn't noticed her—his attention was zeroed in on Gabe.

Jessie used that to her advantage and made a wide loop to intersect them both. Suddenly Vance was headed straight for her. Harmony followed with Gabe not far behind. She took her baseball cap off and called his name as he neared.

He stopped short, focusing on her face, confusion clearly evident in his eyes. His normally stoic expression now seemed just short of crying.

"Oh wow." Harmony skidded to a halt behind Vance.

"Is there somewhere private we could go to talk?" Jessie put the baseball cap back on and tugged the bill down low.

"My car's out front." Vance nodded slowly as if still unsure of the reality of the moment.

The little group moved as one out to the parking lot. Gabe and Vance flanked Jessie, both recognizing the need to keep her from plain sight.

Gabe gave Vance directions to their hotel. Otherwise, the ride was silent. It seemed best to wait until they could finish the conversation before starting it and no one had a clue where to start anyway.

"So, ah, I'm not dead," Jessie finally spoke as she sat on the edge of the bed in her hotel room. Vance's eyebrows shot up. He stood facing her, arms crossed and leaning against the wall. Gabe stood close to Jessie, as if he wasn't entirely ready to trust Vance. Harmony sat in a nearby chair, still staring openly at Jessie.

"Why now?" Harmony asked. "Why didn't you get in touch with us sooner?"

"Because I was trying to stay out of sight and alive." Jessie hoped her friend could understand that.

"I got word that someone was eliminating anyone involved in Jessie's death. She got worried about him." Gabe nodded towards Vance. "I told her to stay put, but she's a very stubborn woman. She insisted on making sure no one was doing anything stupid in her name."

"You shouldn't have come back." Vance shook his head. "If Aleksandar finds out you're alive, you'll wish he hadn't missed the first time."

"I don't want to know if it's you." Jessie rose and went to him, placing her hands on his arms and meeting his eye. "If I know, then Gabe knows."

"And Gabe doesn't want to arrest you," Gabe interjected.

"So why are you here?"

"Because I wanted you to know I survived. I swam to shore and hitched a ride to the car Gabe had stashed for me. I have a new life. I'm happy and well cared for. Things turned out okay for me. I wanted you to know," she repeated feebly, feeling stupid now that she was looking up at him.

He closed his eyes for a second, trying to collect his emotions. When they opened again, they glistened with the sheen of tears. He kissed the top of her forehead and pulled her into a hug. The uncharacteristic display of affection threw Jessie for a loop, but she quickly recovered and wrapped her arms around his thick waist.

"I'm so glad you are okay. But you were right all along. When I saw you disappear in that river I knew—if someone could do that to one person, they could do it to any person. The world is better off without monsters like that in it. And I was one of them for too long."

"Leave," she commanded him, raising her head up to look in his eyes once more. "Leave the country. Go to some island with no extradition laws and live a long and happy life. I have money. I'll pay for you to get there."

"I hope you're keeping your money somewhere besides a mattress these days," Vance teased. "And I appreciate the thought, but Harmony and I can't just pick up and run. She's brilliant, Jess. A mind like that shouldn't be hiding on a remote island somewhere."

"I was hoping she was smart enough not to be mixed up in this." Jessie frowned, stepping back so she could scowl at Harmony.

"Don't you look at me like that." She threw her hands up defensively. "He's right. Those men are monsters. Someone had to stop them."

"I'm not hearing this." Gabe looked like he'd rather be anywhere but there. "Haven't you people ever heard of the police? What ever happened to the idea of letting them do their job?"

"Aleksandar has at least one member of the STLPD on his payroll. I never caught a name, but I can promise you there's at least one dirty cop in that precinct. That's why Jessie wasn't extracted before the raid. She was supposed to die in the melee. They planned to take out a lot of trash with that fiasco."

Jessie's heart broke for Gabe in that instant. He looked like a man whose last sliver of faith had been destroyed as he sank to the bed Jessie had been sitting on. She instinctively met him there, curling up almost protectively against his back.

The gesture was not lost on either Vance or Harmony. Silence prevailed for a moment while each collected their thoughts.

"Are you planning on coming back?" Vance asked Gabe.

"I'll stay with Jessie. I gave Carter my resignation last week. "

Vance nodded as if he approved of that decision. Jessie scowled at Gabe; he hadn't told her that either. She'd known it was coming, but it rankled her that he'd left out something that important.

Jessie's stomach growled, commanding Gabe's instant attention. "We should get some lunch."

"It can wait." She flushed with embarrassment.

"I don't want you getting sick because we didn't feed you," Gabe argued. "Vance can take me to pick up the Jeep and we'll grab food on the way back."

"Do you have somewhere else to be?" Jessie looked from Harmony to Vance.

"Nowhere that can't wait," Harmony assured her.

"Why are you so concerned about Jessie's eating habits?" Vance answered with a question of his own to Gabe.

Gabe gave Vance a look that bordered on threatening. Vance responded with a sigh.

"Come on. Let's go get your car."

"I would appreciate it if neither of you made any major life decisions for me while you're gone." Jessie frowned at them both.

"When are you due?" Harmony asked when they were alone.

"May."

"Gabe's?"

"Yeah."

"You really fell hard for him, didn't you?"

"Guess you were right about my love story and all that." Jessie shrugged.

"I was devastated when Vance showed up on my doorstep, telling me that you were gone and urging me to leave the life."

"I'm sorry I didn't call you. It was all so strange—and scary." Jessie filled her in on the events of the past months. It seemed distant and unreal now, so very different from her new world.

When Jessie had shared her story, she listened as Harmony told her of starting a new life in a four-flat building in South City where Vance could keep an eye on her from a distance. They met in secret and pretended not to know each other in public. For the most part, Vance had become invisible.

"At first, I didn't know for sure what he was doing," Harmony admitted.

"You probably shouldn't say any more than that." Jessie held her hand up. "I'm so sorry for whatever harm I caused you."

"It was easy to blame this on you and Gabe at first," Harmony told her. "But this thing is way bigger than either of you. It would have exploded even if you hadn't fallen in love with a cop."

"I don't want you to hate me."

"I don't. I miss you. I wish things could be like they used to be sometimes, but I don't hate you."

"What are you and Vance going to do?" Jessie asked after another silence.

"Finish this."

"I think you should both leave," Jessie shook her head. "They need geniuses in other countries, too. This isn't your mess to clean up."

"It's not really yours, either. Vance saw it coming long before you got sucked in. It's more his mess than yours."

"And you?"

"Vance is my mess." She smiled.

"Then let us help you."

"You have a baby to take care of."

"Now you sound like Gabe."

"Well, the man has a point. Aleksandar will kill you if he sees you. He really hates you."

"Nice."

"He doesn't know me. He trusts Vance. Gabe's a known cop. No telling who in the department is trustworthy and who isn't so he can't help us. The way I see it, Vance and I are as good as anyone to finish this."

"Harmony, Gabe and I followed you from the campus. If we did, someone else could. I think I've handled the trauma of this all pretty

well, but I couldn't handle it if something happened to you. Not
you."

Chapter Twenty-One

N o. Absolutely not." Jessie stood toe to toe with Gabe, her jaw line hard with determination.

"Who's the bossy one now?" He tried to lighten the mood.

"Don't you get cute with me." She narrowed her eyes. "If you get to boss me around because I'm carrying extra cargo, then I get a say in your life as the father of this child."

"It's not exactly the same, but I see your point," he conceded. "It doesn't change the fact that I can't just walk away from my job knowing there's a bad cop in the department. I owe it to Carter to find out who it is."

"You owe it to Carter? No. The last time we were separated I nearly lost you. No. I'm not okay with this."

"I wasn't okay with coming to St. Louis in the first place, but I'm here aren't I?"

"Only because I snuck away from you—don't try to rewrite history."

"I'm not rewriting history." He rolled his eyes. "I'm just saying that sometimes relationships require compromise."

"You sanctimonious…"

"Jessie…" He cut her off. "Please don't finish that sentence."

"Fine. You want to compromise? We'll both stay in St. Louis."

"No. Absolutely not."

"But we're compromising, darling."

"You are such a brat," he accused.

"Am not." She crossed her arms and glared up at him.

"I really want to kiss you right now."

"Don't change the subject."

"But you're really sexy when you're mad at me."

"Stop it." She shoved at his chest.

With the devil's grin, he grabbed her by the waist and started tracing a line of fire along her collarbone.

"This doesn't change anything." Her head rolled back and she melted in his arms. "My answer is still no."

"Mm-hmm…"

Two hours later, Jessie lay staring at the ceiling wondering how exactly he'd managed to so completely befuddle her.

After Vance and Harmony had left, he'd broached the subject of him staying in St. Louis until things were settled. They'd fought and now here she was—a mockery to decades of the struggle for women's rights.

"One month," he promised. "Give me one month and then I'll come home, whether it's done or not."

"Assuming you don't get yourself shot in that month."

"Ever the optimist."

"I thought you were dead once. I can't do that again. I won't."

"You won't have to. I'll call every day. I'll come home every chance I get."

"And what about the hours in between?"

"I guess that's where faith comes in."

Jessie wanted to tell him her world consisted of what was. Things like faith didn't hold much stock. But the words died in her throat. Instead she nodded and blinked back the tears that threatened. She rolled over, tucking herself against his side. The baby kicked soundly, unhappy with the newly cramped quarters.

"I felt that." Excitement permeated his voice. He moved his hand to the side of her stomach, eager to feel a repeat performance. The baby obliged, obviously irritated to have its space cut down even further.

His grin could have lit the blackest of nights. Jessie smiled at the look of wonder in his eyes, stroking his hair and watching him with no small amount of adoration in her own eyes.

There, in that moment, she felt a spark of what could only be faith—faith that their little family would stand together in the end. If Gabe were the kind of man who could walk away from a responsibility, then he wouldn't be the man she loved. And she wanted their child to have the kind of parents that stood up for truth no matter what. And for those two reasons, he was right. He had to stay.

"Come back to us." Jessie seared the look on his face to her memory. "Swear to me."

"I do as I say." He stilled, meeting her eyes. "One month."

"Hailey and I will plan the wedding while you're gone." She decided as the words tumbled out of her mouth. "Don't leave me standing there without a groom."

"You don't have to entice me to come back." He shook his head.

"Gabe, please."

"I'll be there. We'll make it a Valentine's Day wedding."

"Oh that's so cheesy." Jessie wrinkled her nose.

"Humor me."

"Fine. Valentine's Day."

"Hopeless romantic," he teased before kissing her long and slow.

The next morning Jessie took her time getting ready. She knew it was time for her to go home; she still wasn't ready to leave Gabe behind. She wished she could see Vance and Harmony once more, but each meeting increased the risk they would be caught. So she contented herself with the knowledge that as of the moment, they were alive and well.

She cried the first half of the drive home. The baby kicked like crazy, making her cry all the harder. She stopped at the Pizza Inn at Rolla to have their buffet for lunch, then spent the next half of the trip practicing what she'd tell Milo.

As it turned out, Gabe had already paved the way for her there. Milo welcomed her back without a word and they picked up right where they left off. The first week of Gabe's absence passed quietly enough.

Hailey gladly dove into helping Jessie plan an impromptu wedding, which would be held at Honeybranch. It seemed the most appropriate venue. Ethan graciously stepped in to oversee the process of making the property livable again after years of sitting dormant. Before she knew it, Gabe was back for his first two-day visit. They spent both days turning the main house at Honeybranch into their new home.

He was gone again before she was ready, but not before they moved her meager possessions into the main house.

"I don't like you being here alone." He'd frowned when she'd first announced her intention to move in right away.

"I'll get a pet."

"A dog. A big dog."

"Drive carefully." She'd kissed him and watched him drive away.

The next day she'd stuck to her promise to get a pet and adopted a cat. It was a fluffy gray ragdoll with white paws who spent her time lounging in the sunlight streaming through the big bay windows in the living room.

He wasn't amused. He walked through the door and stopped short at the sight of the gray cat in the window.

"That is not a guard dog."

"But she doesn't drool on me," Jessie informed him pertly. "Oh, but I can't change the litter. It's bad for the baby. Could you do that before you head back?"

He'd grumbled, but he did change the litter. The next day, he left bright and early only to return with a large white German Shepherd.

"No." She refused to let the pair into her house.

"He's cleaner than that creature." Gabe gestured at the cat. "And he has a function… besides filling the litter box."

"His paws are muddy."

"I'll dry them," he promised, pushing his way through the door. "His name is Lobo."

"Perfect." Jessie eyed the animal warily as he sniffed his new surroundings. "Just perfect."

Gabe spent the rest of his time off with Ethan walking the property and drawing up plans. Lumber contractors were hired to clear a pasture. The sale of the lumber was supposed to pay for fencing and a pole barn.

Jessie simply smiled and nodded when they talked farm plans with her. It just wasn't her thing. She was much happier working with Hailey to contact children's homes so they could introduce themselves.

With the work to be done, learning how to be a grill cook, settling into a new home and planning a wedding, the second week without Gabe passed even more quickly than the first.

Gabe was starting to look drawn. He was no closer to uncovering the dirty cop and there had been another murder.

"We hired Hailey's son Aaron to do dishes at the diner. Unofficially, because he's not technically old enough," Jessie filled him in on local news. "But he's trying to save for a new saddle and Milo wants me free to do more cooking."

"He's a good kid," Gabe commented halfheartedly.

"You are a million miles from here."

"I just can't stop thinking about this thing at work. I know Brunner is an idiot, but is he capable of being a bad cop?"

"Maybe." Jessie wasn't sure how to help him. "Maybe not. Stop thinking about it, though. That's when the answer will come to you."

All she could do was watch helplessly as he drove away, the strain of the situation bearing heavily on his shoulders. Being so far removed made her feel impotent, but she couldn't fathom how to help. So she threw herself even harder into the things she did have control over.

Having Aaron work part-time at the diner gave her an idea, which she ran past Milo one day over a late lunch.

"What do you think about hiring some of the kids we take in?"

"Here?"

"Yeah. You're always short-staffed. Maybe we could start a training program for kids that are interested in learning a skill… give them something to put on a job application when they are ready to move on."

"We could take on one or two at a time, I suppose," he mulled it over. "How many kids you planning on having at that halfway house of yours?"

"We can handle ten at first. The plan is to expand to twenty within five years."

"Looks like maybe you need to start asking around. Maybe some of these other local businesses would be willing to take on an apprentice."

"That's a good idea." Jessie nodded slowly. "I don't suppose you could help me come up with a list of people to talk to?"

"I'll think about it a bit... maybe ask around some," he promised. "Now you'd better get going. You have too much to do to sit around keeping an old man company."

"Never." She grinned, nonetheless getting up to kiss him on the cheek before washing her plate and gathering her things. Thanks to a steady drizzle and dropping temperatures, a fine sheen of ice was gathering on the ground and she had no desire to test her driving skills on it.

When she was safely home, she got a fire going, changed into her pajamas and snuggled up on the couch to watch TV. She tried petting the cat, but it gave her a disdainful look, stretched and returned to its spot in the window.

She sighed; the sound seemed to bounce around the big, empty house. Lobo cocked his head and watched her expectantly.

"What do you want?" She scowled at him.

He wagged his tail and inched closer to her.

"I'm not a dog person."

He inched a little closer.

"Seriously. Go away."

He rested his massive head on her lap.

"You listen about as well as your master."

The dog's tail thumped in response.

"Do you know any tricks?"

The dog sighed.

"Okay, I won't bring it up anymore."

The dog's tail thumped again and she scratched his ears. He licked her arm and gave her a look of pure adoration.

"Fine. We can be friends...but don't tell Gabe. I'll never live it down."

It turned out Lobo was a great listener. Over the course of the afternoon, Jessie managed to fill him in on every major event of her life. He seemed quite interested in her current predicament. It was either that or the food she was dishing into his bowl as she wound down her current tale of woe.

He scarfed down his kibble while she picked absentmindedly at a microwaved meal for one. Her brain hurt from all of the planning and worrying so she decided to spend an evening doing nothing. She curled up on the couch with a bowl of popcorn and a mug of hot chocolate to watch *The Notebook*. Somewhere between Noah securing the first date with Allie and the final, tear-wrenching scene, Lobo had worked his way onto the couch. She wrapped her arms around him as she cried; he licked her face with concern.

The shrill ring of the home phone sliced through the air, startling them both.

"Are you okay?" Worry permeated Gabe's voice when he realized Jessie had been crying.

"Fine. It's nothing, really," she promised him. "Are you okay? You sound stressed."

"It's probably nothing." What was meant to be reassuring had the opposite effect. "Do you remember Kevin? The uniform standing out front at Nick's? He asked about my girlfriend today… He was just making conversation, but a bunch of guys heard. I don't know. Maybe I'm just making myself crazy… just be extra careful, okay?"

"Sure," she promised. They talked for a little while longer. From the tone of Gabe's voice, Jessie half-expected him to drive home overnight just to check on her. She did her best to comfort him, but the truth was his call scared her. She was glad for the white dog that shadowed her every move.

After thirty minutes of restless pacing, she called Vance.

"Hey. I just got a call that made me a little nervous and thought maybe you could tell me if there's anything new going on," she told his voicemail. She hung up, not sure what else to say.

Her nerves were a wreck and she wished having a big glass of wine was an option. As it was, she dozed off on the couch in front of a documentary with two phones, a cast iron skillet, and a butcher knife on the coffee table in front of her. Lobo was stretched out at her side, his head resting on her chest.

The vibration of a growl rumbling low in his throat was what woke her up. His entire body was tense as he honed in on an unseen threat in the woods surrounding the house.

Jessie was afraid to move, afraid to distract his attention. She reached for the phone as discreetly as possible. Her hands shook as she dialed Gabe's cell.

"I think there's someone outside." She tried to sound calm, but desperately wanted to weep at the sound of his tired voice.

"Okay. It's okay. I'm going to call Bobby and ask him to swing by. I'm not far away myself. I couldn't sleep. Call me back in a few minutes so I know you're okay."

"Sure. Thanks. Love you." She hung up the phone. Any hopes she had of him telling her it was a wild animal and to go back to sleep were completely dashed.

Lobo hopped lightly off the couch, moving with impressive agility for something so large. He crouched facing the door, ready to leap at the threat on the other side. Jessie sat up, briefly debating her choice of weapon. She finally decided the skillet required less skill and fortitude, so she hoisted the heavy pan as she turned to inch towards the door.

"Jessie?" The voice from her nightmares called through the door. "Jessie, I want you to open the door. If you try anything stupid, your boyfriend here is dead."

The initial feeling of being frozen in terror was replaced by one of confusion. She'd just gotten off the phone with Gabe.

"Jessie, don't listen to him. Run like hell," Vance instructed. The sound of metal meeting flesh was sickening even through the thick door. That was enough to spur her into action.

She traded the frying pan for the cell phone and dialed Gabe's number. Without waiting to see if he answered, she turned the earpiece volume down and slid the phone under the edge of the couch.

"I'm waiting," the voice reminded her from the other side of the door.

"Do you want me to have control of my dog first or not?" she snapped in response as she looped her fingers around Lobo's collar. Together, they walked over to the door.

"You're rather difficult to kill," Aleksandar greeted her when they stood face to face.

"If it makes you feel any better, you came very close." Jessie tried to quickly assess the situation. Vance had obviously taken a beating and now stood at gunpoint.

"So, who's the lucky father? Any guesses? The cop? The pimp? The hit man? Are there any other contenders?"

Jessie didn't bother answering. There were three men on her doorstep. Probably at least one more waiting outside. If she let go of Lobo's collar, he'd take down one. Hopefully the one with the gun pointed at Vance, but Jessie would settle for any of them.

That left one for her and one for Vance. Again, there was a measure of hope being factored in. If Vance was too weak to fight, she couldn't exactly count on the cat to pitch in. Not that she'd ever tell Gabe he'd been right.

"Aren't you going to invite us in?"

"Wipe your feet outside. I just cleaned my floors."

"They're about to get dirty again."

"I don't like you." Jessie stepped aside, allowing them to enter her home. She had a feeling his threat had to do with more than muddy shoes.

Two out of three men had crossed her threshold when a shot rang out and the third fell like a bag of bricks where he stood. Aleksandar and his henchman both startled and Jessie took the chance to let go of Lobo's collar.

He leapt at the man closest to Jessie, pinning him to the ground by the neck. Vance knocked the gun from Aleksandar's hand as Jessie jumped the couch to grab the cast iron skillet. She waited for a break in the scuffle to crack Aleksandar over the head with the frying pan.

He crumpled to the floor. Vance gave the pan an appreciative look before checking for a pulse.

"He's alive," Vance told her as he picked up the gun. "Don't let either of them go anywhere. I'll be right back."

Jessie did as she was told, although she felt a little useless. Aleksandar didn't so much as moan and Lobo wasn't about to let his victim up. The man gargled once and the dog growled in response. All was silent again after that.

Jessie jumped a foot at the gunshot outside. Lobo didn't flinch, sealing Jessie's conviction that Gabe had found her a retired police dog.

Vance reappeared in her doorway with Harmony at his side.

"Nice shot," Jessie complimented her friend.

"Thanks." Harmony cast an uneasy glance back at the man she'd felled.

"Could you get your dog to release this one?" Vance took a step towards Lobo, stopping short at the deep growl that rumbled in the animal's throat.

"You can let him go now." Jessie scratched the dog's ears. He looked up at her but didn't move. "Spit him out now, buddy."

"You don't know how to turn him off?" Vance asked.

"It's never come up before." She shrugged. "Lobo—stop chewing on him. Come on now. Bad dog."

"Forget it." Vance snorted in disgust. "I'll question him like this."

"Sorry." She tugged at Lobo's collar but the dog didn't budge.

"Who's your guy on the inside?" Vance knelt beside the man on the floor. Lobo growled low in his throat.

The man opened his mouth to speak but only another gargle came out.

"This isn't going to work." Vance reached for the dog, who bared his teeth in response. "Damn it, Jessie, call off the dog."

"Open sesame?" She tried again.

"Release," a voice commanded from beyond the door. Lobo let the man go and sat down.

"Thanks." Jessie looked up at Gabe as he stepped into the light. Everything in her wanted to throw herself into his arms but she resisted the urge.

"I'm surprised poor Lobo got to see any action. I figured that cat of yours would be all over something like this." He walked over to where she stood. The cat briefly looked up from her spot by the fireplace.

"I'm so happy to see you I'll let that slide."

"Do you have any idea how horrible it is to listen to something like that, knowing you can't do anything to help?" He pulled her into the hug she'd been longing for.

"You want to come with me when I do this?" Vance asked Gabe as he grabbed the man off the floor and jerked him to his feet.

"Do what exactly?" Gabe arched an eyebrow.

"It's our best chance to find out who the dirty cop is."

"He's not going to know any more than you did," Gabe countered. "And you are not taking that poor fool outside to torture him. The sheriff will be here any second."

"How did you beat Bobby here?" Jessie remembered that Gabe had called him.

"He was tied up at the other end of town." Gabe scowled. "Apparently this is the one night Ava decides to have a crime spree."

"How exactly do you plan to find out who they're working with?" Vance demanded.

"I think I have a way figured out," Gabe answered, taking the gun from Harmony's grasp. "Thanks for holding that for me."

Confusion flashed across her face, followed by understanding. "Anytime."

Red and blue lights flashed outside, signaling the arrival of Bobby. As Jessie listened to Gabe fill him in, she began to understand the direction his mind was headed. In Gabe's version, he'd been alerted to the presence of the intruders by Jessie's phone call, shooting two of them on arrival.

Vance's injuries came from the ensuing scuffle and Jessie still got credit for taking Aleksandar down with the frying pan. The look on Vance's face was one of uneasy trust as he followed Gabe's lead.

Her peaceful home was filled with chaos as EMTs arrived to load Aleksandar on a stretcher. He still hadn't roused, making Jessie wonder if he ever would. She wasn't sure how she felt about being the one to scramble his brains.

The remaining henchman had his throat bandaged before being loaded into the back of Bobby's cruiser.

"I should ride with them in the ambulance." Gabe seemed reluctant to leave Jessie's side.

"Where are they taking him? I'll get dressed and meet you there."

"Don't bother. Once I arrange for someone else to babysit him,

I'm coming home. You should get some rest."

"Like that's going to happen." Jessie stared at the pool of blood on the porch, wondering if she'd ever get it all up.

"Try," he insisted before tossing his keys to Vance. "Follow me to the hospital? You can give me a ride home after you get a clean bill of health for yourself."

Vance nodded, giving Harmony a quick kiss on the forehead and striding out to the Jeep.

And just like that, the women were left alone. Jessie retrieved her phone from under the couch and gave Lobo a fierce hug. He bathed her face with kisses in return.

"Want some coffee?" Jessie straightened and looked at Harmony.

"Yeah. That sounds good."

Jessie reasoned that the baby could survive one dose of caffeine and made a cup for herself, too. They sat at the kitchen island, clasping their coffee mugs and not saying much in particular.

"I'm glad you showed up when you did," Jessie broke the silence.

"That was nice of Gabe to say he shot those guys. I know that was probably hard for him."

"Yeah, I'm sure it was. He'll do everything he can to keep you and Vance from going to prison, though."

"Is it fair to ask him to do that for us?" Harmony understood the internal sacrifice lying would require of Gabe.

"No." Jessie shook her head. "But lots of things in life aren't fair. The two of you going to prison doesn't seem very fair to me, either."

A knock at the door made both women jump. The sun was peeking over the horizon, but it was still too early to expect visitors. Lobo trotted over to the door, curious but not on guard. Jessie trusted his instinct, even if she couldn't fathom it, and opened the door.

"We heard there was a bit of excitement here last night." Ethan grinned at her. Jessie laughed at the understatement.

"You guys didn't have to come over this early."

"Don't be silly. I wouldn't want to sit here alone with something like that fresh in my brain." Hailey hugged Jessie and let herself in.

"Ethan, Hailey, this is my old roommate. Harmony, these are friends of ours. They have a beautiful ranch a few miles from here. You should see it while you're visiting."

"You're so young," Hailey blurted, then stopped short, horrified.

"Not so young. Jessie's just really old." Harmony grinned, setting her at ease.

"Thanks a lot." Jessie swatted her playfully. "Can I offer either of you some coffee or breakfast?"

"Why don't you let me make the breakfast?" Ethan rolled up his sleeves and Jessie gladly conceded.

Chapter Twenty-Two

The calm and reassuring presence of her friends completely changed the tenor of the morning. Still, Jessie felt odd being in the house with bloodstains on the porch and the telltale signs of a scuffle in her living room.

Apparently the Ava police force had never seen CSI because no one seemed overly concerned with their presence contaminating any crime scene. She desperately wanted to restore order to her home, but waited for the all-clear from Gabe. Until then, she simply did her best to ignore it.

"Want to see our cave?" Jessie turned to Harmony after breakfast. "Come to think of it, have you guys ever seen the cave?"

"It's been a while." Ethan's expression told of fond memories.

"I haven't." Hailey sat up a little straighter.

"Want to poke our heads in while we wait for Gabe? I don't think I can sit in the house much longer."

"Sure." Harmony was slightly less enthusiastic than Hailey. Still, once Jessie had wrestled the lock open and ushered the little group inside, it was hard to resist the mysterious charm of Honeybranch.

Giving a tour and recounting the history of Jesse James's second life took Jessie's mind off of dead men and dirty cops. It was dark and quiet and cool in the cave, just as it had been on her first visit five months before.

Jessie tried to call Gabe when they were back in the house warming their hands by the fire. His voicemail picked up just as it had the last time she called. She had expected to see Gabe and Vance before lunchtime and the wait was making her antsy.

"You look exhausted." Jessie noticed the dark circles under Harmony's eyes. "You should go take a nap. I promise to come get you if we hear from him."

"I doubt I could sleep right now."

"Seriously. You'll do him more good if you're rested."

"Maybe just a few minutes?"

"Come on, I'll show you the guest room… can you believe I have a house with a guest room?"

"This place is amazing." Harmony surprised Jessie with a hug. "Soon this will all be over and you can just live your fairy tale."

"If Gabe has anything to say about it, I think you and Vance will have some peace and quiet, too."

"That would be nice."

Jessie got Harmony settled then returned to her guests. It bothered her to think about the work that was piling up on their own ranch while they sat with her.

"Do you want some lunch?" Ethan asked as he rooted through her pantry.

"I just want to know Gabe's okay," she answered honestly. "Ever since he came back from overseas, I worry about him like a mother hen."

"We could go check on him if you want," Hailey offered. Ethan gave her a look that said he didn't like the idea. She gave him one back that plainly asked, "why not?"

"He was probably given strict instructions not to leave me alone," Jessie interjected into their silent communication.

Ethan's guilty expression told Jessie she had guessed correctly.

"It's okay. The bad guys are incapacitated. I'll be fine for an hour. It would actually make me feel a lot better to know Gabe was okay. If you don't mind, that is."

"I don't mind…." Ethan started only to be cut off by Jessie.

"Great—thank you!" she trapped him.

"Fine. But lock the door after me. And I'm leaving my 12-gauge. Do you know how to shoot a gun?"

"Sure."

"You're a horrible liar."

"Point and click?"

"Pump, point and click," he corrected. "Come on. If I'm leaving you alone, I'm teaching you to shoot first."

Jessie nodded. She had no desire to hold a shotgun, let alone use one, but if that's what it took for him to feel comfortable then so be it. She followed him out to his truck, where he produced a shotgun that would convince her not to trespass.

"This--" he pointed, "--is the safety. Move it like this to load the gun."

Jessie furrowed her brow in concentration. It seemed simple enough.

"Once you've got it loaded and are ready to fire, move the safety back. Hold it like this... point and shoot."

"Got it."

"It's got a bit of a kick," he warned. "Pump it like this to eject the shell and get it ready to fire again."

"Sure."

"Your turn." He handed the gun to her. She hesitated briefly before taking it and trying to mimic his stance.

The weight of the weapon was both terrifying and empowering. She took careful aim and pulled the trigger.

"Holy..." She swore soundly. "I see what you mean about a kick."

"You learn the best way to hold it with practice," Hailey reassured her.

"Is everything okay?" Harmony bolted out the front door.

"Yes, sorry." Jessie felt guilty for waking her up.

"That was a great shot." Ethan pointed to the sign they'd used as a target. "So now you just need to pump it and it's ready to go. Be careful you don't accidentally fire it. Watch where you're aiming when it's not in use."

"I'll be careful," she promised.

"Here's a box of shells. You shouldn't need them, but just in case."

"Thank you."

With Ethan satisfied that she could protect herself and Harmony reassured they were not under siege, Jessie stuck the gun in a corner in the kitchen and curled up on the couch with Lobo to doze while she waited for word.

A knock at the door caused her to bolt upright again. Jessie sighed and grabbed Lobo's collar before answering it.

"Captain Carter," Jessie greeted Gabe's boss uneasily.

"Jessie," Carter nodded politely.

"It's good to see you again." She smiled softly and turned her attention to the man with him. She recognized him as the uniform from Nick's. "And you as well, Kevin. It's funny; Gabe was just talking about you last night."

"It's good to see you in one piece," Carter told her with genuine warmth.

"Thank you, sir." She stepped to the side, allowing them in.

"We were supposed to meet Gabe here… is he around?" Carter surveyed the house.

"No, I'm sorry. He's still at the hospital. I expected him back by now. Can I get you a cup of coffee while you wait?"

She didn't wait for a response before moving to make a fresh pot of coffee. She needed something to keep her hands busy. Their presence made her nervous again. Would Gabe be in trouble now? Had she ruined his career?

"Seeing you here, it suddenly makes sense," Carter began conversationally as he accepted the cup of coffee she offered him. "No wonder Gabe was so worried about the timing of the raid."

Jessie swallowed nervously, unsure how to respond. She turned to hand Kevin his coffee and caught movement out of the corner of her eye as he pulled a gun from his waistband. She blinked in shock as he leveled the weapon on Carter, his aim knocked off course at the last second by Lobo, who had lunged at his arm. The bullet plowed into Carter's shoulder, knocking him back off the stool. Kevin swore and swung the gun at Lobo, who went down with a yelp.

Jessie bolted out the front door before he could regain his shot. He was right behind her. The woods offered little coverage this time of year, so she made a beeline for the cave. With the lights off, she was quickly ensconced in total darkness. She knew her way well enough to feel along the edges with a certain amount of confidence that she could make it all the way to the back without falling in a hole.

The journey was slow. She could only hope it was even slower for Kevin. A few times she had to release the wall to stay on the path and during those times she prayed fervently to anyone who might listen that she wouldn't get turned around.

Kevin's curses echoing through the cave told her he was there, following her. Once she saw the distant glow of an LED screen behind her. He was using his cell phone as a flashlight. Knowing he wasn't flying as blind as hoped, she picked up her pace.

After a timeless eternity, she felt the rickety railing that lined the natural stairs up to the shelf Gabe had once told her about. The cold, slick Missouri clay caked to her hands and clothes as she did her best to shimmy blindly through the narrow corridor.

Sometimes the squeeze got a little tight, thanks to her protruding stomach. She crawled at an awkward angle, trying to fit through the hole without hurting the baby. Since she couldn't see anyway, she tucked her chin in effort to protect her face. Gabe had mentioned a bat roost in this part of the cave.

She was so focused on bracing for the bat encounter the sound of the waterfall took her completely by surprise. Before daylight pierced the black, Jessie knew it was close as the complete absence of light lessened. Then the first welcome slices of sun reached her and she prepared herself for the frigid water she would have to go through.

She tried to see through the waterfall ahead to be sure she wouldn't be nose-diving into danger, but couldn't. Space was tight and she had no clue what was on the other side, but going back wasn't an option. Lobo and Carter might die if she stayed put waiting for a cavalry that might or might not appear.

She took a deep breath and thrust herself into the bone chilling cold. Ice ran through her veins as she emerged on the other side, gasping for air. She gave her surroundings a cursory glance to figure out where on the property she was.

The back of the house was a couple hundred feet away. Jessie gulped some air into her lungs and forced her frozen legs into action. She sprinted across the lawn, hoping against hope that the back door was open. As she neared her goal, Kevin's head appeared when he emerged from the front of the cave.

He burst into action, racing for the front door as she barreled through the back. Carter and Lobo were gone but she didn't have time to wonder what had happened to them. She dove for the shotgun, pumping it as he crashed through her front door. Without thinking, she took aim and pulled the trigger.

She pumped the gun again and took aim, her breath coming in rapid heaves as she stood trembling and ready to fire again if needed. It took her a second to realize that the first shot had more than done the job.

Slowly, she set the gun down and sank to the floor. Too shocked to cry and too tired to move, she just sat and shivered. The heat of the house pierced her frozen skin, compounding the tremors that already wracked her body.

"Jessie? Jessie? Oh, thank God. Are you okay? Jessie?" Harmony flew at her from the stairs, falling to the floor to pull Jessie into an embrace. "I have the man and your dog. I took them upstairs. I didn't know what else to do."

"Gabe?"

"He still isn't answering his phone. Neither is Vance."

"Ethan. Call Ethan. I don't know how to reach Bobby. Ethan will," Jessie could barely think. She was so cold.

"Okay. Is his number in your cell phone?"

"Yeah. Or Hailey."

Jessie was vaguely aware of Harmony calling Ethan and the conversation they had. She was so completely overwhelmed. With an injured man and dog upstairs, a dead man on her doorstep and two people she loved missing, she couldn't begin to process what should happen next.

All she wanted was for Gabe to be there. She wanted him to take her face in his hands. She wanted him to kiss her in a way that cleared her mind of anything but him.

She closed her eyes, picturing his face, his arms, his laugh. How blissful it would be to slip into oblivion—to let her subconscious revel in warmer memories.

But there was this stupid, nagging voice in the back of her mind that told her it wasn't fair to leave a nineteen-year-old kid to handle this chaos on her own. She pushed herself up off the ground and placed the shotgun on the kitchen island.

"Ethan didn't answer his phone. I left a message." Harmony seemed dangerously close to losing her grasp on calm.

"Cell coverage is horrible in these hills," Jessie rationalized. "They could just be in between pockets of coverage. I know the closest hospital is in Springfield. That's about an hour away. How bad is Carter?"

"The wound itself isn't bad, but he's lost a lot of blood."

"Is Lobo?"

"Hurt, but I think he'll be fine."

"Okay. Let's load them into the Plymouth. We'll head to Springfield and keep trying to call on the way."

The urge to panic was shoved firmly aside. She pulled on her boots and coat, ignoring the layer of mud and clay that covered her. Together, she and Harmony went to check on the patients. Lobo whimpered softly, but stood to greet Jessie. He kissed her face as she knelt to thank him for saving her life twice in twenty-four hours.

Carter was pale but awake. His pasty complexion worried Jessie. Harmony had used a sheet to staunch the flow of blood. Making it to the hospital was a long shot, but staying here was a death sentence.

"If you lean on me, do you think you can make it back down the stairs?" Harmony held an arm out to Carter, who nodded weakly and accepted the help. Jessie followed behind them, her dog limping at her side. She grabbed a pillow off the couch on their way out.

Once the cop and the dog were situated in the back seat, she fired the old car to life and the makeshift ambulance headed for the main road. But not before cranking the heat up.

She had a white-knuckled grip on the steering wheel as the car sailed around the roller-coaster roads. They nearly lost the back end on a particularly sharp curve and Jessie backed off the accelerator a bit.

Ice still covered the roads, invisible but effectively turning the winding blacktop into a skating rink. Harmony revealed her Catholic upbringing by the litany of hail Marys she was sending skyward in between attempts to reach someone on the cell phone.

"Oh dear Lord." Harmony squeezed her eyes shut. "Tell me

again why we didn't just dial 911."

"I'm pretty sure there's no 911 service in Ava. And I'd be shocked if they had more than two ambulances in town—both of which headed to Springfield this morning... from my house."

"Don't you think they'd be back by now?"

"Do you have their phone number?" Jessie snapped. "This seemed like the fastest way, okay?"

"No, no. It's fine. It's fine," Harmony was most likely trying to convince herself as much as Jessie.

The phone rang and both women were torn between weeping and cheering.

"Hello?" Harmony answered, mouthing the name "Ethan" at Jessie as she listened. At the first break in the conversation, she filled him in on their current status.

Jessie could hear Ethan's response from the driver's seat. It was obvious he blamed himself for leaving. Harmony listened intently to him then hung up to relay the information to Jessie.

"There's a hospital on the south end of town. They're all there. We're supposed to call when we get close and he'll have someone meet us at the emergency entrance."

"Did he say where Vance and Gabe had been?"

"No. He said they're okay, but I got the feeling that was up in the air for a bit. I'll feel better when I see them for myself."

"You okay back there?" Jessie glanced in the rearview mirror. Carter's eyes were closed. At first glance, it looked like she might have lost him. "Harmony, he's not dead, is he?"

"No." She twisted in her seat. "He's still breathing. But he doesn't look good."

"Great," Jessie groaned. "I do not need Gabe's boss to die in my backseat. That would be bad."

"I think we're almost there. Look... there's the exit Ethan told me to watch for."

Harmony navigated Jessie to the hospital, calling Ethan again when it seemed they were close. An army of medical professionals met them at the door, but Jessie only had eyes for the man standing at the front of them.

He looked ready to climb out of his skin he was so frustrated with waiting. She eased the car into park, taking a second to close her eyes and take a few deep breaths while Carter was removed in a flurry of activity.

Gabe was there, at her side. He opened the car door and knelt to the ground beside her, taking her hands in his. They stared at each other for a full minute, their eyes saying all the things tumbling around inside that they just couldn't voice.

"Come on, let's get you inside." Gabe stood, pulling her out of the car and into his arms. "Harmony, are you okay?"

"Physically? Yes." She smiled a little shakily.

"Room 204."

Harmony needed no more than that. She was out of the car and off in search of Vance.

"Lobo." Jessie pulled back on Gabe.

"Ethan will take him to the vet."

As if on cue, the car was being moved. She hadn't even noticed him. Knowing Lobo would be taken care of, she allowed herself to be led inside.

The ensuing flurry of medical care left her a little dazed... dazed and wishing she'd married Gabe sooner. She knew her life savings would be gone when they were done. If it weren't for the baby, she would have insisted she was fine. As it was, she'd gladly hand over every earthly possession to know the baby was okay.

Once the doctor informed her "Your daughter is fine," she found the first real measure of peace in her day. They had shooed Gabe out of the room, but she could see him. Worry etched every line on his face and his eyes never left hers.

"She's fine," Jessie mouthed, watching as the weight of the world melted from his shoulders at his comprehension of words. A smile broke across his face. Jessie's own smile was muted. Now that she was warm, now that the baby was safe, all she wanted was sleep. The last of her strength slipped away and she closed her eyes, if only for a minute.

Chapter Twenty-Three

G abe's face was the first thing she saw when her eyes opened again. At the slightest movement, he was leaning over her, brushing the hair from her face.

"Why am I hooked up to all of this crap?" Jessie scowled at the IV protruding from her hand.

"To keep you hydrated. They were afraid you'd start contracting if you got dehydrated."

Jessie's scowl deepened. That didn't make sense to her. It seemed like overkill. She just wanted to go home. Only home had a dead guy in it.

"Kevin. Kevin was the dirty cop. He's at the house. In the living room."

"Carter told us. Sounds like you, Harmony and Lobo really saved the day."

"He's a good dog."

"I'll let that slide under the circumstances."

"Thanks."

"Don't worry about the house. It'll all be cleaned up before you go home."

"I killed a man."

"A man who would have killed you and our baby."

"But I killed him." Jessie squeezed her eyes shut, trying to rid herself of the image.

"Apparently while Carter was getting an update from me, Kevin killed Aleksandar and jacked with my steering wheel so I wouldn't notice it until the first big curve on the way home. We flew right off the road in the middle of no cell coverage. Vance hit the windshield. I had to walk for help."

"As long as you had a reason for not calling."

"Very funny. You shouldn't have sent Ethan after me."

"I was worried about you. He taught me to shoot his gun before he left."

"Obviously." Gabe chuckled at that one. Jessie thought about reprimanding him for the tasteless joke, but she liked the sound of his laughter too much.

"You're not going to be in trouble at work because of me, are you?"

"You saved Carter's life. I don't think he'll be out to give us trouble anytime soon."

"When can I go home?"

"Give it a night. I want to be sure you're both okay. Besides, that gives our cleanup crew time to work."

"A hotel is cheaper than a hospital."

"Now's not the time to worry about that. Worst-case scenario, we take out a loan against the land. We'll figure it out."

Jessie nodded. It was odd having options. She was used to being limited to the cash under the mattress and the whims of others.

They talked for a while longer before Jessie drifted off to sleep again. She vaguely overheard Gabe turning away visitors, insisting that Jessie needed her sleep. She wanted to reassure her loved ones that all was well, but couldn't quite muster the energy to wake up.

By the time sunlight was once again streaming through her window, Jessie was more than ready to leave. She drove Gabe crazy with her insistence that they unhook her and send her home.

Eventually the IV was taken out and she was given permission to shower and dress. Hailey had brought her clean clothes early in the morning, sneaking past a dozing Gabe long enough to give Jessie a hug.

"Lobo's going to be fine," she'd whispered. "He has a broken leg, but no permanent damage."

"Thank you," Jessie whispered, hugging her back fervently. "Thank you so much for everything."

"You two learned to whisper in a sawmill." Gabe opened one eye.

"I'm leaving, I'm leaving." Hailey held her hands up in

surrender.

"Jailer," Jessie accused.

Now, as she showered and dressed in fresh clothes, she felt squeaky clean and eternally grateful for a friend that was willing to cross grumpy Gabe.

"Is Vance going home today?" Jessie asked as she sat on the end of her bed waiting for her walking papers.

"He left an hour ago."

"What? That is totally unfair!"

"Yeah, well, he's scarier than you are."

There wasn't much to do with that information other than pout...which she did. Just when she was ready to stage a coup, a nurse came in with paperwork for her to sign and a wheelchair.

"I feel ridiculous," Jessie groused as the nurse wheeled her through the corridors. "This isn't necessary. There's nothing wrong with me."

"It's hospital policy, ma'am," the nurse patiently informed her in a voice that hinted she'd had many similar conversations before. Jessie couldn't get past the fact that the woman had called her ma'am.

"People treat me like I'm a real person now," Jessie observed as she settled into the car.

"You've always been a real person, Jess."

"I was never ashamed of who I was," Jessie continued. "But I knew what other people thought. Most of them looked right through me."

"Then they were the ones missing out." He reached over to stroke her cheek with his free hand.

"No, seriously. It's weird how people treat me now. Like I'm good by association."

"Association with what?"

"You."

"Wow. I don't see it that way at all." He shook his head. "Any fool can follow the rules. It takes a special kind of person to keep a kind heart through the worst this life has to offer."

Jessie didn't know what to say to that so she changed the subject. "Is the Jeep totaled?"

"Pretty much." His shoulders sank.

"I'm going to miss it."

"I think maybe I should get a truck. Now that I'm a country boy again and all."

"As long as I can keep the Plymouth. We've become friends."

"I wouldn't dream of parting you."

It struck Jessie in that moment how far she and Gabe had come. Suddenly she wasn't worried about losing who they were to marriage. Instead, she was excited find out who they would become together.

That knowledge caused all of the worry and tension of the past month to melt away, leaving her almost buoyant as they pulled down the now-familiar gravel road. Her home was filled with laughter and friends who'd gathered to wish them well.

She knew rumors of her past would have spread with all of the goings-on over the past days. That didn't seem to deter the people in her living room now.

"You took ten years off my life this week, young lady," Milo admonished as he wrapped her in a bear hug.

"You old goat, everyone knows you're going to live forever," she teased him back.

Her house was actually cleaner than it had been before it all began. Looking at it now, it was hard to believe there'd been a body in her doorway 24 hours ago. She didn't know if she'd ever be able to thank everyone for all they'd done.

A part of her would always miss the vibrancy of Cherokee Street, but she was deeply in love with her new home. Maybe one of these days she'd get around to painting a mural on the side of one of their outbuildings or tiling a mosaic on the trashcans for nostalgia's sake.

From her vantage point on the floor with Lobo, she could see Harmony leave the room visibly upset. Jessie waited until she could extract herself discreetly before following. She found her sitting on the front porch swing of the log cabin, her arms wrapped around herself for warmth and comfort.

Jessie eased onto the swing beside her, sitting in silence and looking out over the property. It was already starting to transform; it was slowly coming to life. She could almost see it bustling with activity as it would be.

"He's leaving," Harmony finally broke the silence.

Jessie didn't speak at first as she tried to process what Harmony was telling her. "Going where?"

"He doesn't know. He's decided to be some vigilante or something. He's going after the rest of that human trafficking ring."

"That doesn't make any sense. He loves you; I know he does."

"Yeah, well, I offered to go with him. He wouldn't hear of it." She stopped, watching as Vance approached from the main house.

"So, ah, what's with you becoming Batman?" Jessie folded her arms and leaned back in the swing to look up at him. "I was kind of looking forward to none of my loved ones being in immediate danger."

"I wouldn't say Batman, so much." He cracked the smallest of grins. "I mean, I'm not a billionaire and don't plan to wear a costume. And I won't have cool gadgets...."

"Why are you doing this?" Jessie interrupted.

"For you." His eyes met hers. "And for all of the ones I didn't help."

"I get it," she admitted. "It's not so very different than what I'm doing here, I guess."

"I was kind of hoping that if I ever needed a safe place to hide a girl from the mob, your doors would be open."

"Always."

"So you're okay with this?" Frustration seethed in Harmony's voice.

"I get it." Jessie shrugged, unsure what else to say.

"It doesn't change the way I feel about you." Vance took a step towards Harmony. "All I'm saying is the world needs you in a lab somewhere solving its problems more than it needs you being a vagrant with me."

"At least finish school," Jessie interjected. "Then if you choose to go with him you know it's what you really wanted and not just the heat of the moment. Then you won't end up a Bread Co wife."

Harmony nodded, seeming to consider Jessie's words. "Will you at least stick around for my wedding? Just one more week," Jessie asked him. "I was actually hoping you would give me away. If that's not too weird, I mean."

Jessie wasn't sure, but it looked like there might have been a sheen in Vance's eyes before he ducked his head.

"Sure. I can do that."

"I'm cold." Jessie stood up. "And after yesterday, I don't have a whole lot of tolerance for being cold."

She left the couple alone on the swing and went to find Gabe. He had mentioned going back to the hospital to check on Carter and she wanted to spend time with him while she could.

Despite her insistence that she'd be fine, Milo, Ethan and Hailey refused to leave her alone while Gabe was gone.

"Last time I believed you it didn't work out so well," Ethan reminded her.

"Very funny." She made a face at him. "Be nice or I won't buy any more horses from you."

"You know you're hooked."

The banter continued well into the evening. Gabe returned with takeout for everyone. After dinner, they were finally alone. He no longer cared about his sister's disapproval and refused to leave her side.

She made him carry Lobo upstairs when they went to bed, earning some gentle ribbing from Gabe.

The remaining days to their wedding were a blur. And then the morning itself came. Jessie woke to sunlight streaming through her window. Rose petals had been strewn about the bed and room while she slept. A note was pinned to the pillow where Gabe had been the night before.

"Time to make some new memories," she read aloud as she scratched Lobo's ears.

All in all, it was the kind of sunny day that made Jessie glad for things like faith and love.

Epilogue

Darcy took a few hesitant steps towards her father, her arms held up in a silent request to be carried. She had her daddy's dark hair and her mommy's big blue eyes and baby doll face. The combination was striking; Gabe suffered through many jokes about the day when his little girl would be old enough for boys to come sniffing around. To his credit, he took them well enough.

Jessie stood leaning against the old Plymouth, watching the pair as they played in the yard by the old log cabin. It had been a busy morning at Ma's, but the new kid learned fast so they managed to cut out a little early. It had been almost a year since Honeybranch had first opened its doors to a teenager suddenly without a home. They now had 15 kids living there, all in various stages of readiness for the real world. It had become apparent early on that a few things needed to be re-thought, so the property now had three distinct areas.

There was a lodge for girls and one for boys, with Gabe and Jessie's home directly in between the two. They might not be able to control any blossoming romances between the two sides, but they certainly didn't need to add fuel to the fire.

So far, most of the kids seemed pretty intent on getting their feet under them. Being faced with a life on the streets had startled them into reality. It turned out Jessie and Gabe made a perfect couple for guiding them along the way.

Every so often Vance would show up with another frightened girl in tow—someone rescued from slavery without a home to return to. They took up residence on the girls' side and were given a safe place to heal emotionally and physically before rejoining the world.

Ethan and Hailey had become indispensable. Their business

sense kept the place afloat when Jessie's next big dream threatened to make it stumble. They always seemed to be able to come up with a way to finance each new venture.

"Hey, there's Mommy." Gabe picked the toddler up and turned her to face Jessie.

"Harmony called today," Jessie told him. "She promised to spend summer break with us."

"Good. Someone to help with the cooking for a change."

"Ouch." She laughed. There was a certain truth to his words. She always made him do the cooking.

Lobo appeared from the woods at the sound of her voice. He barked and danced around Gabe, begging him to throw the tennis ball he'd scooped off the ground. Darcy held her father's leg with one arm and tried to catch the bouncing dog with her free hand.

The mouth of the cave stood just behind them and Jessie couldn't help but wonder about all of the lives that had crossed that exact path.

She could almost see the ghosts of Frank and Jesse James riding their horses down that hill straight into the inky black opening. Or drunk men laughing as they wheeled a piano into the belly of the earth to create a hidden bar during Prohibition. So many stories with one common thread. Lovers' break-ups and make-ups. Class fieldtrips and the Klan. A prostitute and a cop....

Author's Note

While Jessie's story is fiction, she was in a situation too many children face as they age out of the foster system. There are organizations that have been established to transition teens from the foster system into adulthood, but the need is still great.

I often encourage my readers to use their talents to leave their mark on this world—to make a difference. This book is my small way of doing what I can to be a voice for the voiceless.

One cause I believe very strongly in is the fight against modern-day slavery. Every day around the world people from all walks of life are enslaved, just like Jessie and the girls she encountered. Statistics show there are more people in slavery today than there were during the height of the transatlantic slave trade. Women and children are especially at risk.

It's an atrocity on all our heads if we hold silent. Sometimes with a problem this large, it's hard to know where to begin.

Fair Trade is a good place to start. By ensuring the products you purchase weren't made by the hands of slaves, you speak with your consumer dollars. And that voice is loud. Learn more about Fair Trade at www.wfto.com.

There are also many excellent organizations out there who dedicate themselves to making a difference. One I trust and respect is World Vision. Please consider making a donation to their Hope for Sexually Exploited Girls fund. Every dollar helps. You can learn more about World Vision at www.worldvision.org, or by clicking one of the World Vision buttons on my website.

About the Author

Heather Huffman lives in Missouri with her husband and their three sons. In addition to writing, she enjoys spending time with the family horse and their pack of rescued dogs. A firm believer that life is more than the act of taking up air, Heather is always on the lookout for an adventure that will become fodder for the next novel.

Connect with me online

www.heatherhuffman.net

Twitter: @Heathers_mark

Made in the USA
Charleston, SC
20 October 2011